HALOBAND

C. TURNER

L. LASERRE

This is a work of fiction. All the characters and events portrayed in these stories are either fictitious or are used fictitiously.

Cover Art: Shutterstock

Published by Innersky Books
www.innersky.ca/books

ISBN-13: 978-1-989493-34-2

Chapter 1

Gym class, bright and early, every Tuesday and Friday. I L-swipe the chip in my wrist. A holographic panel the size of my hand pops up, shows me weather, solar radiation index, storm warnings, time, date. I'm only fifteen minutes late.

Karie gives me the palm slap. "Whatsup, Ellan?"

"Not much. Too early to rise," I say. "Need some sleep. You?"

"Could be better." Her chubby-cheeked face crinkles in a sympathetic grin.

We hustle to the locker rooms. Soccer practice is scheduled for 8:30am. Normally this is a good thing, but our school's earned a reputation as a rough place, tension never far away.

Zandra intercepts us in the end section near the showers. She struts toward us with her two besties and manages to jostle both Karie and me as we're digging socks, runners and T-shirts out of our lockers.

"Clumsy much?" I rasp.

"Yeah." Karie glares through slitted eyes.

Zandra's dressed in a suede jacket and skin-tight pants. The sides of her head are shaved and raven-black waves of hair spill over her gleaming brow and down to her sleek shoulders. The bully that she is, I have to admit, looks devastatingly beautiful, and as intimidating. Her figure's stacked, as the guys would say, in all the right places.

My kickboxer's fists tingle for a showdown. One thing I never reveal is how well I can fight. These lamebrains might think I'm a coward, but that's their problem.

I pick up my tank top and runners and chuck the rest back into the locker. If it comes down to it, I can take her out with a mean kick to the ribs. With my speed and training, that's all it would take, even though she's got twenty pounds on me. Nah, easier to just ignore them. Like a pack of pesky dogs they'll stop yapping and go away.

"Karie, quite contrary, you look scary," Zandra croons. She gives Karie a shove. "Spit it out, I know you have something to say."

I'm ready to snap the lock when I see Karie contemplating a rash move.

I grip her arm. This situation can escalate fast. "Let it go, Karie. Isn't worth it."

Zandra tucks in her elbows and flaps her arms like a chicken. "Yeah, back off...bok, bok, bok." She contrives to bump hips with me. "You and your flat-chested girlie friend can go make out in the shower. We won't mind."

Hoots come from her entourage of followers, Bess Gee and Kyla Little, another couple of ignoramuses. I ignore them, but Karie's fit to be tied, clenching fingers fast turning white.

I don't care. It is all kind of comic drama except for the people I know who are bullied or don't fit in. The ones forced to work harder to make their way and keep a low profile because of scary creeps like Zandra.

Karie's voice drops to a sullen murmur. "One of these days we're going to kick those girls' asses, right?" A crooked smile tugs at her lips.

I return the grin. "Yeah, we will. But maybe not today."

Karie and I make our way to the steel double doors that lead to the playing fields at Visgate High. Not before scooting past the caf and its sickening sweet odors of refried beans and hash browns.

Out in the yard, there're a few dozen teens milling around, rallying each other and trading high fives as we assemble in our designated spots. A separate field is arranged for the guys. Ms. Gates, our thick-boned gym instructor, has the soccer balls laid out by the north net. She's bouncing one from hand to hand as she prepares her morning pep talk. The horizon's smeared with a dull yellow of perpetual smog, while an acid-wash blue dominates the zenith with the promise of a scorcher at high noon. Our outdoor fitness time is scheduled early for a reason. Isn't wise to be out in the sun during the height of day for too long. The rays are strong enough to bring on severe burns. Ten to two is considered high risk. Neither is it cool or practical to wear caps while running full tilt on the field.

The grass turf's a bit wet from last night's rain.

While the distant drone of a helicopter brushes the sky, I stoop to palm the ground, looking out upon our disparate team of eleven stragglers. Beyond the stone fence it's a battleground of rubble, skeletal girders and old memories—a graveyard. I recall Ms. Gates telling us the small sports field came into existence after they tore down the block of crumbling tanning factories sometime after the Cataclysm. There are still some remnants of the oldest buildings beyond the north wall. No one goes there, unless they want to get in serious trouble. We're content to play team sports here and use this questionable oasis as a track and field meet.

Of all the sports, track and field is my favorite. But we only get to practice during the fall.

Soccer season's in full swing. Okay, I can run with it—no pun intended.

"Okay, up and at it, ladies." Ms. Gates claps her hands. "Hustle up!"

Our team separates into groups. Eleven on one side, eleven on the other, and a handful of others on the sidelines. Karie, Leta and I are on the same team. Thankfully all the other girls who don't like me, like Zandra and Bess, are members of the opposite team. It's bound to be rough going. When Gates isn't looking, any chance to land an elbow in the face or a kick in the shin while sliding by with the ball, is fair game.

I'm a naturally competitive person, I'll admit. I like winning. But not the scuffs and bruises. Kickboxing has toughened me up enough for the inevitable collateral damage.

Zandra has the ball and at the moment has daggers set aside for me. Probably because a guy she likes has been making eyes at me. Maybe Joey for all I know. While we're milling around, she wheels and chucks the ball at me. I see it arc out of the corner of my eye so I duck, but it slams into Karie's chest, knocking her over.

Karie gets up, snorting out her wrath. "Hey, watch it, you dumb bitch."

"Oh, sorry," Zandra coos. "My hands slipped."

Karie scoops up the ball and hoofs it back at her. Zandra catches it hard on her shoulder, deflects it away, but I can tell it stings.

Ms. Gates comes running. "Hey, enough of this horseplay. It's a collaborative team effort, not a battleground."

Could have fooled me. I snuffle out a cynical grunt.

We shuffle back into our positions and cream them as payback. Zandra's not happy about it and she's mouthing ugly words at me. We've been rivals ever since primary school. I'm not sure today's aggression is because of Joey, but I'm captain of my team and she's captain of the other. A bit of rivalry's expected, but this kind of grudge mentality is stupid.

Still a half hour to go for drill practice, passing and penalty kicks with Ms. Gates, but I cut out early on an extended washroom break. After changing back to jeans in the locker room, I hit the library in an effort to bone-up for an upcoming presentation. I stare fixedly at the small collection of books stacked in the ten or so aisles. All have been published only within the last thirty years. Not at all useful for what I have in mind.

I pull up a stool at a bistro table overlooking the scraggly quadrangle. Pale light winks off the school admin office windows that face the library. I reach for my makeup kit. I apply more mascara, though I don't need it. I'm pretty enough, though I'm thinking I'm only a shade above plain with my long oval face and V-chin, willowy build, innocent eyes and sun-browned nose, but Karie and my other friends think I'm gorgeous. *Look at your slender figure and height, girl,* they say. All natural beauty I've inherited from my mother.

I swipe my wristlet and search the web for information about any semi-historical events, but only discover recent entries. Only so much on the 'resurgence of commerce and technology after the Cataclysm' I can fake my way through today if Mr. Peters calls me to speak. The material's dog-dull.

I still cringe as I stare at that pale grey, button-sized chip under my skin, knowing that every few years the devices are surgically removed and upgraded to the latest technology. They're our means of communication and link with the digital community. Fewer lost children with their enhanced tracking capability. Greater 'social cohesion', so they say. With Starcom networks able to service millions of the units in real-time with the new 6G+ systems, they can feed us big data, record our location on a minute-by-minute basis, and tabulate our profile. Business as usual.

This is getting nowhere. I'm no further ahead on this project than I was when I stepped into this damned library.

I crinkle my brow, tug at my lip. Then I remember Bram, my hacker brother, who's promised me a password to sites off the grid…the grey net, or dark net or something. Hopefully, it'll help me find more interesting material for this assignment. I'll bug him again tonight.

I look at the clock. I realize I'm ten minutes late for science class. "Shit." With a muffled curse, I boot it out of the library. I'm down the hall past the east wing and wrench open the door. Maybe not the smartest move, if I'm trying to be invisible.

I stumble into class a little breathless, wondering what punishment Peters'll dole out. But he is late too, so I pause and breathe a sigh of relief.

Chapter 2

Welcome to Room 3B, science class for disinterested teens. Some shuffling in the back today centers on Torv, class bully #2 who holds the freckle-faced, braces-and-smiles kid, Hock, in a headlock in his muscular arms while dragging knuckles across his scalp. Ouch. It makes a dry, scraping sound. A drawn-out moan comes from Hock. Some are laughing. Some aren't. Torv's best buddy, Vin, is pissing himself laughing.

Ordinarily I don't push my nose in other people's battles but this incident with Zandra has inflamed my blood. I stalk over and grab Torv's arm.

"Like beating on kids weaker than you?"

"When they steal girls' lunch money, yeah, sure."

He shakes off my hand and I hesitate. Since when did he become a vigilante? But then who am I to talk? I make my way to my seat in the third row, face set in a scowl. Let the holo monitor deal with Torv. I admit, he's a striking rogue in his dirty-blond, bad-boy sort of way, but he scares me. A scar on his left cheek runs toward his nose, a visible indicator of rough dealings in the past. Makes him look sexier, but scarier. A lot of kids would like him better if he'd just take the roughhousing out of doors rather than terrorizing kids in the classroom. No secret that he runs with the *Spikes* on the west side of town.

Puerto Rican, Mexican? He's deep-tanned, with a cat's grin and half-inch dark thatch of beard and matching mustache. His golden bronze-dyed mass of hair is tucked back with a red headband.

Mr. Peters, our science teacher, at last glides in with a heavy sigh on his lips and a bundle of papers under his arm. He shakes his head and drops it on his desk before he marches to the back.

"Knock it off, you two. First and last warning."

He looks comical with his flushed face and baldish head with cauliflower patches of yellow crowning his ears. He flicks a switch on the baton looped in the belt of his white lab coat. A figure materializes out of nowhere. The image coalesces into finer detail. A sporty, phys-ed type with black ponytail, brown piercing eyes and tanned physique, hands on her hips. She has an unnatural glow to her skin and seems to shimmer with every move. Enter Nelly, one holographic robo assist, or holo monitor. Torv immediately releases Hock. They both go silent.

Peters mills about, a smug breath whistling through his teeth. "Very good. Now can we begin?"

"No objections, Teach," says Torv.

"This morning's agenda." Peters slaps the viewscreen with his baton. "A lesson on metamorphic rocks, followed by class presentations. We'll start the day with a geographic overview of igneous intrusions, then some looks at the dwindling insect population. Following that we'll have an introduction to light and its refractive properties."

Groans. Face palms.

A real treat for us today. I look over at Karie with a deep sigh.

While Peters slides into his sleep-inducing monologue, I stifle a yawn. The images on the screen come and go: lava on a scorched mountainside, middle-aged geologists with hardhats pointing out warped strata on a dry riverbed and snapping closeups of the fossils that help confirm the rock's age. Peters points his laser baton at whatever object fits into his lesson.

Ben Gilsen puts up a hand and asks a semi-serious question about the probability of ancient sea beds forming the sub-stratum.

Peters is about to answer when Vin mutters, "All geeks should have the boots put to them." He brushes back the dirty red dog's muff of hair on his scalp and makes no attempt to control the easy grin on his bland, pink face.

Peters draws a deep breath. "It's part of the curriculum, Vin. Pay attention."

All of the images are available on wristlets to review at a later time, so at least we don't have to take notes by hand. Taking notes is optional, but not wanting to pair myself with the unpopular geeks, I opt not to. I continue to do covert research on my wristlet, trying to brainstorm material I'm supposed to present today, but I can't concentrate. I haven't even picked a topic yet. Not good, Elly.

Forty five of us crowd this classroom. A lot, but it could be worse. The classes are way too long for me—two hours. Sheer agony. Math and English next. But what can you do?

I peer over at Nelly who stalks the aisle. I'm never quite comfortable with that machine-like presence lurking. She graces me with prolonged eye contact and I force a stare back.

I can't help recall a few years back when two teachers had to take time off from knife wounds. Before that, many were getting rotten stuff chucked at them. So the school board contracted Starcom to engineer some electronic monitors to watch over us. A lot of prototypes built, so I heard, but the Starcom whiz kids figured it was more economical to employ holograms with basic AI, than have a physical robot.

Enter Nelly, or some machine like her… An effective deterrent against classroom eruptions and disruptions. Authorized and programmed to step in to offer 'assistance' if needed.

They've been in the schools for one and a half years. Real charmers, if you ask me. Keeping an evil eye on everything, like having some fire-breathing parent or security guard hovering over you every minute. They programmed these things to interrupt the teacher too, in case the lesson plans could be 'improved'.

Much to Peters' contempt, that was happening now. He hates them, mainly for this last reason. I can only guess his silent wish is that Nelly, the dumb bot, can stay out from underfoot, and only appear whenever Torv, Vin or any of the other troublemakers act out. I've tried to figure out how they work, but not sure I've succeeded. For sure, not a physical robot. Its CPU and processing power are located in some central basement or cloud space somewhere. Hidden sensors scattered about the room relay all the necessary information to the central store.

The overriding certainty is, all events are recorded and Peters can hit the hot switch any time he likes. I've seen it happen only once, and it wasn't pleasant. Blood, broken teeth, fists flying. Security guards running in to drag three kids off. One kid even had brought in a spray can of toxic paint and started dousing everyone. The kid was high or having some meltdown. Either way, shit disturbers like Torv have learned to dial back the aggression while Nelly is active. Though hotheaded impulse can always push them over the edge.

Speak of the devil. She turns and interrupts, pointing a manicured fingernail at the current image. "Don't forget to mention, Mr. Peters, that igneous rocks make up the largest intrusions in North America."

"I won't, Nelly." Peters grits his teeth, squares his shoulders and is about to flip to the next image when he chances to turn his head. Vin and Torv have taken to tossing paper airplanes at each other, like a couple of primary school kids. It's enough to make me laugh.

But I don't.

Peters flings down his laser cane and calls a halt to the lesson. "Okay, enough of this for now. Let's begin the presentations." He peers over at me. "You're up first, Ellan. And Rosa, you'll follow."

Panic kicks in. My mind blanks. Not even enough there to flub my way through a half-assed rendition of the resurgence of commerce. And I've been trying to cram information in my head all morning.

A paper airplane glides through the air to stick in Peters' ear, held there by wide tufts of yellow hair.

He glares at the back row. Nelly tags at his heels as he troops down the aisle. He looms over Torv and Vin, brows drawn, his shadow a mile long.

"You bozos again?"

Loud words and smacks erupt from the side as a kid gets pelted with something in the back of the head. Looks as if it's Hock and he's bawling like a baby. Maybe a rotten apple, or tennis ball, or some such. Vin has a chimp-like smirk on his face. Torv looks all innocence as he pats his knuckly hands on his brown leather jacket. Damn, he looks good: lanky in his ripped up jeans. While Nelly goes to investigate the infraction, Peters loses his cool. A full-fledged fight breaks out.

What luck, just the diversion I need.

"You two delinquents plan on learning something any time soon?"

"Nothing in it for us," Torv says. "Sic your bitch robo on us all you want."

"Higher education ensures greater chance of getting a job."

"Can get a job any day, Mr. Peters. Cement mixer, road repair rat, bag boy, corner store sweeper, you name it. My old man tells me I have to get through this year, then—" he spreads his hands in an I-don't-care gesture "—I can do whatever the crap I want."

"Easy as that, just putting in time, eh?"

"Whatever you say, Boss."

Peters casts a sly glance over at the holographic figure of Nelly who shimmers with energy.

"Two counts of transgressional language, Torv," the AI Holo Assist says in a sweet, patronizing voice, "'crap' and 'bitch'. Final warning."

Vin gives a snarky laugh. "Shows disrespect, Torv. You should be ashamed of yourself."

Joey puts in his two bits. "Yeah, Torv. Nelly oughta taser your lazy hide." He's got his hair shaved to peach fuzz at his ears, his dark wavy curls frizzed up three inches over the dome of his head. Looks like a beat wave musician, but he's actually a wannabe, doesn't even play an instrument.

The usual snickers trickle from the other kids. Nelly's polite imperiousness is always a scene.

"Nell's hell to the rescue." Torv laughs. "Hey, Teach, how 'bout I demo how to make one of these airplanes? More practical than your B.S. lecture."

Peters tries to get control of his class, but is failing badly, judging by the hoots of laughter. He turns to me, and says rather harshly, "Ellan, you're up. Get on with it."

I sit there, paralyzed.

Peters, twitching in his white coat, seems angrier than ever. Wonder why.

"I'm not ready." There's a nervous hitch in my voice.

He nods with cool impatience. "That's a five mark deduction. Tomorrow is your last chance."

"Sure."

The girls who are not my friends trade triumphant sneers. I don't give Zandra the pleasure of showing how flustered I am, though it takes every inch of reserve to keep my head up. I don't fit into their social cliques. Never will. I like track and field and kickboxing. They like wristlet social media and gossiping. They moon over guys and are always going to raves and proms. Not that I never gossip, but it's a low priority.

"What's your topic?" Peters snaps me out of my daydream.

I fish for an idea. "Time travel to distant planets." It's all I can come up with.

He looks at me through half-closed lids. "Please be serious."

"Can I tell you tomorrow, Mr. Peters? I've a cool idea I'm working on."

He shakes his head with an air of great sadness. "Same old, same old. At your peril, Ellan."

I let out a tense breath. For now.

As sweat beads my neck, I note Ben Gilsen has his eye on me—brows arched in curiosity, or is it concern? I can't help but blush. He's tall, slim, blue-eyed, blond-haired, got a clean-cut, classic look, a great bod. I'll admit I've had a small crush on him since first year, but he's never seemed to notice me. Until now.

Or maybe he has and there's been a flicker of interest I'd completely missed. Karie always tells me I flunk out when it came to reading boys' signals.

Vin mutters something rude in my direction that I can't quite catch. Joey takes exception to it, and his throat flushes pink, perhaps in jealousy, and a mist comes over his eyes. "Knock it off, jerkoff."

Vin leans forward, his yellow teeth showing. "You going to make me, asswipe?"

"Settle down." Peters groans. "This isn't a grade three remedial class."

"Language warning #1." Nelly lifts a finger at Vin.

While Vin turns toward Cody, another of his cronies, some wet slop of a lettuce and mustard sandwich comes peeling towards Vin's head.

Vin gives Torv a shove. "What's the idea of smacking me with that? You looking for a fight?"

"Wasn't me. Was that turd over there—" Torv jerks his elbow toward Joey.

"Oh, really? Gomer over there's going to get his head kicked in then."

He springs at Joey like a panther. But Joey is up, intercepting him in the aisle, a knee into the gut. Joey's well prepared, being part of my kickboxing club. But a fist catches him above the eye. I wince. He cries out.

The Robo Assist veers in. Twin rays zap out from her navel, catching both boys in the chest.

Peters pinches the bridge of his nose and closes his eyes.

Joey ducks, crouched and breathing heavily. He looks up at Vin in unbridled contempt from a wild, red-rimmed eye. "Hey Vin, slick your hair much?"

"Why don't you shut the hell up? Or you want to lose an eye?" Vin squares a fist and throws himself on Joey again. Torv and Cody are just shaking their heads and laughing in the back.

Vin rasps, "You want to be sucking grapes out of a straw, you dumb shit?"

Nelly comes hustling at them down the aisle. "Language infraction #2. Physical aggression. Immediate expulsion from class."

"Like hell."

A yellow ray shoots out from her navel and stuns Vin, doubling him over.

"OW!" He rubs his gut. Joey picks himself up, but he backs off, not keen to get himself thrown out of school.

Vin takes a swing at Nelly, but his fist goes right through thin air, leaving the shimmering hourglass figure of little Miss Priss intact. Dumb idiot. As if he didn't know Nelly is a transparent nothing.

Nelly responds by zapping him again and the classroom goes berserkers. Now she is tasering him out of the classroom and down to the detention office. Vin tries to veer off, huffing and swearing, but gets jolted with another beam.

"Alright, dumb bitch. I'm going," he yells. Nelly's sensors are not confined to just this room. The whole hallway's bugged with them so Vin has no chance.

Looks as if science class is a write-off. Peters, slumped at his desk, hand clawing at his hair, dismisses us. We are stunned but overjoyed. We wander about the halls.

Yet even with the 'excitement' of the morning, the day drags and I'm useless during Math and English, daydreaming, mind wandering, still worrying about tomorrow's deadline.

Before heading out for the day, I pad by the community posting board where students can pin events and bulletins. My 'better air-circulation-in-the-classroom' petition has got more hits. Fifty-two signups now.

I read the headline with a hint of satisfaction. *"Want to breathe cleaner air? Sign up if you are in favor of regular classroom duct cleaning!"*

Still too few signups to make a difference, but a step in the right direction.

There's the usual hasty shuffle through security. Kids pass by me eager to get through the scanners. Telltale clicks and lime-green flashes break out on our wristlets. No weapons or contraband today, folks, not packing my luger...I wink at the security officer. The 6G+ system keeps chugging away. All tags meticulously monitored.

Mom picks me up in the courtyard, looking drained from a day of meetings with the public. "How'd the presentation go, Elly?"

"Oh, fine," I lie. I've gotten good at that. I don't like doing it, but it saves us from an argument. Especially tonight. Mom's big rollout at the Starcom convention is on tonight and long story short, I know neither my brother Bram nor I are going to get out of it. More time down the drain when I could be researching a damned topic.

Chapter 3

All of us are silent as Dad drives Bram and me to the Convention Center downtown. None of us are relishing this event much, except maybe Bram, resident tech-lover, who works at Starcom, courtesy of Mom.

I stare out the window. To either side lurk abandoned buildings which speak of yesteryear's population. A withering one. Towers of crumbled stone, buildings grown to disuse. Black-streaked monuments of another era, weatherwashed with age. This is Old Levenbrook.

Nobody talks about this black hole in our history, a shameful place of past purgatory. As children we grew up hearing that the world was a 'bigger place' once, but civil war reduced us to this reality…come and gone, wiping out many lives. The only services that the city government maintains are the police force, the public works and a functional transit system. Corporations manage everything else, like the 6G+ towers. Twin antennae poking up from gunmetal rectangular boxes everywhere, like an infestation of alien rabbit ears. They cluster at street corners, cling to lampposts and hydro poles along with a host of surveillance cameras. No square signpost or traffic light is immune from them. The electric trams, service vehicles, even the city cop cars run with strange aerials on top, for whatever reasons I can't imagine.

A familiar feeling of déjà vu grips my senses, as if I've been here before in another time, another life. Feelings like this I keep well hidden, even from Mom, Dad and Karie. Especially from Mom.

We pull in beside the Hilton Hotel. An in-your-face glass cube with a slew of fake willows and marble fountains out front. We make our way in. Mom has already arrived a few hours ahead of time. Two valets dressed in white suits with black belts and wide bell hats usher us down some escalators to a cavernous assembly hall buzzing with energy. Upbeat corporate inspirational music echoes from the surround-sound speakers. There're some three hundred people gathered. Important people, I realize, from the city council members, bigshots from Agra and other companies, and people from the press. We're late. The show is about to begin.

Bram and I take seats in the second row with Dad at our heels. Bram kind of bumbles his way along, muttering apologies to the people already seated. He's this gangly, dark-haired and shaggy guy, shoulders somewhat hunched from being eternally stooped over a computer. People wonder how it is we are related. I always say, *Bram takes after my dad.*

Mom acts as hostess on stage. Four corporate figureheads are sitting in plush-blue easy chairs at the front. Rotating display screens glow with 3D renditions of the new haloband goggles in different colors. The ads are strategically placed on the walls behind the guest speakers. Such is the glitz and glimmer of hi-tech gadgets at these promo gatherings. Mom flashes us a sharp glance when I wave to her. She's dressed to the nines in an immaculate white dress with black stilettos. Auburn hair coiffed up, cheeks flushed, shining with carefully-applied make-up, taking in the whole audience. Her ear buds and silver mic clipped to her lapel are remarkably well concealed. In comparison, I'm dressed in a simple caramel-colored dress to match my eyes…far too frilly for my tastes with its long twined rose vines, but I'm doing it for my mother. I'm proud of her. I feel nervous just looking at her, imagining what it must be like to be in her shoes. But she carries herself well, with such a sense of authority and charismatic fervor, I know my worries are for naught.

Mom, how can I ever impress you when you're always setting the bar so high?

Maybe that is the problem. I have too much of her in me.

She approaches the podium and her husky voice grabs everybody's attention. "On behalf of Starcom Enterprises, I'd like to thank everyone for attending." Mumbles and scattered clapping drift from the audience. "I'm Viv Weis, hostess for the evening and head of Consumer Relations. It's a big night for us all! The long awaited Haloband is here!" Applause. Lots of it. Mom is impressive. Stunning in her white, shimmering silk dress as she points to the digital ads.

"Tonight I'm pleased to announce the future of virtual reality with video superband and universal 6G+ speeds!" She peers across the audience, a sparkle in her eyes. "Who would have known it could be yours by donning visor and ear pads and letting the wizardry of haloband do the rest?" More applause ripples through the auditorium. Mom holds up her palms to quell the cheers. "Our engineers have been working around the clock for the last three years to perfect this technology. At last the launch date has arrived." She sweeps an arm to the four seated to the left of the podium. "I'd like to introduce the people who made this possible. Mr. Hal Menzes, Senior Production Manager, Mrs. Liz Farell, Technical Engineering Consultant, Mr. Tian Darley, General Manager at Levenbrook. Now, let's welcome our CEO, Stan Rane. Founder of Starcom, visionary and philanthropist. He'll say a few words about this brilliant technology, having just returned from the nation's capital."

A tall, distinguished-looking man with rugged jawline, coal-dark eyes, and shock of steel-grey hair steps up to the podium. "Thank you, Vivian. This is indeed a landmark moment. I'm pleased to confirm, as of tomorrow, Haloband technology and all affiliated smart devices will be commercially available in public retail outlets at a low introductory cost." He rests his hands on the podium and leans forward. "This technology will supersede the standard tech of palm technology, wristlets and old handheld gadgets. We have worked hard with government sponsors and national interest groups to promote a highly beneficial product for an ever-demanding modern society."

Vivian beams and speaks into her headset, as if on cue. "First off, what would this benefit be, Mr. Rane?"

Stan nods and with a gracious smile, lifts a hand. "Our technical researchers have compiled a list of benefits—" Rane proceeds to read from a gold-leaf sheet, the title which he is not shy to share, "Wow!...4D Realizations of the Improbable, Your Impossible Dreams Come True.

"Users forget their troubles, tune in with their feelings, stimulate the creative centers of the brain, plumb the secret depths of their innermost desires... The list goes on. In truth, haloband is the ultimate life changer and mood lifter!"

Another round of applause sweeps the room. I reluctantly add my clap, clap to the pool. Rhetoric and self-assured hype do little to impress me.

As if cutting to the chase, Rane beckons Liz and Tian to the podium with a grin. "Before the demos and words from our design team, I will take a few questions from the press." He lifts another hand as if inviting a response.

A short-haired reporter stands up with a gold-plated nametag pinned to her blue business suit. Her wristlet menu is exposed and opened to full size. "These are bold claims, Mr. Rane. How can one device do all this? Is there a guarantee along with the purchase?"

Rane's lips curve in a smile. "I will defer to my engineering staff. Liz?"

Liz smiles. She pushes back her thick braid of burnished gold as she mounts the podium. "Though HB has its roots in smart technology, it has resident feedback circuitry which monitors heart rate, pulse, pheromones, blink frequency—every bit of body language available. While processers work in real time to seed the AI scheduler, the VR algorithm selects the next appropriate activity or story that the user desires. We use the word 'Story' to identify these impulses, or experience-enhancers, because we all have 'stories'. Each impulse is unique to the individual's taste and his or her response signatures." She pauses for a breath. "So, if Martha likes vegetarian cooking, she may end up with a one-on-one celebrity chef on a major talk show prepping spanakopita. Or if Dan likes car races, he may, for example, end up in an Indie 500 race with the latest and greatest champion drivers. Likewise, a horticulturist searching for the next super genus of plants, may be on a tour with renowned scientists to the most remote jungles, to Madagascar, to the Amazon. The possibilities are endless."

The reporter pauses, a puzzled frown on her flushed cheeks. "I'm struggling to understand. All these applications seem incredible for one pair of hi-tech goggles."

Rane intervenes, "More than a pair of goggles." His coal-dark eyes flick to the press woman's lapel. "My associate Liz will elaborate."

Liz nods. "Haloband communicates with the wristlet that monitors our body signals. On receiving the data, the HB further indexes the wearers' desires and fantasies. It creates a real-time profile and updates it over time—to reengage the wearer, as it adapts to his or her every preference."

"Amazing, if possible."

"Truly. Let's view some video clips for the audience to better understand." Liz signals to my mother. On cue, she starts up the video show on the overhead screen.

The Imax-like screen is impressive enough to draw us in, give us vertigo. We're in a virtual helicopter, getting a bird's eye view over the ocean. Then we descend at threatening speed into some seaside cave, hovering inside a vast grotto-like space. The audience grips their leather armrests. Then we turn to look out upon an endless spread of aquamarine swells. Sea birds swoop in and out and call to each other. The splash of dolphins resounds as they weave in and out of the gentle waves.

The audience settles down with a collective, contented sigh. We are all instantly relaxed by the seascape's majestic ambience interweaved with soft, bewitching synthesized tones.

More scenes stream by, of rugged mountains, whitewater rivers, lush forests, glidebys over volcanoes, then on to new supermalls of the future. Spacecraft, futuristic high tech parks, playgrounds, sports stadiums. It's a special type of screen. Coiling mist seems to swirl right out at the viewer. Tree branches waving in the wind appear at nose distance. A tossed football arcs by so close I reach out to grab it. Within fifteen minutes we are lulled into a state of relaxed receptivity. The screen is some new high tech that somehow makes 3D look 4D without glasses. It's also had a hypnotic effect, as if there were much more than water and birds in those moving pictures. It's but a prep for the haloband demos to come. Or so Liz intimates.

The last image dims, and morphs into a simple picture of the haloband, with blue visor, strap and ear bands on a white background with the text: "Wow...The Future is Now!" in bold print beneath. Mom calls an end to the presentation and invites us to enjoy the refreshments at the sides and to try out the demos. Everyone is sufficiently hooked.

As Bram, Dad and I stretch out our legs, there's a moment of busy confusion as others also rise from their chairs. Many are eager to be the first to try out the devices. The key speakers wander down from the stage to mingle with the guests and answer questions. Security people man the exits, their legs braced, arms crossed over chests, ear buds in place. A comical image flits through my mind of them all wearing halobands like crimson berets in a parade.

It's a harsh transition from an enlightened euphoria to everyone talking at once, and the babel of sound hits me like a sledgehammer. I wobble on my feet, slightly dazed.

Mom weaves her way through the crowd toward us. She joins us with a look of barely-contained excitement.

"Great presentation, honey." Dad plants a kiss on her cheek.

She beams. "Glad you liked it. How was it overall, Lars?"

He shakes his head and grins. "Couldn't have been better. We're all aching to try one of the devices." He nudges me in the ribs. "Aren't we, Ellan?"

"Of course we are." I give Mom a big hug, trying not to look as distracted as I feel, considering that my presentation is due tomorrow and already is five marks down.

"Way to go, Mom." Bram pats her on the back and is quick to beetle over to the demo tables.

"Lars, hi!"

Dad turns, squinting to take in a leggy brunette dressed in high heels and a skin-tight black dress. She holds a martini in one hand and flashes him a wide-eyed smile, as if almost conspiratorial.

Dad coughs and reaches out a hand. "Lois. Glad you could make it. This is my other half, Viv. Viv, Lois is my coworker in sales. She's our best shipping agent."

"Pleased to meet you," says Mom. Though she looks far from enthralled to see this woman in her tight dress, with her animated, suggestive movements, as she draws another deep draught of a martini.

"Congrats on your rollout," Lois compliments. "You must be proud."

"Oh, we are all proud and excited."

"I'm sure. Can't wait to get my pair of goggles."

Mom nods and casts her a bland grin. I roll my eyes. Obviously my mother is little enamored with the high-pitched laugh and the dramatic way she has injected herself into our family group. Dad picks up on the awkwardness of the moment and caresses his goatee, tries to put forth some witty words which are falling flat. The briefest body language passes and hints at something clandestine: the quick gesture of hand, flicker of eyes, suggestive move of hip, which speaks volumes to my mom. Her strained silence tells me she senses that more has been going on behind the scenes than just sales and shipping protocol. Dad chats about inconsequential things like office deadlines, schedules and such, though he looks tense, as if someone has been prying through his personal belongings.

The moment passes as Dad exits gratefully with a simple, "Ladies?" and sweeps his arm to shuttle us toward the hors d'oeuvres where a demonstration section of halobands lies. A series of the units in clear plastic bags for all to use rest on a black counter. They're mostly blue and white, some gold and white. A blue visor to cover both eyes, the ear tips connected to a stretchy band that wraps around the head and holds white ear pads in place.

Behind the counters, three hostesses in black suits outfit guests with the visor and headband.

Some people, already accoutered, are smiling, their mouths agape. Some are mute, others flush-faced, giving thumbs up signs.

Dad ushers us forth while Lois goes to chitchat with another woman in a nearby group. She seemed to revel in making us feel uncomfortable. It's weird. But then this whole ballroom full of glittering people, flashing teeth, plastic smiles and fancy suits reminds me of a fairyland. People talking and laughing and indulging in the latest scandal and gossip while casual interplay and innuendo carry on.

Not my scene. Glad to make like a rabbit and split. I plead fatigue and a need to rest as exams are coming up. Dad offers to escort me home.

"No worries, Dad. You and Mom enjoy the rest of the evening." My Dad—the big supply manager at Cramco Electronic—acquiesces.

"Sure." He shrugs. "But don't you want to try the halobands, Ellan?"

I look at the long line at the demo tables and crinkle my face. "Nah, next time though. I have to get back and finish my research. I'll take the tram home."

"Another project?" my mom barks. Her sharp glance veers my way. "Thought you just finished one? Wasn't it due today?"

"Ah, yes, technically it was, but—"

She shakes her head and sighs. "We'll talk about that later."

Now it's my turn to sidle from foot to foot. I make a hasty exit. Hopefully Mom'll have forgotten about it by the time the hubbub of the evening is over. Though that was unlikely, knowing her stickler-for-detail brain.

Chapter 4

The last sunlight peeks through the rain clouds as the tram whirs over the silver-steeled rails...past the towering ice-cube of the C-Sec police headquarters and its adjacent firehouse, then onto Jefferson Square. On past the public fountain where looms a monolithic court house with masthead flagpoles and its façade of grey-washed pillars.

The central core is left behind along with the ruddy glint of sunset off metal and glass as the last raindrops reflect prismatic light. The wheels clack while the passengers stare in lassitude, protected in our insulated bubble.

Winds pick up, dark storm clouds rumble closer and send a volley of rainsplatter on the metal roof. I bare my left wrist and swipe on the button-sized disc under my skin. A small oval screen pops up. Frowning, I recheck the weather. All clear for tonight and tomorrow, no major windstorms or floods. There shouldn't be, it's well past spring. But one can never be too sure. Unpredictable weather patterns seem to be the norm. There're a dozen other things I should be doing, like research for my presentation today, but I'm not inspired. I tap the screen again. It dissolves back into a speckling of light particles.

At last the tram creaks to a halt outside Tallahoe Station. An air whistle blows and the doors hiss open, letting me and a few other passengers down onto the cracked, weed-ridden pavement.

Once home, I shuck off the fancy dress and break into my grubbies: a loose pair of faded jeans and a thin black sweatshirt with a grey hoodie. *Well, Ellan, it's now or never. Either finish this project or flunk out and stop whining about it.* I settle down to my scuffed-up Apdek laptop—which I prefer, because of its simplicity—and start knuckling down, pulling up website after website, searching for content that may actually be stimulating enough to get me to finish this assignment. I tentatively coin it, 'Blast from the past'.

Nothing interesting shows up.

'Economic decline' yields various irrelevant and forgettable results.

'Viral outbreak' comes up with '202k people infected in China, few deaths'.

China, oh, yeah, they call it *Xinjian* now.

'Civil unrest in America' yields a two-page article of the uprising some three or four decades ago…the uprising is 'contained by the authorities' and the 'instigators imprisoned for life'.

I pause and massage my forehead. How much of this is truth, lies or propaganda? What can I read that can be trusted?

'Climate crisis' comes back with 'no evidence to support gas and oil corps are culprits in global warming' and 'temperature rise has been held to 0.1 degrees Fahrenheit per decade, nothing to cause alarm'. The article is further tagged with, 'the outcries of the few are from a few ultra-socialists, green freaks and conspiracy theorists', reports Bonito Donn of the *Globe and Grist* of…" the city's name has been edited out.

I clutch my hair in frustration. I'm getting nowhere. Where's a viable source of compelling information when I need it?

Things are going from bad to worse. Nothing but generic articles, the usual clichés and manicured bylines about some alleged civil war that broke out thirty years ago and a sudden outbreak that coincidentally wiped out half of humans worldwide.

I grit my teeth.

A few hours later, a scuffling noise comes from down the hall. Bram? I pad down the hallway to investigate. A sliver of light shines under the door to his man cave. Twenty years old and still living at home. I can hear Dad downstairs, mixing a drink at the bar. A familiar tinkle of ice suggests scotch on the rocks, his favorite. I knock and enter Bram's room without invitation.

He's at his desk in front of his holo screen with one of those gold haloband units on.

"Bram, glad you're back."

"Yeah, why?" He lifts his visor so it perches beak-like on his forehead. His pale eyes turn toward me and narrow in suspicion. They have a strange, spaced-out look like someone who's just taken a hit of bayludes.

"Enjoying your new toy?"

"I'm wearing it—if that means anything. Yeah, it's pretty whacked." He blinks. "Why the small talk?"

"Special interests project due tomorrow. Haven't started it."

"So? Looks like you're screwed. What do you want me to do, cheer you on?"

"Remember, you said you'd help me."

"Did I say that? You gotta try this thing out, Ellan, it's—"

"You said you'd give me access to some juicy sites."

He turns back to the monster extension display at his desk that has a red wire hooked to his visor. Weird. I wonder what hack geekery he's up to. His setup is so ahead of my old laptop with the LCD screen, it's not funny. I can tell Bram is super distracted, itching to get back to his new toy, the headgear and goggles. If he could have a love affair with tech, he would.

I sidle closer, thinking of how to get him to bite. "Come on, I know you can work some magic with computers."

"I'm not going to do your effing project for you, if that's what you mean." He elbows me back.

"I don't expect you to. You have to know how to get into sites that I can't access. I can't get any data on my topic."

"What topic are we talking about?"

I hesitate. "The past."

He rolls his eyes. "No wonder."

"What's that supposed to mean?"

He pauses, rubs his jaw and purses his lip. "There's another way perhaps." He fiddles with the wire going from his visor to his computer, and taps some holo keypad to bring up a lamp black screen with some small white text on it. Up pops an image of some bearded guy looking like an old wizard, blindfolded and pointing a finger straight at the viewer. "Visit this page. Then close it when you're done. Okay?"

"What is it?" I crane my neck, but he's already closed the window.

"No need to know, Elly. I'll send you a link to your wristlet."

"Sure, sounds good."

"And don't dare share this link with anyone. Promise? On penalty of death."

I shrug.

"Promise?" His voice is two degrees louder.

"Sure, scouts honor."

He looks at me crosswise. "Just get your stuff and then get out."

"Yeah, I heard you the first time." I frown in annoyance. I ask no questions, just scoot back to my room. Yet, I guess his 'privileged' access has something to do with Mom and her connections at Starcom. Definitely through my mom, and her executive position. Bram, as everyone knows, is no small hacker.

I hunker down at my desk and use the password he sent me, only to bring up a page with the image of the old blindfolded guy. A prompt below reads, "NAME YOUR POISON". I cannot pass this screen without entering something, so I enter the password again. Nope. No go. I enter "LIARS". It is not a skill-testing question. The word, or I'm guessing any word besides the password, unlocks the portal, simply called 'Darkweb'. There's a larger, slightly weirder icon of the same blindfolded man sitting on a throne with an air of the erudite, like some grand wizard. This time, half his blindfold has slipped down. A piercing, wily eye stares back at me from the screen. I frown, type a few general searches: 'Armageddon', 'collapse of the world', 'apocalypse'.

My heart skips a beat.

Up comes a grainy video feed of a woman with a primitive camera, whom I can't seem to make out, the picture is so blurred. But she is running for her life. Across a public square, from black-vested soldiers with shields and visored helmets, wielding tear gas and pressure explosives. The caption underneath reads: "Underground freedom fighter, Ignatia Frehan aka Abighail Ayet, spokeswoman for the *United Liberation Front*, gassed and pursued by militants. Frehan, reporter for the 'Underground Beat' independent news blog *samaritan.org*, reports the 2027 crisis in the Bengal riots. Similar events of brutality are happening worldwide. The video goes all snowy. The caption under the vid is replaced with:

"In the chaos that ensues, history was rewritten. It is neither what we think, nor what it will ever be."

The words fade away as the feed goes dead.

I probe more of the *darkweb*. Figures, numbers, images, jump out at me at once, like a procession of zombies. My eyes strain to absorb the forbidden details. Can all this be for real?

Minutes pass.

The sounds of clinking dishes and voices pull me out of my reverie...Mom and Dad buzzing around downstairs, angry again. Dad's drunk and Mom's frazzled from the evening.

"I know you've been sneaking around, Lars. Why don't you admit it?"

"No proof there. Just your overactive imagination, Viv."

"Listen to yourself, you've had one too many. You're slurring your words."

"Listen yourself. You've had a stressful day, I get it, but let's take a time out, have a few glasses of wine, watch a flick—"

There's a crash of a cup on the counter. "Screw the flick. As if that Lois episode wasn't enough. What do you do at that job of yours, sneak quickies in the closet?"

"Who? Lois? She's just a natural flirt. Anyone can see that. Been after all the guys at the office."

"I bet."

"What? You want to follow me around all day and find out?" I hear Dad's voice grow to a drunken snarl.

"No, I've got better things to do with my time."

I plug my ears in an effort to block out the negative energy. I turn my attention back to the darkweb.

Viruses mutating, wiping out major populations. City transit grinding to a halt. Governments toppling. Airports shut down. Borders shifting. America, one of the few nations that is not completely overrun by outbreaks, faces global warming melting point.

Massive spread of GMO seeds affecting plants and animals nationwide. GMO calamity gives rise to monster bees. Trees grow bark as thick as fungus. Accelerated growth of trunks deemed nothing less than alien.

Fires rage in Australia and Africa. Storms ravage the west coast. WCL (West Coast Labs) inundated by floods. Experimental seeds loosed into streams and GMO byproducts into the atmosphere.

Proxy Inc, subsidiary of WCL, is victim of intense and protracted storms. Lead scientist, Ian Tilbury, believes the toll could be devastating even years down the road. Prosecutors say company officials at Proxy are being held accountable for the carnage.

Man-made viruses continue to plague the globe: from continued overuse of antibiotics and vaccine experiments. Immunity passcards failing. Sources report that regions as far as Germany, Saudi Arabia and Thailand are seeing tens of thousands dying.

New 5G+ causes public outcry. Cancers and cellular damage skyrocket among city residents and animals exposed to high doses of EMF and microwave radiation.

As my brain reels, I watch another clip with a shaky camera, a grainy vid whose audio cuts in and out. Frenzied shouts erupt as a figure records footage, waving arms and rallying people. It's the same woman whom I'd seen earlier.

My jaw drops.

The scene opens as a line of soldiers in riot gear push against a crowd of protesters in Houston. Artificial barriers separate the military from civilians. A boiling sea of people push against heavily armed authorities. Gas grenades explode within the masses who flee the smoking gases. Some fall and are trampled. More clouds of stinging smoke erupt like fireworks on the Fourth of July.

Then, long arcs of flame erupt from behind the shields and land within the crowd. Dozens of people burst into flames. The victims flail their arms and legs in wild exotic dances of death.

Police and army officials employ tear gas, tasers and finally flamethrowers to keep violent protesters behind the artificial barriers. Black helicopters circle in a gunmetal sky.

An announcer's voice begins, "Citizens lash out at the rollout of the latest 5G+. The new tech introduces even higher levels of EMF into the air which are reputed to damage tissue and interfere with cell function. Underground reporter, Ignatia Frehan, is seen as a thorn in the telecom megacorps' side."

A woman is highlighted on the clip. She rallies protesters who threaten to crush the police line. Some protesters lob cans of burning kerosene into the police. Uniforms burn. More blasts of flame surge into the masses pushing them back. Men and women erupt in flames. Screams grate against the camera's audio. Police apprehend the highlighted woman, but she melds back into the masses. As men and women flank her on both sides, the entire group, ten or more, burst into flames.

A headline reads, "Ignatia Frehan fatally burned. Inquiry is underway into her controversial death." Another reads, "Tens of thousands attend Frehan's funeral in Princeton, New Jersey."

My pulse hammers.

The vid pans to what looks like the charred remains of bodies. I look away. I can't take any more. My heartbeat is thudding in my ears. Too much information. Why do I feel so crushed by these revelations? The last glimpse of Ignatia's face, the one panned in on with the pale eyes and high cheekbones, was unapologetic defiance. A born and bred martyr. It haunts me.

She looks so much like me. Brown hair, slim, searching eyes, serious look. I shake my head as I experience a déjà vu moment of being her in another life. Crazy!

Be careful what you delve into, Ellan. Once you get a glimpse of the dark side of hell, there's no turning back. Fingers trembling, I copy some of the media to my wristlet and am about to do as Bram suggested, exit the page, when my eye trains upon one final side headline: 'Rebirth after the fall'.

I learn that, after the crash, Starcom was built from the ashes of mega corporations I'd never heard of: AT&T, Google, Huawei, IBM, a bunch of others. Oil and energy companies, national banks and factory farms merged into another conglomerate called *Agra*.

I'm stunned. These truths, or fictional conspiracies, have never been revealed to me or anyone I've known. Why? How is that possible? I'm trying to figure out what it all means.

I'm too exhausted from the day already. It's 4 am and I've been cramming for this presentation for three hours now. Yet I force myself to assimilate all that I have discovered and organize it on a spreadsheet. Some of the darkweb photos and live vids I can sneak into the presentation. Just snippets of telling images, fires, buildings, and protestors running for their lives. Enough drama to spark my classmates' imaginations. Peters, on the other hand, is going to go apeshit.

Chapter 5

Pale dawn creeps over my duvet too early. I sneak past Mom's room, beetling down to the kitchen to mix myself some instant cereal, but my eyes are bleary, dark-circled like a raccoon's; I've had two hours sleep.

I hop on the early tram like a zombie and nudge shoulders with the commuters. My head's buzzing. I have no time to actually condense this project into something presentable. It's going to be a wing-it thing.

As I pour over last night's horror show, two things continue to trouble me. How does covering up the past serve anyone's purpose, and how has it been done?

Sure, there've been crackpots in Jefferson Square. Guys with megaphones spewing conspiracy theories about corporate hypnosis, government think tanks and secret labs, but they have been shut down in quick time.

Was it a sham? Or did the powers-that-be feel responsible for a failure to protect their citizens?

No, something else. Something more sinister.

I thought back to the violent uprisings I'd seen on the darkweb. The police and army using tear gas and flamethrowers to quell protests. Why such heavy force? What were they afraid of?

Everything seemed peaceful nowadays. The few public uprisings or demonstrations I'd witnessed in my childhood were swiftly contained. Instigators loaded into police vans and shuttled away in a much more streamlined manner than that savage age of the past.

One thing's for sure, I'm looking at the city with different eyes. The concrete seems greyer, as if there's a hidden lie everywhere I look. I mean, people are walking down the street, going about their business, but there's an unspoken eeriness lingering about the core...in the small puddles from the evening's rain, the shadows of the back alley, even the ornamental trees clambering up past the glinting glass of the government buildings, with their genetically modified fronds drooping and palm leaves swaying in the wind. But it's well hidden, only now dimly visible to my eyes.

I make use of my time in the library before I step into class, half in a trance, my mind still a million miles away.

I vaguely notice Karie. My wristlet buzzes. I open the home page to see a bunch of unread messages. I tap my avatar, a lone gull, to hide the mainstream, low-grade posts that somehow always filter their way up into my stream. Many more have piled up since I last logged on.

Vin is nowhere to be seen. Probably got suspended. Can't say that I'm grieving. Joey's got a black eye from their scuffle. I'm touched he stood up for me. Troubled though, as I didn't ask for it in the first place and I don't want to owe anybody.

Torv is looking cheeky per usual and hotter than ever. Ben Gilsen remains indifferent to everyone, except Zandra who he's clearly ogling. Karie, Leta and I exchange knowing grins.

Several kids wear halobands. They circle around each other and chatter with enthusiasm about the gadget. Trish and Zandra are wearing them. So is Lonny.

As soon as Nelly materializes though, everyone goes silent and the halobands come off. Some stash their headgear away, looking all innocent. Nelly has that effect.

Peters seems almost distracted as he stands before us, searching our faces with his laser stick clenched in hand. Maybe at the absence of Vin?

His eagle eyes fall upon me. "Ellan, I hope you've got something to present. You're up."

I nod, though hesitation has me biting my lip. I make my way to the front while readying my wristlet. I heave a deep sigh. Forty-some faces are looking at me. I'm not used to the attention and can feel my pale cheeks burn and the butterflies flit in my stomach. *So now it's show time. What are you going to say? The light or the heavy? Screw it. The heavy.*

Peters tosses his baton from hand to hand. "What's it on? Think I asked you this before."

I hold my head high. "An examination of the social and physical impact of historic events."

Peters pauses, his face curling in a frown. "A provocative topic, if not rather odd. But your choice. Carry on."

I begin in a quiet voice, emotionless, hypnotic to my ear. "Facts of the Past. I'd like to highlight some alarming truths and put them in context to what we've been learned at school. We can dispute them, or we can wonder if they are true and even get enraged by them. We study history, but we're told that there has only been a 'Cataclysm', with no further details or evidence outside of vague myths of public record. I did some digging."

Peters's starting to get edgy already. I can tell by his pursed lips and glinting eyes. "Very well, Ellan. What did you find?"

"A boatload." I take a forced breath. "A few decades ago, savage bush fires raged in Australia and burnt a billion animals: koalas, kangaroos, dingoes, and countless other forms of natural wildlife. I've brought pics." I sync my wristlet to the overhead projector. Scenes of burning forest thirty feet high flash across the screen. Fleeing animals and vehicles pan the periphery. All eyes turn to the licking flames.

"There were two known species pushed to extinction." The kids' eyes moon at the tragic unfolding scene. I hear whimpers from some of the girls. "Shocking, I know. Meanwhile world leaders, including those of the Australian government, turned a strangely cool eye while tucked in on their Xmas vacations abroad."

An outcry rises from class members. Yalee, the resident dreadlocker, half afro-American and Nordic, hops out of his seat at the back and raises a fist.

"Calm yourself," says Peters.

I flick to the next clip. "Extreme cold snaps in the northern states and Canada—floods worldwide, record high temperatures elsewhere, destructive migrations in Venezuela, crop failure. All signs of extreme climate change and global warming shucked under the carpet by governments and corporations. The funny thing is, I noticed all this was suppressed from regular Starcom web searches. Invisible. Yet only one who is clever and knows where to look has access to the feeds. You can see the footage yourself. Why aren't these facts readily available?"

"Where did you get this data?" Peters snaps.

Determined to continue, I ignore his furious gaze and show graphic images of a pandemic that wiped out millions, the makeshift morgues with stacks of numbered coffins awaiting cremations. Then I flip to the GMO seeds that proliferated and altered the flora forever. Next, I pull up a brief clip of police aggression against angry protesters opposed to 5G+.

"As you know, we run 6G+ now. I wonder what it's doing to our bodies, and why our clinics, owned and operated by corporations, are so full of ailing patients, many terminal. Already one in three women can't conceive and the sterility stat is higher for men. But again, that information is not publicly available."

There are sharp whispers from the back and shocked exclamations. Even Torv and Joey have stopped horsing around and are listening. Others, too, sit quietly attentive, some bristle with confusion.

"My grandma's dying of thyroid cancer!" one girl yells. "In a Starcom clinic."

"And my teenage cousin is crippled with rheumatoid arthritis at Agra's," seconds another. "My aunt's goddaughter has already been told she'd never have a baby."

More heartfelt claims echo throughout the classroom.

Peters grows distraught, flushed to the ears. He holds up a hand. "Settle down. People, as they age, get sick. Viruses and diseases get stronger. The gene pool changes. We can't blame natural selection and survival of the fittest on governments and Starcom, especially without scientific proof."

"So what are these videos then? Casual entertainment?" someone yells.

"Yeah!" cries another.

There are more grumbles and murmurs. As I flip to the next clip of a sweeping view inside a forced labor camp, Peters surges forward and manually kills the projector. "Enough! What are your sources, Ellan?"

My lips curl at the corners but it's anything but a smirk. "There are sites out there, Mr. Peters, if you know where to look."

"Where?"

Zandra pipes up, "Darkweb."

My cheeks flush with anger. There are exhalations of shock from the class.

Karie shares the same look of consternation I felt while sneaking peeks at death and destruction in the wee hours of the night. Mom'd be pissed if she ever knew I was exploring darkweb sites.

A shadow falls over Peters' face. "Browsing darkweb's illegal, young lady, if you don't know it already. Forbidden. Against the law."

Somehow, my mother's mood of confidence from the night before's Haloband rollout has infected me. "I could be just exaggerating or reporting fake data. Are you going to report me?"

It was a stupid thing to say, but I had dug myself into this corner. So how to *undig* myself?

Nervous giggles trickle from the students. A cherry red blush mottles Peters' features.

Nelly the hologram breaks her silence as she sweeps over. "A level two infraction. Recording."

The muscles in my shoulders knot. "As I said, maybe I'm just making it up, Nelly."

"Recorded."

Peters blows out his cheeks and clicks a button on his laser baton. Nelly's figure shimmers out. Many students gape in astonishment. It is the first time we've seen him do that.

"You'll thank me for that, Miss Weis," Peters says in his reedy, lecture-hall voice.

I nod. Incomplete evidence is inadmissible in court.

At least I was smart enough to raise doubts about where I got the data. They'd have to search the whole web to prove I wasn't lying. And then, would they want to admit the truth in public?

Peters is still trying to shut me down and control the class that is descending further into chaos. Half are talking over each other and rising from their seats. Torv's up and shadow-boxing Cody. Zandra's got fists planted smugly on hips. She looks over my way with a satisfied leer, aware I'm in big trouble. But I remember Ignatia Frehan's heroic death and I'm overcome with a fierce wave of passion. I wave my hands and yell at everyone to hush.

"Listen!" I cry. Before Peters can stop me, I push on. "Ever since a new technology came out, 5G radio towers, there were more and more cancers and dysfunction in the human body than ever. Then viruses, or what they claim were viruses, broke out. *Cupiolo* epidemics wiped out 65% of the human populations. Go figure. Oddly Africa was mostly spared where the technology was not rolled out in such damaging proportions."

Peters turns and glares. "Evidence for that is not conclusive. Nothing was proven either way. Epidemics have been around since the beginning. They take human lives without regard to race, sex or gender. Recall the Bubonic plague, the cholera and flu pandemics."

I don't like Peters' cold defensiveness. Almost suggests collusion, or denial, if you ask me. I wonder how much he really knows. He strikes me as an intelligent man, the kind who would probe and dig if he had the inclination, but who is not ready to ask questions. Right now he's not looking like a man prepared to lose his job over a student's wild conspiracy theory.

His face resumes that reddish, fleshy look, as the kids seem to favor my arguments over his. He clears his throat, as if it's his duty to uphold the establishment. "Worse things have happened to those endorsing such wild sentiments," he mutters.

Pulling at his chin, he recovers his composure. "Thank you for your intriguing contribution, Ellan. You may return to your seat." He casts me a withering gaze.

"Everyone, quiet down!" He raps his baton on the desk. "Clare, you're up next."

Peters seems eager to keep things moving and attention off the forbidden data I've laid bare. He's combing his fingers through the ruffs of wheat-colored hair over his ears, though whatever small control or distraction he's won is scant.

Clare's flushed face and bird-like movements are testament to the pressure she's feeling trying to compete with the sensationalism I've created. She starts in uncertainly, smoothing her slender fingers on her white dress. Nobody's listening and at last after ten minutes of a boring treatise on 'The Pros and Cons of Alternative Diets', she sits down in a huff. My brain only half registers her spiel about mineral salts and enzymes, iron in reconstituted beef, the benefits of freeze-dried celery and protein in GMO soy.

Four more students go after me. Everyone called up speaks in nervous voices, no one relishes public speaking. Peters' chronic habit of interrupting only adds to their distress. Kids are giving me funny looks. Even the girls who don't normally like me, like Bess and Kyla—they're giving me decent space, flashing me sideways glances, as if I'm now a person in a different category, maybe less of a persona non grata. I can almost catch a whiff of their confusion over the smell of their heady perfume.

I spend the last hour of class fearful that the vice principal will bust in and escort me away, but nothing of note occurs.

The period's over and the bell rings before we know it. My palms are still sweating from the adrenalin rush of the presentation.

I sigh in relief. Fifty minutes respite. I wander down the fluorescent halls in a semi-daze to drop my stuff in my locker. My brain barely registers the naked chests of hot, muscle-bound guys I have taped on the walls. The buzz of voices and activity in the halls don't penetrate my awareness. Karie's excited voice intrudes on my reverie as I look up on the way to the cafeteria.

"Wow, those were some choice vids, girl! Some butt on you, to mess up old Peters like that."

I'm quick to shrug it off, feeling now that I've created a slew of new problems for myself. I may have to deny everything I said. A rebellious part of me doesn't want to, though.

I feel a presence at my back and I turn sharply. Torv. He seems to have made a point of sidling up to us with a few lanky strides.

"Those words you said, and the clips—they were good." His voice is sincere, complimentary. His lips part and tongue dips to trace a curve on his lower lip. A look of admiration, also challenge.

I move a step faster, tugging at Karie's arm. She just grins and gives me a wink, as if I've found a new admirer. Still, I feel uncomfortable under Torv's gaze, something akin to a mouse being eyed by a stealthy tomcat. At least he's not eyeing me as lasciviously as before.

We pass by the school bulletin board. No new signups for my 'duct cleaning' petition. I frown. Maybe it's too plain. People have posted their fluff over its edges. I adjust a few words with my pen and pin it up higher, then straighten the curled edges of the greyed paper.

Karie shakes her head. "I don't know why you bother with such causes, Ellan."

"Life is what you make of it, Karie." I brush her a grave look.

"I hate maxims but I'll give you a point for that."

I snatch a fresh card in the box and start writing a new sign. "*VOICE OF THE PAST. Discussion group. Are you curious about what happened before you were born? Thursdays, 4:30. Meet in room 10B off the indoor gym.*"

"Nothing ventured, nothing gained," I murmur. It'll probably get shut down by Ms. Hent but in the meantime, I might get some curious people interested in our *secret* past. "Karie, I know you'll at least come."

"Don't hold your breath." She turns with a wry grunt. "I'm not as brave as you are."

Karie and I are heading back toward the caf and the crowded hall of our lockers. On a sudden hunch, I look over my shoulder. One of the admin staff is reaching over to tear my paper off the wall. A cold chill surfaces on the nape of my neck.

I hustle Karie along.

No worries, Ellan, just repost the damn thing tomorrow.

Chapter 6

It's the middle of the day and we're in math class, the worst. I feel like school is closing in on me and it's all about math, especially this weird one called calculus. Something with the limit as F at x goes to zero. There're a thousand other things I'd rather be doing, like getting my eyebrows plucked. I'm more about geography, plants, nature and history, which are sadly lacking in our curriculum—things the teachers hedge around or downplay. Instead, they offer us vague stories about civil wars that don't seem to add up after the things I saw on darkweb. Hopefully my classmates'll be thinking twice about the lies they feed us of the past.

Gilsen is reaching for his Haloband with the gold strap and white goggles. So is Trish, and hers are actually draped over her eyes, making her look like a Martian, but Mr. Singleton reams them out for using them in class. "Get those off, you two. Now!"

I smile a pretty smile. Soon there'll be a rule we have to check our halobands at the door before heading into class.

More messages appear on my wristlet. One from Leta catches my attention. *'Chilling stuff. You raised quite a stir. Ready for the popularity boost?'*

I message back, *'No, not in a million years.'*

People are still giving me the wary eye. But I'm saved by an unexpected diversion. From the hall comes a piercing echo. An emergency alarm. Not seconds later, three figures in bubble helmets and protective suits barge in through the heavy door. My heart skips a beat, thinking they are coming for me.

No. Just a surprise drill. The principal's voice crackles over the mainspeaker. *"Do not panic. This is only a drill, repeat, a drill. Follow what the technicians have to say."* I exhale relief. Only exercises of what to do during an outbreak, or what to do in case of a violent storm, tornado or flash flood. There've only been two real cases that I remember. Both were contained, thanks to the UHO (United Health Organization). Relief technicians in space suits had administered spray, vaccinations, hauled off the sickest kids, the ones coughing, some hacking up blood. We'd all been sent home, told to stay indoors and to return in two weeks. A thousand people had died in the city, including Tommie, one of my closest friends. It crippled me. I have a slew of recurring and painful memories about that.

A stinging wetness floods my eyes. I remember his laugh, his brown eyes, his innocent way of speaking and looking up at me without pretense. Saying something profound, even funny, without trying to be.

The drill eats up an hour of math which doesn't bother me in the least.

All the while I'm assaulted with a peculiar feeling, as if I'm floating on air. I should be crapping out for stirring up a hornet's nest and exposing a sliver of darkweb, but I'm not. I almost feel exhilarated by speaking some truth that others have not heard, or been too scared to talk about for so long. Strange, long-buried memories pop in my head: as a child, calling out relatives at the dinner table when they said stuff that didn't add up. Dates, places, people's names. Seeing the shocked looks, awkward pauses and nervous laughs. It's uncanny, and yet, all so weirdly synchronistic at the same time. The masked rebel in me grins. Maybe I murmur a word or two. Kids around me mutter and give me brow-furled looks, as if I'm talking to myself. Which I kind of am.

As a child I was always making up stories of good versus evil, in my head mostly, and sometimes sketching out images, weird stuff, like a talking tree or a magic dog. My talking tree could give advice to people, tell their fortunes. My mom was delighted by it. She pinned my crayon drawings, like the one with the green tree and the giant brown dog, on the fridge with magnets. She would ask me questions about them. *What does Rusty have to say? How did the tree guide the little girl out of the forest?*

No lie that presentation has stirred up something within me. Philosophers use words like purpose and destiny, but how is it that I get an almost boiling feeling in my gut when I recall those pics of Ignatia being scorched? Why do I feel such a breathless glow when I'm stirring up the pot, calling people on their lies and misdirection? Maybe I was always cut out to be a truthdigger like Ignatia.

Dream on, Ellan. When I realize how silly that sounds, I shake my head in disgust and huff out a breath. People around me turn again. They think I'm losing it. Perhaps I am. Yet I can't deny that this recurring sense of déjà vu still strikes deep chords somewhere in an old part of myself.

My brows crease in a frown as my mind grows reflective. Today is much too serious a day.

The principal seems to agree as she calls me down to the detention center in between classes. Ms. Hent's middle-aged monkey face is caked with too much makeup, like a cadaver at a morgue, as she sits before me at the head desk. My heart quickens and I start to think that Peters didn't shut down Nelly fast enough.

"Ellan Weis." She beckons me with a finger. Her curled lip and tone of voice says it all. "First request is to delete all the offending material from your wristlet."

I shrug. "Sure. But what about it is offensive?"

She clears her throat. "Obvious, isn't it? The past is just that, the past. No one knows what actually happened in the cataclysmic years. That video footage, I don't know where you got it, but it's fake. A lot of images circulated around the time of the Cataclysm. C-Sec warned us to be on the lookout for any misleading material passed around the school. We don't need old hates and civil strife broadcast—material twisted by anarchist media sources—to confuse and undermine the state."

"You mean perpetuate lies by giving us a void instead. Pretend it never happened?"

Her eyes flash and she slaps her hand on the table. "Watch it, Miss Weis. You do yourself no service to criticize us and tell us what we should or should not do. There are school rules. You'll have to follow them or get out. You're lucky I don't report you to C-Sec headquarters myself. But I see too much potential in you. So do Mr. Peters and Mrs. Sandford. You're an A student and both teachers have put in a good word for you. They say you have a sharp mind and the tenacity to 'dig'. A rare quality in students."

I nod. That makes sense. However there's no use arguing with these people. They can't see the importance of knowing the truth above all. What good are straight A's and a sharp mind if you don't have any truthful ground to stand on? I'm ready to tell her but I nix the idea. I was wasting my time here. "Can I go now?"

"Yes, see that it doesn't happen again." She levels me a crisp stare. Yet I can see the outward relief masking the anxiety under her skin. In the shaky way she smooths out her papers and wipes the sweat from her forehead.

I'd riled her. Just like Peters and the kids in my class.

I feel an inner smirk coming on. Maybe that was my calling. To stir the pot, wake the dozy passengers up from their dream. I shake my head, realizing my conundrum. I'll never stop delving in the darkweb. Even if it burned my fingers. It was a vehicle to the truth. I knew it! I was too much about the truth.

A hot thrill brews in my chest, and yet a horrible fear at the same time. It was like standing on the edge of a cliff, looking down upon the rocks poking above the foam in a roiling sea. It was one thing to dream about being a truthsayer like Ignatia, quite another being one.

* * *

Mom messages me and says she'll pick me up after school. I tell her not to bother as I need some time for jogging and my kickboxing class's been moved up.

Her forwarded message is curt. She hates the sport. Thinks I'm going to get seriously injured one day. There's no real answer to that, outside of, 'well, life's full of risks'. Yes, it could happen, but I'm developing skills that could save my life.

I see Joey trying to corral me at the front steps. Damn. Probably to offer me a ride to practice tonight. But I need some time to myself and some air, so I pretend not to see him.

Callous, maybe, but sometimes one needs to look out for #1.

I take the tram to Wellington station and get out. The air always seems fresher here. Few people live this far east. Only some low rise tenements with big aerials on top, a public square and a few shops. The dipping sun struggles between hazy banks of cloud while a thin line of yellowish-grey hangs on the skyline. Old veils of pollution that hark back to times before the Cataclysm. The tops of trees yellowed and scorched brown by solar radiation and a thinning ozone layer.

I put on my headband, roll up my jeans to the knees and start eating up the pavement in long, leggy strides. I take the long way home, via Tydon Park, a maze of wooded pathways and long tracts of greenery—well *yellowery*, considering the heat wave and the drooping leaves of the reconstituted oaks. I pass a small pool where a school of three orange koi huddle in the murky water. These ones have enlarged gills, as if to compensate for the lack of oxygen in the acidity of the pool. They look like lubberly submarines. I pluck off some cedar buds from the nearest low-lying branch and toss them in. The fish are grateful at first, as they come over to investigate, but ignore the offering. Two flick their tails ever so perceptibly.

I adjust my sweaty headband. This spring is hotter than ever. Stifling.

Already we'd had our usual battery of storms, heavy winds and rain. The late afternoon sun beats down on my head like an angry god.

I pick up the pace and my legs burn for oxygen. My double-soled, white *Roxy* runners are getting into a rhythm, as I feel the tension ease out of my joints. The park relaxes my jangled nerves. No one really knows how the trees grew five-foot diameters. We'd just accepted their breadth as normal. But those darkweb headlines give me more clues…make me start to think that maybe it was true that secret gene research experiments had gone awry. That cross pollination had set off a series of mutations across the nation. The truth has gotten hushed up somehow. Or lost through time, probably the former.

Crazy! Look at these trees. I always stare in wonder at the transplanted GMO-seeded birches and pine I pass. Some trees are over a hundred and fifty feet high. At their bases are massive trunks, giant ferns and shrubs that grow as tall as signposts in one season only to get drowned in floods or uprooted in high winds. Nothing seems to escape persecution by the weird weather patterns of the day. Times where it can snow in the middle of summer or spike to sixty degrees in the middle of winter.

I'm cruising full on. This strenuous workout is perfect conditioning for my upcoming kickboxing session. New sweat pours off my skin.

Passersby think I'm crazy when they see me shadow boxing one of the big trees. But screw them. I'm the one who has to keep my body fit and immune system strong to survive in this noxious world, not to mention repel attackers should they leap out at me.

I make it as far as the periphery. Tydon's a vast, welcome sanctuary. I visualize the sprawling map we have pasted on our kitchen wall. To the east, the forest continues for a few hundred acres. I take the western route, past a small field of experimental wheat with long, spiky shoots. They shiver in the wind, engineered to be resistant to the storms and climate fluctuations.

I go the full stretch, take the Haberdack Loop back to the trailhead and break out of the trees. It's a straight haul down Forrester's Ave where I make it back home an hour later. I'm sweaty and feeling energized from my brisk jaunt, ready to jump into the shower.

C. TURNER, L. LASERRE

Chapter 7

Dad's home in his study, a gloomy scowl on his face and drink in his hand as he scans his reports. Mom's out. I bypass the family room, padding quietly over the carpet to hit the kitchen where I slap some leftover pizza in the toaster oven. Wincing at the shrill ring of the timer, I head upstairs to my room, triple cheese slice in hand with a tall glass of lemonade in the other. Bram is still geeking out in his room. His door's slightly ajar and through the gap I see him wearing one of those crazy HBs. His head's nodding and he's making small cooing noises. I smile and shake my head. Geek. There's a different flavor of geekdom every day. This pair has a different color, bright red, so I'm guessing the Starcom managers must have given him a special set from work.

A quick shower and change of clothes—cut-off jean shorts and light, hooded sweatshirt. I'm wolfing my food at my desk. My cluttered room is well-equipped with pinups of hunks and some goofy old teddy bears on the bed. I trip over one fallen to the floor as I'm on my way out. Gotta split in case Mom gets home early.

Mission accomplished. I scoot past a bakery and two hair salons. Past the mini mall, though there's an area where the old brick buildings are crumbling and deserted with broken windows where squirrels nest and the few birds native to the city can fly in and out. Gives me the creeps, this neighborhood, as if old memories and ghosts still linger here. I wonder if this shadowy neighborhood holds secrets like those chained in the darkweb. It's almost as if I can feel the lost souls here, the ones who died in pandemics, revolutions or uprisings, or EMF or GMO poisoning. Another shiver. Sometimes I think I might be psychic—then other times I think I'm just full of B.S. or have too vivid an imagination.

As I pass the old United Church off Brundles, and the Order of St. Bartholomew's Tabernacle, a new age Christian sect, I gaze at the powerful 6G+ antennae that spike our beleaguered city like porcupine quills. If what the darkweb says is true, I cannot fathom the absolute madness that keeps them standing there so proud and tall in our insular community. Especially while everyone goes about his business, as if blissfully unaware of their capacity for affecting our immune systems.

I imagine the transmitters' invisible electro-magnetic rays and what havoc they must be doing to our cells over time. I am young, and haven't felt the full effects. At least not yet. But what of the elderly sequestered in clinics, dying of chronic illnesses? And my parents who are older, and burdened with chronic fatigue, have trouble sleeping and drink away their troubles every night? Even they know something is wrong but have not tapped into the information I have, except my mom recently.

It's a twenty minute jog from our place to the kickboxing club off Adelain. A light rain patters down, leaving an acid stench over the city. Gusts of vagrant wind tuft the draggled hair tucked under my headband. It is good there is wind. It blows some of the toxins away, but more often than not, blows them right back the next day. If I dare to stay out too long under the trickling drizzle, a redness will appear under my skin, even blisters, and I'll itch all night. So for that reason, I hope the weather doesn't turn ugly. My feet follow my brain's command. I keep a slow and steady stride after the earlier workout, then pick up the pace. It's good prep for the grueling ordeal to come.

People ask me why I kickbox. Well, aside from there being a certain art to the moves, there's the thrill of the fight and the feeling of power and victory. Violent, yes, bruises and sprains and sometimes worse, but it gets the lead out of my body. Brings out the bottled emotions, pent up frustrations…There's also a degree of satisfaction. If I am honest, I can take my angst out on a punching bag—or a sparring partner—if I was having boy trouble, or parent/teacher trouble.

The added bonus, I can defend myself in case someone tries to rob me or a guy tries to get too frisky with his hands. I don't like being touched without my permission. And then there's anger management. What am I angry about? Everything. School. Hormones. Benny Gilsen, the cutie he is, doesn't even look at me. What is it with guys these days? A good-looking girl gives them all the hints and they just blink and stare in a vacuous daze. Not like I haven't given him any hints.

Plus something isn't right at home. Mom and Dad aren't seeing eye to eye. Something's eating at them, ever since that Lois thing. I'll see Mom look at Dad, as if it's daggers she's hurling. And not because it's that time of month. I know she doesn't get angry for no reason. My mom isn't that type of person.

The club's a single cinderblock one-story unit. We've a 19' x 19' ring raised three feet above the ground. To the side, padded walls and mats stretch under four punching bags for students to work out on. Long rectangular windows at the top let in light. Today only a grey light. I hear the beginnings of another brisk rain pattering on the tiled roof even as I walk in.

There's already the bustle of training going on. Grunts, jabs, hooks, knees to thigh, feet squeeching on the mats. A healthy dose of locker room smell of sweat and aggressive energy to go.

A couple of guys going fast with jab, cross, hook, uppercut and roundhouse combos. Another crushing it against the wall. Two girls with toned abs doing high kicks with medicine balls. Conn, another motivated trainee, getting in tight, right cross punches and left hooks to Max's arm pads while Illie does his basic hop with cross swing on the jump ropes.

I lift two fingers in greeting to other members of the club: Rack, Hue, Joey, Jenie and Fret. Nods and waves. I'm late as usual. There're twelve of us here today, though there're about eighteen of us registered. It's a coed club where we spar with each other as equals, since the tournaments are always mixed.

Angelos, our trainer, is there by the ring watching everybody's progress. He's a stickler for discipline and a taskmaster, a man whose wiry 5' 8" frame belies his impressive strength. He was some champion in his day. In Levenbrook at least. He must be forty now. An old man, by fighters' standards, but still a skilled trainer. He can move like a lynx and come at you like a bull from all angles, land three jabs on the sides of your head before you can blink. His cool eyes fix on you, like a big cat. But deep down, there's gentleness. A straight shooter. Always know exactly where you stand with him, whether your technique sucks or whether the training and your self-discipline are actually getting you somewhere. That's why I like and trust the guy. Otherwise I'd be hoofing it out of here, because this club is pretty hardcore. I've had my share of criticism from the man, as well as words of encouragement. He gets us to spar with one another while he watches and dissects, picks apart our weaknesses, praises our progress and strengths. Sometimes he jumps into the ring to demonstrate what he preaches. When he does, it's always an educational experience.

"Joey, you up for some bag practice?" I level him a challenging look.

Joey nods and holds one of the unused bags while I put on gloves, a nice bright red pair, and start punching the bejesus out of the bag, getting the odd switch kick in. Before long my lightly-tanned skin is shining with sweat and my breath ragged.

I motion to Joey. "Your turn." He grins and opens up into the bag. I hold it tight. He's got a strong punch and a half decent roundhouse. I can feel myself pushed back by his staccato blows, even as I dig in both feet. Cross-eyed Huey's sparring with Jenie, a stocky blonde, right next to us on the mats while Rack's got arm guards on and drilling with Fret.

After waiting my turn, I hear my name called. This time it's Jenie up with me. She's built solidly, got short, bleached spiky hair, square-shoulders, narrow hips, a somewhat mannish composure, though she's anything but. All the guys are eyeing her. We trade grins, insert our mouthguards and don leather-padded headgear—mine deep brown and hers white—then duck under the ropes.

I warm up with an exaggerated show of shadow box jab and high roundhouse kick, landing in my shuffler's stance. Just for show, but hey, it feels good and gets us both chuckling. I put my fists up in front of my face and I'm bouncing on the balls of my feet, moving in a wide circle around her. By all means, she is no meek opponent. If her powerful right connects, look out. She's got a year on me, maybe twenty five pounds and enough strength to crush me. But what I lack in power, I make up for in speed. I keep my feet moving, doing my rocker shuffle. She echoes my moves. She stays far enough way for me not to make an easy attack. I convince myself I have a good chance to feint her out and avoid her hardest blows. Anticipation. That's the key to winning or losing a match. Many times I've had stars twinkle in my head before I start to waver and feel myself tumbling even after a few glancing hits—at least before the ref calls the round.

Left, left, right. My left leg back-roundhouses out at Jenie's thick right thigh.

She grunts, takes it well. Then counters with a left leg snap and I move in to block her right fist coming at my cheek. I duck, lifting my elbow to block. She anticipates. Catches my next move but gets knocked back to the ropes on my follow up, a sneaky left. Her grey eyes pinch into a grin. Angelos jumps into the ring and pushes us apart.

"You ladies are just toying with each other. Like a bunch of playful pups. Ellan, you've got to do better than that. Move faster."

"I'm already moving faster!" I protest.

He ignores me. "Jenie, you should have tried out for tiny tots. You keep going left instead of right. That last kick was pathetic. Hollow, like a kettle drum. Boom, boom. You're not feinting enough. Quicker punches, less time trying to figure out a next move. Kickboxing's not pretty. Move in with all your weight. Like this—" he does a quick left jab that turns into a right combo that has me staggering back before I can block his second hit. "See?"

I let out a rattling breath. "Hey, what's the idea of using me as a punching bag? Wasn't ready."

"That's the point. No one's ever 'ready' in a real fight. More quick jabs. Less overthinking. Move in as if you've got it all figured out, without hesitation, with confidence. Don't wait for the other guy to get settled. You lose that way. And forget the fancy feet. You're moving like you're on a dance floor. This is not a rave. You should have been making fist combos."

Jenie nods. I growl out a sardonic laugh.

"Try again!"

So we go at it again while Angelos steps away to inspect another pairing on the sparring mats.

Okay, good. I feel better when he's not hovering.

While Jenie circles, I keep her back with my strong right leg. She ducks a high hook kick, my heel passing a half inch from her chin guard. While she's recovering, I catch a movement out of the corner of my eye. Fret's holding the bag while Rack launches in with a vicious eight combo, all his weight into the bag. I like the shape of his rounded shoulders and gleaming biceps. He's got a sheen of sweat on his slightly oiled skin. Joey's not bad either, but I think Rack's got him beat.

As my mind wanders, Jenie smacks me hard in the ribs. A tingling now in my left side. A warm throb in the upper right thigh as she lands a follow-up switch kick.

I'm thinking how some of the guys go easier on the girls, not just because it's more chivalrous but not wanting to look like bullies either. Angelos always says this is wrong. He claims it's a suicide mission to underestimate any opponent, whether based on weight, age or sex. So the guys learn not to take kid gloves to me. Jenie's sure not.

Angelos returns with a look of exasperation on his face. He pulls me out of the ring and pits Jenie against Rack. They do a mock round. Rack's fresh and pumped. He scores five points on her two in the space of a few minutes.

Angelos puts me back in the ring, with Rack. This surprises me. There's some grumbling from the sidelines. I've had my turn and there're eight others waiting to go. Angelos just does this rippling thing with his shoulders, like a mock defiant shrug. He does stuff like that. Riles up people's emotions. Incites animosities and petty jealousies among us, then when the moment's ripe, he pounces, puts us in the ring and works one against the other while we're at our worst, steaming mad. His way of putting the 'screws' to us. *"You're only as good as your weakest mental moment. Once your opponent figures out how to unnerve you, you've lost."*

I'm already off balance, with my mind wandering all over the place. Rack, of course, is picking up on this and is already sticking it to me. Hard.

My muscles strain. I do a tinkerbell dance, doing more blocking than hitting. No good with a guy as capable as Rack, with all that muscle and speed. He's a slugger and I'm an outboxer, staying out of harm's way. No contest, he's more than my match. But I hate to give in. I hate Rack knowing that he's always going to win, so I dig in my heels and grit my teeth. I want to prove him wrong, give him a clear signal that tables can be turned. I duck under a swing, one thrown too casually, lean in and punish his ribs. He's pushed back to the ropes. Rather than beat me back with fist and knees, he does a cocky little walk around the ring in arrogant Rack fashion, holding up a gloved hand as if to say, It's alright, folks, nothing to see here. Maybe just giving me a chance to catch my second wind. Whatever.

Angelos pretends not to notice. He's watching everything from the side like he's trained us to do, even while reaming Fret for being such a gorilla against the bag and not practicing his footwork. "Any idiot can punch a bag to death. Can you dodge nine out of ten hits?" I'm momentarily distracted. While Fret's not looking, Angelos lets one loose, and Fret's head snaps back. Fret licks his lip. He's ready to tell him to f-off and smack back but thinks twice about it. That makes me smile. But the smile is wiped off my face when Rack's big blue glove connects with my jaw. I catch the glint in Rack's green eyes before I stumble back, ears ringing, barely able to scoot away from a crippling kick and stagger to the other side of the ring.

Angelos is now shaking his head as he sees my awkward recovery—or blunder. But I'm able to hold my own. I get one good switch kick in Rack's left side just above the kidney and a left hook to his shoulder, but he's still advancing, making me run around the ring to keep away from his strong right leg. My breath's catching in my throat. I can smell my own sweat, and Rack's, which is more pungent, a sweet-sour mix. We trade some fists and stupid words, me trying to goad him into a mistake, but he's not biting. More amused than anything, he stays away from my taps and jabs, using my own tactics against me. Anger pushes its way past my patience.

My inner coach tolls in my head. *Keep that healthy distance, Ellan. You're an outboxer, not a swarmer! Wait your chance, especially with the heavier hitters like Rack. You do less well with sluggers or swarmers. They hit hard and knock you off balance, particularly the swarmers who get an early advantage by coming in fast and hard, psyching you out and punishing you hard against the ropes.*

I make some more dumb mistakes, even though my mind is screaming at me to settle down. Why can't I just let him poke around a bit and think he's winning, then when he's off guard, sucker him into an awkward position and clock him in the head? Kinda hard when I'm this agitated and while everyone's watching. I'm feeling the pressure, more self-conscious than ever. The heat rises up my spine. I land another good right to his chest but he counters with a hook kick to my right thigh. And that hook has me reeling back.

Angelos throws up his hands. "Okay, enough. Another clown match. You managed to recover well, Ellan. I'll give you that. But you got distracted by whatever meathead stuff is cycling through your brain. It's your worst enemy. Wandering mind—I can see it a mile away, from the way your eyes move. Also some negative beliefs. You think you can't win against Rack because he's bigger, faster, has more muscles and experience. Wrong thinking. It will bury you."

Rack just smiles.

"Wipe that grin off your face, Rack. You're just as bad as she is. You think you can toy with her and she has no advantage over you. Think again. You're one of these big lazy, puffed up domestic cats that ends up getting trashed in the back alley by the sneaky tomcat. You're going to lose big time one of these days."

That prediction has Rack's brow furrowing and a sliver of a tongue tracing an uneasy line on his upper lip. The quiet laughter from the guys around the punching bag doesn't help. Angelos gusts out a weary breath. "You need to feel bad so you'll think harder. Listen, you're both good fighters and I'm proud of you." He gives us each a fatherly thump on the back and smiles. "You two are going to spar again next week, and I'd like to see some more kazoo from both of you."

"Sure, Angelos." Rack turns with a wry grin.

We both bunt gloves and duck under the wire.

"No, Rack, I want you to stay in. Ellan you're out."

I feel slightly put out at that. It's unresolved between Rack and me. This time I'm grateful for the time out, thinking maybe I should have eased up on the jogging. But my competitive half wants instant revenge on Rack. A chance to redeem myself.

I've only vaguely absorbed what Angelos has been saying. My mind's still bouncing around, over darkweb, 5G, Peters' warning, Hent's slap on the wrist, the halobands. Angelos is right, but my head's still spinning over too many things and there's a ringing in my ears.

Rack is pulled out soon enough. Angelos's words have unnerved him too. He puts Max and Conn in, old rivals from way back to pre-teen years.

Angelos yells something at Max from the side. "Not with the elbows! Keep them tucked in. This isn't some turkey shoot or duck strut. Get with the program." All the while he's half munching on a sandwich and taking a drink of carbonated water, making jokes with Fret. It looks really bad from say a new arrival's perspective, but I know it's all an act. Soft words pad a fighter's ego, Angelos says.

Max is hitting Conn hard with powerful legs and his strong right, but Conn is just taking it, tiring Max out. Everyone can see it. Even me.

"No finesse. You guys are hobos. Get out!" Angelos jerks a thumb over his shoulder and climbs in the ring. He calls over Joey who is less sloppy. "Watch us. Lose the clumsiness." He and Joey start a clean fight. Joey's light on his feet, not falling into the obvious traps. *Yet.* He's putting on his best performance, being in the center ring with the big boss, dodging Angelos's wicked right hook. Most of the time. Angelos is only going at it half power, or maybe a third. He stops the play and points out where Joey could have done better. Maybe anticipated faster. But Angelos's just as quick to yell out, "Good move, J-boy! Remember to keep your head down and feet moving and fists in front of your face at all times. Could save you from a knockout one day. Now, another round!" He and Joey amp it up and some cheers rumble from those of us watching.

I find myself entranced as the two fight. The remaining hour goes by faster than a chance rainfall as we watch and do more sparring and exercises. I'm sore, my arms and chest are aching. I'm feeling down because

I'm still distracted and not absorbing much of Angelos's lesson. Sure, my ears are hearing all his advice, but my mind's not taking it in. I'm sure I'd go back in the ring next week and just do all the same stupid things over again.

I don't hang around the club long, not keen on many of the guys trying to hit on me. I'm not really into them in any visceral way, except maybe Rack, he's kind of a heartthrob, but I know for sure he has a girlfriend. Still doesn't stop him from flirting with me.

Men.

Joey swaggers over in his half trot as I'm exiting the steel doors. He's dragging a towel over his glistening shoulders. "Nice moves, Ellan. Some good hits back there. Need a lift back?"

I look over at his beat up car, a dirty brown *Bel-aire* hand-me-down from his father who runs an auto-body shop. Joey, one of the few kids who has his own wheels.

"No thanks, Joey. Need some air. I'll jog back."

"Doing a lot of jogging these days."

"Yeah, it's catchy. It's how I blow off steam. See you tomorrow—at school."

"Sure. Suit yourself." He walks off, slightly miffed. His back is stiff, probably nose out of joint too as all the guys are watching and I can see that it's important for him to be seen with me and to have me accept his chivalrous offer. They know I've blown him off, and that was a bit hard to take, male ego and all—but he'll have to suck it up.

C. TURNER, L. LASERRE

Chapter 8

By the time I get back home, Mom's pretty uptight. She's sitting on the family room couch, looking no less stunning in her white dress and tight-cinched belt, drink in hand, wristlet in full spread showing charts, color stats, images of haloband ad conferences. Thankfully Dad's not around. Guess this haloband stuff is ramping up from her end.

She snaps off the screen and—I'm guessing she'll be on her way to another public talk about haloband soon. She starts tapping her fingernail against the glass. Hard liquor, no doubt. Her eyes are slightly dilated, so I can guess this is not her first drink of the day.

"Mr. Peters just informed me about your outrageous presentation. Wanna talk about it?"

"No."

"Where'd you get access to that information?" Her hazel brown eyes glint with accusation.

"Mom, before you get all mad, let me ask, what do you remember about the world when you were young? Growing up, I mean. What was it like?"

She hesitates, squirms in her seat. Her cheeks flush as if such is taboo territory. "I remember my mother and father hiding me, protecting me from the roving bands. We hid out in a shelter after the riots."

"What happened to them—Gran and Grandad?" I'd asked her this before, but she'd always hedged.

She bites her lip. A different kind of glaze besets her eyes, one that alcohol had no influence over. I can see her struggling with a painful memory, as if weighing the cost of lying versus the relief of sharing what went on decades ago. It's a sensitive issue long overdue—especially now that I know more about what really went on in our forbidden past.

"They died. Victims of some epidemic—the Sion plague before vaccines were made available. We huddled in shelters. I was moved from warehouse to warehouse, raised by caring souls in the communes. Thousands of us. Those were tough times, Ellan. Little food, even less hygiene. People were lucky to have some rags for clothes and shoes on their feet."

I swallow, trying to absorb the horror of it. An empty pit forms in my stomach, at the thought of my mother, all dirty, her hair ragged, running barefoot through the cracked, mob-ridden streets, a gaunt, emaciated urchin without proper food.

"Sounds horrible."

"It was. We were all crammed into community centers by the military. Half the population worldwide had died practically overnight, so we were told. People would suddenly gaze into space then topple over. The country was in chaos, everything shut down: power, telecom, bridges and borders. Helicopters and fighter jets flew overhead. Mass panic to get supplies, fuel, weapons, food. Looting, riots, destruction. Knife-fighting in the streets."

Her eyes stare away, unfocused. She sucks in a breath, forces her delicate features to show a composed face. "I was so young, I didn't think anything about it. I thought life was just like that. By the time I was five or six, they started to rebuild things. Schools, roads, power grids, radio towers. But there were big changes."

So, she was part of it. Meaning the Cataclysm happened about thirty five years ago, if she's forty-two.

"How much do you know about Starcom?"

"What do you mean, Starcom?"

"Where did they come from? How did they start up?"

Her hand flicks to her semi-permed hair, red mouth set in a firm line.

When she doesn't answer, I make it easier for her. "Ever hear of a company called Google? What about Huawei? AT&T?"

She downs her glass. Lipstick trails on the rim. "Where'd you hear those names?"

I wet my own lips. "Same place I heard about 5G and GMOs."

"No, I haven't heard of them."

But I knew she had. She just didn't want to talk about it. *Funny, she'd talk about her bleak past, but not about her own company.* "I heard Starcom came from those dead megacorps."

Her face kindles in fascination, as if such a fairy tale hits closer to the truth. "Where Starcom comes from…Maybe," she said. "But it was a long time ago. Who's been feeding you those names?"

"Nobody, just rumors at school."

"Yeah, right." She makes a hoarse noise in her throat. "Better stay off the darkweb, Ellan. People don't like mention of the past."

I let it drop. From what little she divulged, she'd confirmed some of my darkest suspicions.

"People have gotten into big trouble dredging up old ghosts, things bigger than themselves. There's worse trouble for spreading rumors than you can imagine."

"No worries, Mom. I'll be more careful."

Her cherry-red lips chink into a frown. "Don't 'no worries' me. I'm going to change my password." She taps her wristlet.

Go ahead, Mom. I'll just get Bram to find a way around it. There are always other bits of dirty work I can get him to do for me. He can open all kinds of back doors.

* * *

I can't sleep—not that insomnia's anything new. I've had a sleep problem since I was a child. Maybe a coincidence? No, I don't think so. Karie and other friends have it, to varying degrees of severity. The clinics are full of people with problems, from migraines to attention disorders to mood swings to chronic fatigue. We've been told it's just part of growing up. But could it be because of this 6G? The debilitating aftereffects of our toxic heritage? My mind is churning. We've been duped. Misinformed. The darkweb tells us truths of a magnitude we may not be ready to hear.

There's more to my stress. Zone competition's coming up. I like kickboxing and its adrenalin rush, but real combat under lights and crowds puts me on edge.

Morning comes too early. About a quarter of Peters' class is absent. Why am I not surprised? It seems HB has caught on too fast. Everybody's got a date with their new gadget.

A slow, dull day. I'm watching the clock. Not surprised Peters's slapping me with another project, deeming my last unacceptable and stricken from the record. Sure, have it your way, Petie.

It's a Friday night, and Joey's invited me to a rave. I'm allowed to stay out late, just not too late.

I catch a fleeting glimpse in the bedroom mirror as I'm practicing my dance moves. Snapshot of a twirl, a quick hip roll, like one of those gaudy models on public net. Black blouse, black-dyed jeans, accentuating my sleek curves, boyish hips. A luxurious mat of wavy hair veils my face and hangs down past my shoulders. Joey comes early to pick me up. He's got his jet black hair oiled back and is wearing hip khakis and a bright short sleeve tie-dye. Looking not too shabby. Hot, I'd say.

We're at this party at Nord's over on Baymont. Music thudding away, kids in small groups drinking, piping, vaping, a bunch of us dancing on the monster living room floor with the wild lights flickering on and off. Nord's got a pretty good setup here. A sense of good fun too: strobe, a mini rave box, AI sensor-controlled. It tells the central unit to base its next picks on the mood of the house. How cool. Tables, chairs, all've been cleared away. His parents are gone for the weekend. I start to move to the beat like a gypsy child. "Right on, girl!" Karie slaps palms with me. We mirror each other's movements then get lost in the beat before I lose sight of her. We are all in our own element, our own head space. It's dark, kind of dusky crimson and ultramarine dark with all the dry ice and stuff floating around. I see Ben Gilsen's here, June, Leta, Darrin, Zandra, others.

Nord's novel feature has added a new dimension to the room. The floating strobe that lights up the dancers moves about the room like a psychedelic sci-fi beach ball. I weave and dance around it. A mystical globe with a mind of its own. It touches me and instantly bounces off in another direction, this time toward Karie. How the hell does it move? Magnets or something? The touch is soft as a balloon, warm as a midday sun.

The beat switches to a deep jungle rhythm. I whip back my hair, thick and damp, sweat clinging to my pores. I'm feeling alive, like a queen, liking the way the black fabric clings to my hot skin. Can make out Joey's Italian, hook-nosed features in the smoky dark, alternating green and dull crimson.

June, a hip brunette, bops over and gives me a hit of something I don't know what—sadies, seebies, bayludes? Either way, it was whack and I'm now floating on my heels, weaving amongst the crowd of others, wax idols on a pilgrimage, doing my thing, doing my own dance with my long brown hair flying out, ever conscious of my own individuality, every muscle in my body moving to a crazy beat coming from the diamond-shaped speakers at the front of Nord's sanctuary. Like we are all some collection of mutant, animated wax dolls. Crazy, Ellan...jiving in a primitive ritual from somewhere back in the mists of time.

Joey glides over to me, his dreamy grin surreal. Only under the strobing lights do I notice the beginnings of a small, tapered goatee on his chin. He looks as if he's doing fine.

"Sexy and supple as ever." His wide, glassy eyes scan me with no small admiration. "I think you were born to be on a dance floor."

"You no less, Joey. Hey, this music of Nord's is way over. Trippy light too."

"Whack for sure. Wanna dance?"

I shrug. He nods and we start weaving in and out to fast tempo-beats in a psytrance-dance.

There's banging at the door, some hints of swearing and shouts. Two figures push through the far edge of the dancers, leather jackets down to their thighs. Torv? And that dropout Vin?

What the hell are they doing here?

Torv fakes a grin and moves in on the floor as if he's the MC, nodding and checking out the scene. His voice carries over the crowd. "Well, well, Nordie. Looks as if we have a whack party here. Thanks for inviting us." He grabs a drink from a kid near the DJ stand and tosses it back in a single gulp, hands it back to him. Vin follows his lead, upending another kid's drink. He grabs another glass for Torv and shoves it into his hand.

"Hey, no one invited you," rasps Nord.

"Say, that's why we're here, Nordie, so you can correct the problem, sound good? Gives you a second chance to redeem yourself. Know it's rude not to invite your fellow classmates?"

"Beat it, Torv," Darrin sneers. "You're not welcome here."

"Think I'll stay awhile, Dare-boy. He saunters over, grabs a pipe from one of Zandra's friends and starts smoking it.

There's a tense moment. Everybody's waiting, to see who stands up to him.

Even Zandra leans in with an interested look on her face. She's got one hand on a well-padded hip, a leer of anticipation as if secretly relishing a fistfight.

No one's up to pop Torv and his bully friend. Joey's balling his fists though. Ben Gilsen's as quiet as a mouse, and me, well, I'm just still in a dance trance from the jungle music, the heady dry ice and the bayludes.

Gilsen's friend, Xavier, a good couple inches taller and with more bravado than bulk, steps up to block Torv's path. Vin drives a fist his way. Xavier's ready and blocks the blow with his right elbow but Vin clubs him in the side of the head. Xavier goes down and Darrin edges in to take on Vin but Torv chucks a drink into his eyes and knees him in the gut. A muffled cry gurgles from Darrin's throat, as he lies doubled over now. Vin, with a chimp's grin, steps over to take the boots to him while Torv rounds on Gilsen.

In three quick strides I'm there, I don't know why, maybe it's because of Gilsen. I coil to strike, the instinctual reflex of years of training. The bony edge of my right foot thunks hard into Vin's ribs, smashing him to the ground.

Vin's up on his feet, hissing fury. Man, he's super-pissed, spitting through his teeth. "Stupid bitch. Like to play dirty?"

Torv is standing back, laughing. "Vin, you're such a pussy. Can't admit she hit you fair and square?"

Vin's making some animal grunts, fingers clenching into claws.

I raise my fists, assume my fighter stance. All of the daze is zapped out of my head. Fight does that to me. I pivot on the balls of my feet, protecting my ribs as Vin rages in for a fast punch, a swipe, anything to knock me down as I did him. Even high, I know he's no match for me. I'm already leaning, twisting my upper body, looking over my shoulder and let loose a savage spinning hook kick. It's dark and the strobe is disorienting me. But my heel catches him wide on the shoulder just shy of his chin and he's staggering back, stumbling into Torv.

"Go home, dropout," Karie yells.

"Yeah, loser." Leta thumbs her nose.

Vin lashes out a fist, a blow aimed for my teeth but which I catch on my left forearm. I drop into a half crouch to roundhouse him high in the ear. He staggers back, dazed as my heel lands safely on the floor.

"Come on, Vin, lighten up. Pick fights you're going to win." Torv pulls him back.

Vin whirls around with a look of venom in his eyes. "What, you laughing at me, horseface?"

"No." Torv slaps him on the cheek and pulls him away as Joey moves in, fists balled. Torv pushes Joey back, at the same time elbow-jabbing him in the teeth. "What you looking at, bitchface?"

The side of Joey's lip, now budding in blood, curves into a smile. "Just wondering which of you lowlifes is going to beat up on a girl."

"No need for it," says Torv. "We're all friends here, right?" He grins, a smirk as wide as his bared knuckles.

Joey thumbs his split lip. He holds his ground. "Bet she could take you any day."

"Yeah, and bet she could drop you even faster, monkey brain." Torv slides over to me, flicking his eyes over my toned and poised body. "Well, well, Elly the fighter. Not only an activist but a scrapper. Who would have thought? Ain't that strange? Where'd you learn to fight?"

I don't like the way he's raking eyes over my wiry frame, as if all memory of our recent interaction is forgotten.

"Maybe you'd like a round with me, learn something new?" He smiles, as if in invitation.

Joey grunts and moves in. His muscles tense. Torv elbows him back. My feet are quick to rocker-shuffle two paces closer.

Zandra sneers, "Looks like you've met your match, Drego. Think you better go home." There are chuckles exchanged among her and her friends.

Torv gives a brittle laugh in my direction. "Think you can handle me?" This is a different Torv than the one I remember softening up after my presentation. Zandra's taunted him to get me battered and he can only accept the challenge or lose face. I don't like this Torv, or version of him. He's creepy. He's not a kickboxer but...if the rumors are true about his fighting ability, I could be in trouble. He stands with too much confidence, anchored like a ship, even with everyone against him. His deep chest, significant muscle, unwavering gaze and thuggish aura are unnerving. Angelos's words come back double-time in my brain: *"Never underestimate any opponent. Only fools do. Avoid a fight if you can, but don't sell yourself short if you can't."* Angelos's dead-right but I'm sure Torv's equipped with enough to make me eat blood if he wants.

I lift my fists and feel the feedback loop of adrenaline firing my body. Torv responds with a ripple of shoulder and roll of head. We trade some test jabs then I go full in. He's got this stupid grin on his face as he blocks my left hook and counters with a right which I barely dodge. Shit, he knows how to fight.

He closes in and I feel my head jerk back with a grazing blow aimed for my jaw that only skims my brow. That grin again. Fortunately there'll only be an angry lump there—much worse if his knuckles had actually connected. It's different without headgear and gloves. More to lose. More pain at each strike. I get him with a couple of switch kicks high to ribs left and right that has him grunting and wheezing. His cocky grin has faded. Now he's moving with a little more caution while the ravers ring around us like happy children about a campfire. Their shouts and taunts fade into a hollow background murmur. But part of me is aware of everybody and everything, even Vin, the slug, who waits ready to pounce, his beady eyes ogling my breasts and hips. But Joey's keeping him back.

I run my tongue over my lip, circle around Torv the opposite way, dip back, hook him on the side of the head. His eyes are kind of crazy now, as a new realization hits him. *Look, a new toy to play with. Something worth the chase.* It's as if he relishes this cat and mouse game—exotic, violent, a dance of its own, as his head dips in a kind of tribute: *Hey Touch*é*, baby* or *'Not bad'*. But there's a hint of danger there, as he rubs his fists and charges me, as if he's through making nice.

Joey muscles in and pulls us apart. "Enough, you two. Crazy or what? No need to break each other's faces."

My heart brims with pride that he's ready to jump in and take Torv.

Gilsen and his other friends edge back. They outnumber Torv and Vin, but they all know Torv is part of a street gang operating out of the slum sections of town, and if they try to beat on him, they'll likely get their heads kicked in later by a band of toughies. All which makes my act of challenge even the more insane.

But maybe not.

Torv shoulders Joey aside and studies me with fresh curiosity. He's not winded or fazed. Me, I'm kind of trembling, but I try to hide it. There's a big difference between being in a sparring match and a real fight.

"More to you than meets the eye, Elly. You've got grit. More than I can say for these pussies." He spits a wad of phlegm down at Darren and Xavier, both still face-hugging the floor. "Come on, Vin. This party sucks."

I'm still locked in fighter's poise, dazed, keeping my breath in check, while the beat of the music hammers on, dimmed now by the AI monitor, as it recognizes the dance energy has chilled.

Nord and Gilsen shadow the two bullies to the door, giving them the glare, walking them out but maintaining enough space to avoid fists and feet.

I feel Karie's arm snake around my back. "Good show, slugger. Someone's got to stand up to those bullies. Teach those punks a lesson."

Joey slides over, nodding, "You want to quit this scene?"

I shrug. "Sure." The music had started up again but the mood has been lost. "What about Darrin and Xavier?"

Joey points. "Nord's got them covered." A couple of guys are helping them to the bathroom to get cleaned up. "Hope they'll be all right. They both got smacked pretty hard."

I bite my lip, look away to where Ben Gilsen is sidling back over to his friends by the sound system and its diamond-shaped speakers. He's looking in my direction. If he sees me take off with Joey... "What you got in mind?"

He follows my line of sight to where Ben and Zandra are toking up. Ben's got his arm around her. "Forget Gilsen. He's out of your league."

A flicker of anger has my teeth clenching. "Thanks, Joey."

"I didn't mean it in that way. The guy's a wuss, wouldn't even help you stand up to Torv. You saw him."

I look away, not wanting to believe it. It was true. "Yeah, maybe." But I still feel soiled and low, somehow cheated. *The guy I've had a crush on is a preppie coward.*

My fingers rub the growing lump on my brow. So much for keeping my kickboxing skills under wraps.

Chapter 9

Joey and I step out into the electric night air, crisp enough to bring clarity to my throbbing head. The streets are slick after a fresh rain. The staccato patter of raindrops falling from eaves and balconies in back alleys is like an echo of the beat from the party.

"Hey, Joey, yo!"

We both turn to the slap of the closing door. Zandra's coming down the steps after us.

Joey nods and looks a little flustered. "Zannie. What's up?"

She flicks back her oiled, raven hair, her teeth flashing under the house lights. "Me and Kyla and a few others are heading over to Ben's. Might be a new rave over there, now that Drego and his mutt have spoiled this one. You in?"

Joey pauses, does a funny thing with his shoulders—a shrug then a little shake of the head. He glances away. "Maybe later, Zan. You guys heading there so early?"

She catches his quick but surreptitious look in my direction. Zannie's over-made-up face sours. "Why, you thinking of bringing that anorexic mongrel with you?"

He hesitates, sucks in his lip. "Maybe. What of it?"

She spazzes out, gusting an explosive hiss. She launches herself at him, knocking his shoulder, then storms back into the house, classic Zandra.

I am amused by it all, though it has my blood racing. Zandra is not an enemy to be taken lightly. Then again, we've always been enemies. Right from grade two.

"Well, that went over well." Joey exhales, his head bowed.

"Don't worry champ." I reach over and give him a hug. "Thanks for that, Joey. You're a real friend. Nothing better than seeing that witch squirm."

"Ha. I'll bet." He grins. "Let's go."

We beat it to Joey's brown *Bel-aire* parked across the street. Both of us get in.

"Can you believe that Torv asshole?" He slams the door shut. Always drama with Joey.

I shrug and stare out the window. "Okay, where to now?" The stars are faint twinkles under the city lights.

He smiles a disarming smile, pulls at the ruff of his goatee. Sweat trickles down his cheek following the line of his sideburns. He wipes his fat lip. "Oh, something different. We can head over to my place. No one's going to miss us here." Only the thrum of a few raindrops from a passing cloud on the windshield punctuates the silence between us. The streets are black. Water in the gutters glitter under the cold light of lampposts. "I got one of those halobands," he says casually. "Two actually."

"Oh, those. They sound boring."

He shakes his head, as if anything can be further from the truth. "Nord says he tried it, thought it was whack."

"*Whack,* as in awesome, way over or something to stay away from?"

"All of the above."

I purse my lips. "That's great, Joey, if Nord say's it's whack, then it must be whack." No small sarcasm in my tone.

"Then let's do it."

Back at his place, we grab some drinks and head to the basement, the 'rec-room' as he calls it, the place where he hangs out. It's all decked out with cool instruments and stuff, vintage guitars, basses, drums from some pre-Cataclysmic days. Where he got them, I shudder to think. Most of the stuff is illegal or banned. All I know is his father's a music buff. Never met him but heard about his passion.

The room's set in a weird L-shape with a blue sofa-bed along the far wall. It serves as his bedroom too. The night table beside it is full of pizza crumbs and the bathroom's around the side. The laminate floor is cold on my socks. The plaster ceiling is far too low for my tastes.

He jams on some music, pretty heavy stuff with a grunge, garage feel. I sip my beer, looking at recording packets and rock posters pinned on the bedside wall. Some long-haired guys and bald women strumming guitars, banging drums by a white-foamed winter fountain.

"Far out."

"That's *The Bor Angels,*" he remarks with no small pride.

"Shoulda known." I jerk a thumb at another poster. "What about the bands before then?"

He shrugs. "There weren't any."

"My point exactly."

"Electrogrunk came into being about twenty years ago," he says with sage emphasis.

"Just like everything else." He can see I'm not buying it.

"There's been classical and various country and folk singers way back but—"

"When? Where? It was so long ago. There's a huge gap in time."

"Yeah, because of apocalypse."

The apocalypse, yeah, aka the Cataclysm. Everything stops then everything is suddenly rebirthed. BS.

Joey turns and his profile is limned in the plum-colored glow of his nightstand table lamp. The distinct hook of his nose catches my attention.

He notices my scrutiny and a languorous grin comes over his face. He drifts over and settles beside me on the couch, traces a finger along my forearm.

"The grad dance is coming up."

I look at him, one eyebrow cocked. "And?"

"You want to go?

My left shoulder hikes in a shrug. "Maybe. You formally asking me?" I lift my arm away from his wandering fingers.

"Well, if you have somebody else in mind… Has someone already asked?"

"No."

His eyes brighten. He scrubs at his palms. "No rush. Take your time, Elly. Lemme know what you think. Come on, when has Joey Lazino ever let you down? It'll be a blast."

I'm not sure what I think. The romantic schoolgirl in me is thrilled to have the attention of one who truly likes me enough to put himself on the line for a shit-kicking, and a possible rejection if I say no. But me and Joey, not sure whether it's in the cards for us. I consider him more as a friend than a lover. Tricky to say that. I don't want to crush his hopes.

I can see him leaning in. Funny how there's always this breathless, pseudo-psychedelic sensation in the air before a guy makes a move on you. But he surprises me. He reaches over and presses one of the HB headsets in my hand. A blue visor, four inches long that slips over my eyes, fastened by a stretchy black elastic strap looped around the head.

I hadn't looked that carefully at the rollout: some of these devices are designed like goggles, others have the more voguish look of tinted visors. Joey flips on his own haloband and leans back on the couch, legs apart, mouth open. His head tilts back. He looses a big rattling breath. "Wow! This is whack, Elly. You've got to try. Put yours on!" His eyes seem to go cross-eyed. I can vaguely see them through the thick, tinted shades. As if he's some exotic Siamese cat about to howl at the moon. I pull off his glasses and sit back in a huff.

"Hey, watch it. I'm right in the middle of a hot tub…with some nymphs…warm fingers massaging my back."

I shake my head. "Yeah, right."

"Your turn, Miss Skeptic."

Hesitation has my hand sweating. It's as if my fingers are pulled back by strings. Joey reaches out to patiently fit the haloband over my head. The visor dims the light. Two black pads cover my ears.

Odd. Amazing. I can hear Joey speaking garbled underwater words to me while at the same time I can hear a whooshing sound like waves washing up on a shore. A calm blue sea slowly materializes in the foggy wash.

A menu of three options appears, each their own 3D floating cube: a flaxen-haired queen with a silver crown and wand in hand beckoning me, a pine tree dusted with snow at whose base lies a nearly-frozen pool (a merman is stuck in the ice with striking golden eyes and ice-blue beard). The last's a pirate's skull and crossbones over a pit of smoking embers. None of this is like Joey's fantasy. Somehow the device has already identified me as a different user. My fingers curl into fists. How does it do it? Hair? Head and ear size? Body heat? Pheromones? Some on-board hi-tech sensor? My head spins as I try to figure out the mechanics.

As my gaze lingers on the merman, a wash of coalescing light dissolves the screen and everything around me. A surround-sound-like psychedelic symphony grows in volume. A seascape materializes. I can only stare in wonder. Its hypnotic grandeur is eerily reminiscent of the opening night's haloband rollout.

Can this be real? I feel calmed, bathed in a tingling warmth that rises from my toes to the rest of my body. Okay…weird, but weird in a titillating way. I'm swept up in a reality so powerful it overcomes me as I crest a sparkling wave. I'm swimming now with dolphins in the warm water over to a beach of snow-white sand where a gorgeous merman sits on a rock, trident in hand.

Mesmerized by the play of light, sound and sensation, I swim faster.

Now I've become a character in a kaleidoscope of scenes. I'm a mermaid, with fins for legs that help me kick faster. Impossibly I'm wearing a wreath of white gardenias and coat of coin-sized fish scales that tinkle with every thrust.

The dreamboat merman is closer now and I see his lustrous mane of hair, dark lashes and welcoming smile. He points his trident at an option menu which features a cruise ship or a golden palace. I blink, then feel my cheeks warm. My gaze dwells on the glittering white ship, the Queen Annabella. Immediately I'm on board. The wreath is gone and I'm a mermaid no longer. My nerves tense from the suffocating crowds and buzz of voices. I've never been on a cruise ship before and I don't like it. It's too big, too frenetic. Instantly a magic carpet with golden wings transports me to an older ship with three hardwood masts tossing on a blue sea, like something out of antiquity. It creaks with dozens of high billowing sails, lost in time. I've never seen such a vessel before, so I conclude the device must have sensed I'd like this ship better. Is that possible—

A whistling like a boiling teapot grows in my ears. There's a strange warp in the air and Joey suddenly appears on the aft deck in the form of the merman. He's flopped on his fish-scaled belly looking up at me, but I know it's him from his unmistakable almond eyes and olive-skinned complexion. I shake my head in bewilderment. What—? Has his VR device overlapped with mine? How can he be in the same experience as me? I'm tense with excitement to the point of giggling like an overstimulated child.

The ship morphs into an exotic court adorned with golden statues, attended by half-naked bronze-skinned men. Women wave fans of peacock feathers around us and offer libations. The scent of jasmine and rose petals is heady in our nostrils. We're to be married or something. As soon as the ice-cold nectar touches my lips, we time travel. No longer princess and merman, but dancers at a rave.

A part of my mind must conclude that this is nutso, all this jumping about, regardless of how real it feels. We're in a familiar environment. Nord's place. Hot and dry-ice hazed with the dampness of exertion. Fast, heavy beats synched to the strobe lights. Joey's there. Gilsen, Karie, Zandra, and others. It's all too fantastical to believe. Our halobands, in proximity, must be picking up each other's signals and morphing the scenes. But is such possible? Can the device tap into our memories, pick up signatures of our secret desires and morph the scenes?

No, some trick. Either I'm hallucinating or those bayludes are tripping me out.

And yet, here on the dance floor, everything seems perfectly normal when nothing is.

I give myself over to the dance and the music like I always do. My tension eases up as I start to surrender to the universal language of rhythm. The sweat and the humidity and the tribal sense of belonging. At first the music starts off heavy like *The Bor Angels*, then moves into a series of trance beats in hypnotic procession, as if the haloband knows exactly what turns me on. But then maybe I'm subtly picking the music by my body signals when the unit gauges my reaction at each tonal beat? I'm moving in and out around the others like a wax idol as is my style.

I don't know how it does it, but the circuitry seems to know. My likes, dislikes, my moment-to-moment desires. It's uncanny, almost disturbing. As if it knows my next move, my next thought. It's as if some invisible avatar watches me from above, catering to the coming and going of my desires. Every micro-blink, stare, trembling breath, move I make, no matter how minute. Each choice I make narrows down my other options to perfect my profile. That's it! That's how it does it. But how can it do it so fast?

All this passes in my mind in a flash as Joey approaches. We dance, we twine. We're back to back, doing a funky move, moving to the ground low then back up again. Then we face each other. He's in his tie dye shirt and cargo pants. Real or simulated? I shake my head, blink, confusing reality with VR, but I'm feeling good, as if buzzed on some mellow drug. The setup almost mirrors Nord's place before the fight. A bunch of us, like Karie and Leta and Zandra and others, are pulling on pipes, drinking, dancing...

A fight breaks out. A real one with blood and broken teeth then it's over and the blood is mopped up and Torv and Vin are hauled off in a C-Sec van.

Joey sidles up beside me. He grabs me and we twirl into a contorted, erotic, sexual dance. My heat rises, a flutter of pleasure from loins to breasts. I pick up the tempo. We jive forward so our body heat radiates off each other. Joey makes a sound of rapture, the strong line of his jaw dropping, lips parted. He leans in; he slides his tongue into my mouth. I push him away but come back for more, as if this time following a deeper primal urge, egging him on, daring him to try something bolder.

I'm shocked because part of me, the one not in haloband, realizes how starved for affection and the physical act I am.

Joey, in a fit of mischievousness, reaches past the blur of the smoky, exotic clamor to hit the XR rating button along the side on the panel that controls the scene. I see this out of the corner of my eye, semi-stunned.

"Hey, what are you doing?" I scream at him.

"Relax." He gives a smug grin. "It's all make believe."

"It's not make believe."

"It's called shadow-bingeing."

"Whatever the hell. No way."

My voice drops to a fierce whisper. Is this part of the script? I'm overcome by a wave of passion. We're back to the dance. His hands slide under my shirt, my slender fingers probe his bare ribs, while his hands cup my breasts. "Ahh." A soft sigh of pleasure escapes my lips.

We are buck naked now. Sweat is pouring off our skins. Twined, like ancient gods and goddesses. Locked in intimate embrace.

Wow! I can't believe this. My heart is hammering, going a mile a minute. We are just about to engage in an irreversible, carnal act when I hear a tinny sound, like some faraway ring or buzz. I feel a vibration.

Another reality intrudes upon my fantasy…my communicator wristlet vibrating. My eyes close. I slump, knocked out of the moment's illusion.

I fling off the visor. My chest is heaving. Sweat pools at the base of my throat.

It's Mom, more pissed than ever. She wonders where I am.

Joey pushes up his glasses onto his brow, his skin and cheeks flushed. "What the hell?"

I lift my wristlet to my mouth with a sheepish expression. "Hi Mom, what's up?"

"Great timing," Joey hisses. "Blow her off, Jesus."

My mom's angry voice floods through the receiver. "Where in Christ's name are you? You were supposed to be back hours ago."

"No worries, Mom. I'm over at Joey's."

"Well, get your ass back here."

There're more angry words with threats of being grounded as I sign off, still in a semi-euphoric daze. I lie back on my side, feeling like a person split in two. One in this world, one in the world of the haloband.

The moment's lost, and I'm kinda glad it is, as I didn't want to commit to anything, even though my heart is still racing. I squirm away from the visor as if it's a poisonous asp. I stare at the blue shiny plastic for a long moment, both hating it and marveling at it. How can something so innocuous-looking create that much sensuality? The thing looks as if it has no electronics in it all. But I know different.

Joey's baffled at my hesitation. "What's wrong?"

He's totally not getting it. I've been skeptical of this thing right from the start. I want to know how it works and what it does.

A sudden realization hits me. The device somehow connects to our wristlets. So, it can cross-reference our Citizen IDs and access any profile data already stored there. That's what the engineer, Liz, was hinting at back at the rollout night. I'd missed it the first time.

Joey's cozying over to me, stroking my hair. "Come on, Ellan. Let's try it once more...we were interrupted rudely from a beautiful moment." He wraps his sweaty arms around me in a sloppy embrace.

I wriggle out of his grasp. "I don't think we should use that thing, Joey. I get a bad feeling about it. What's it doing to our bodies? Our brains? I mean, like, it's an all-encompassing turn on, but—"

"Huh?" He levels me a blank stare. "What do you think that stuff June fed us back at Nord's is doing to our brains? Can it be all that different?"

"No—well, yes. Just some little voice in the back of my head says we should be wary."

"Nah, you're just being paranoid."

"Maybe. But I can't just blow off my intuition." The darkweb has given me no less reason to be skeptical.

He nods, reluctant to stop twiddling with his visor. "Sure. Let's watch a flick or something."

"Nah, have to get home."

"Fine." Joey flaps a resigned hand.

A wave of relief washes over me. But there's still a thrill lingering in the pit of my stomach—for a brief replay sometime in the near future.

I don't like that urge. It rides the crest of a darker feeling, one at the cusp of a bad dream.

Chapter 10

I'm in my room on a late Sunday evening. My mind keeps dwelling upon the clips I saw on darkweb: lethal viruses decimating whole populations, 5G horrors, extreme weather shifts racking the earth. I can't deny it, I'm still curious. I pull up my beat-up laptop and start to type in the dark web window, but the page isn't responding.

In dismay, I frame some standard web searches: 'devastating fires, kid rebellion, bacterial outbreak', anticipating nothing'll come up.

Sure enough…nothing.

The few bogus pages that do pop up are laughably light on facts. I know those articles and images I saw the other night were real. When had they started to filter our web? I can only conclude, a long time ago.

My frustrated sigh falls on deaf ears. This is a dead end.

I trip over to Bram's room, knocking loudly.

No answer. The door's unlocked. I poke it open a crack.

"Bram, you in there?"

There's a rustle of feet within. I see a flash of movement.

Okay, this is too embarrassing. I catch Bram and his two friends, Carl and Rabin, dancing around in a circle, hand in hand like Ring around the Rosie. Shirtless. All wearing halobands.

Carl's got no height and a light build with sandy sideburns. His pinched face has the harried look of a rodent caught in a trap. Rabin's got a shock of short dark hair like Bram, but with silver-dyed bangs and an apologetic smirk on his thin lips.

I step in, both aghast and laughing my ass off. "Excuse me, everything all right here?"

Mouths gape in blank astonishment. Self-consciousness masters illusion. They pull off their visors, snatch for their shirts, Carl first, then Rabin. Rabin hastily explains, "We were just—"

"New experimental headgear. Smart device headbands," says Bram. "The Starcom people let us take them home. They're a blast."

"I'm sure they are. Say, I need another favor, Bram."

"Yeah, like what?" he grunts, immediately suspicious.

"Information. Like old man Peters rejected my last project and I got another one due. I'm just not getting the data I need to fill in the gaps using the standard Starcom searches. Peters's on my butt after I made him look bad last time round."

"No doubt." He shrugs. "So, go back to the darkweb."

"It went 'dark'. I can't login anywhere."

"That's because it's protected. It's got a failsafe timeout." He nods, smirks as if nothing can be more obvious. His eyes narrow to dark slits. "What do I get out of it?"

"For starters you don't get me ratting on you to Mom, what you guys are doing in here." I shiver. "I don't even know myself." *Freaks.* "Don't you ever invite girls over?"

"Compared to this visor, they're boring."

I shake my head in disgust.

Bram licks his lips. "You can't logon because the passwords change every sleep cycle, according to a very secret random sequence. You'll have to cipher Mom's password again."

"Don't tell me that. Where does she get them anyway?"

"How the hell do I know?"

"You're the big cyber geek here, not me."

"Yeah, well, it's all relative, ain't it, Sis? I'm not the fountain of knowledge, much as I'd like you to think so."

"Just ping me the link, okay? With a new password."

He sighs. "Listen. Keep your undies on. Do some paper edits or something. I'll send it up to you on your wristie. Carl, Rabe and I are right in the middle of something. Please don't barge in here again."

"Play your serpents and dragons, whatever. Or just circlejerk yourselves to sleep."

He springs up, his face creased in a snarl. "Get lost." He shuttles me out the door and slams it shut. Back to their weirdo VR. *Freak geeks.* But then again, what kind of freakshow was I doing with Joey the other night?

I scramble back to my room, eager to try out the new password. Bram's not quick in sending me the link, so another hour is spent digging around with fruitless searches on our garbage web.

When my wristlet pings, I enter Bram's link into the web browser. The black screen appears. My fingers start tapping, starting with 5G-Starcom-Google.

Multiple headlines appear, in no specific order.

Networks crippled. Failing hi-tech co's merge in desperation to form New-Age-Of-Poverty-and-Plague (NAPP) firm.

Experts agree it's that or fold. Dozens of megacorps given collective new name: Starcom.

Google search engine filtering more and more. Bing, Niaspec follow.

Excludes or bans sites from search results, in accordance with new US government restrictions.

Top sites ranked in favor of ad revenues versus content and general usefulness. Public outcry reaches a maximum. Citizens looking for alternate search engines. Freenet Kayla is a popular pick. The global giant from Mountainview makes no comment on the alleged ranking scandal—this from a report privately contracted out to Oregon company Dallstream Tech.

Ignatia, in a documentary, had made the bold statement that the Chinese government had already been filtering their search engines since its inception. Emphasizing that the 5G download speeds were a joke, considering most of the factual information had been suppressed.

I sit back, rub my eyes.

A story comes to mind. When I was seven, perhaps six, I remember asking my mom, "Why are there no birds in the city?" She looks up at me with surprise, a tinge of embarrassment and guilt. "Well, dear, the towers keep them away. Many of the geese, gulls, pigeons and hawks flew away long ago when 6G came in. That was before you were born."

Somehow they know the city's not the place for them. "So what about the people? Us, Mommy? Why do we live here? Why don't we fly away too?"

"Well, for starters, we're just more resilient. Or *stupid*," she says under her breath. She checks herself and clears her throat and changes the subject.

On a whim, I type, 'Why no birds in the city?'

A headline comes up,

Birds and frogs disappearing. Bees, insects dying.

5G+ linked to birth defects, cancers, sleep dysfunctions and increased autism diagnoses.

And there, a picture of a beautiful falcon that does not exist in our world anymore.

A lump amasses in my throat.

What—so the darkweb, aka free, uncensored web, used to be the norm? Had it always been like that? What was the turning point that brought such a dark change?

Could it be? A slow phaseout or erasure of history? The concept is so staggering, it makes me feel nauseous. I inhale, take several deep breaths. A shudder passes through my shoulders. It makes no sense. But then it does...

An article I had read stated it was possible, before the Cataclysm, to fly around the world for less than a few thousand dollars. Yet in our current situation, international flights are prohibitively expensive. Only high-ranking officials, CEOs and millionaires can afford to fly abroad.

My fingers start tapping again. But as my eyes goggle over the flood of data on pesticides, carbon monoxide, plastics contaminating the earth, I can take no more. I flop back in my chair, my brain numbed. The video drones on about *therighttoknow.truth,* about widespread oil spills and radiation leaks from nuclear reactors in Japan that contaminate large tracts of the Pacific Ocean.

I mute the volume. Even three or four years ago, I didn't understand why all the fighter jets were flying over so often. Nor could I understand why the sky was so yellow or the winds blew so strongly, or so many forest fires were followed by intense torrential rainfalls, mysterious cold snaps in late summer then unseasonable thaws in the middle of winter. Have weather patterns always been so extreme? I'm not sure, after browsing the darkweb articles.

The problems I've had sleeping... 6G. Could radio waves that far back have sickened us over the years, diminished our ability to fight disease? That, combined with the accretion of man-made poisons over the decades. The idea appalls me. Then another thought strikes me.

Many die young...the average life expectancy is 67. Darkweb says it was longer back then in the pre-cataclysm years, like 75 with a 20% infant mortality rate. Even that is much higher now, like 30%. How do the remaining 70% survive? Could we be resistant? I'd already learned the dark truth that one in three women is infertile. Maybe I'm one of the 33%, or will be in the near future.

The magnitude of the stats hits me again. It was always accepted as part of life that the corporate-sponsored clinics are full of patients suffering from various forms of cancer and related illnesses. But is it natural? Or helped along by the 6G towers…and the toxins of the past? The theory is too shocking for my tasked brain to manage.

I hear the doorbell ring and I'm jarred out of my grey haze. I palm my head. I'd invited Karie over for a girl night and I'd completely forgotten. Sure enough, I hear my dad opening the door and her clomping up the stairs. She tumbles in, doing the mock entrance, hip outthrust, her vamp-black hair teased up and smelling of fresh apples in the woods, a bubbly excitement to her.

"Say girl, working again? Why so dour?"

"This A-hole project. This research's getting to me."

"More darkweb? You shouldn't play around with that stuff. I've heard you could get hauled off by C-Sec."

"That's what Bram says." I bite my lip, recalling Hent's chilling warning. I wonder how far she would actually take it. "Hey, ever notice how there're no movies earlier than twenty five years ago? They just drop off the radar, out of existence."

"Maybe they got destroyed during the Cataclysm."

"No, silly, they've been wiped out. Deleted from time and mind. You're as bad as Joey."

She shakes her head. "Full of conspiracy theories, aren't you? Lighten up."

We change the subject, talk about girl troubles and boys. She braids my hair which is all loose and tangled. Bored with that we let loose, grab a few of Dad's scotch bottles from the liquor cabinet. It makes me wince, the peaty, fiery taste—not Karie, who's got more weight on her than me and can handle it—but mellows me out. The horror headlines are receding into the background.

"Need some more entertainment and action in our lives, Ellan. Less of this hanging around on a Sunday night with your bestie."

"Tell me about it. Those last two guys I went out with last month really tanked. Cold gropings in the dark. Drunken fantasies. Ben Gilsen is still looking good these days. Too bad he turned into a chickenshit while his friends were getting beat down."

Karie flashes me a curious smile. "You know, word around town's you're a guy stealer."

"A what?"

"Well, you know Fae has had her eyes on Joey for a while now, and so has Zandra, the queen witch."

I grimace, hand on hips. "I didn't steal him. He asked me out on a date—to the grad dance."

"Really?" Her eyes kindle in amazement.

"It was kind of an afterthought. Not so amazing."

"Oh." She frowns. "Somebody must have seen you two together or Joey spread rumors."

"Great. Well, he has been hanging around me a lot. And we did leave the rave at Nord's together. Not to mention we almost got it on the other evening."

"You what?" Her eyes go wide. "Details, please."

I turn my head with a sober intention of keeping her in the dark. I'm hardly listening. Thinking about how there's going to be more backlash and bullying at school to deal with. But after several insistent naggings, I confide in her.

"We were over at his place, fooling around with those halobands. Things got out of hand, kind of weird."

"Lot of people getting into those headsets. Guess you'll have to suck it up, girl. High school can be mean."

"I've got enough to stew over."

"Don't look so glum. What are you fretting about? You're 5' 7", slim, gorgeous—and available, if you don't count Joey."

"Well, nice of you to say, Karie, but I don't have your high opinion of my sex appeal, but again—thanks."

Karie nods, hangs her own head. "I'm the dumpy one, Ellan, with limp dyed-black hair, freckles, mooncalf face."

"You're just as cute as me, Karie." I click my tongue in admonishment and pull her over toward me. "We're our own dragons when it comes to looks and self-esteem."

She twirls a stray coil of her teased hair. "Yeah, maybe you're right. I'm just lucky to have someone like you to flatter me." She laughs. "Counter the inner critic."

"Wow, did you come up with that, or is it the liquor?"

Karie smirks and I move the subject along.

She cocks her head. "What's that laughter?"

"Just Bram and his geek friends, geeking around as usual."

She strokes her shiny black hair. "They cute?"

"Carl and Rabin?" I can't stifle a laugh fast enough. "Depends by whose standards. Rabin's not bad, if you don't mind the innocent, gawrsh, aw-shucks type. You're not missing much, Karie. All I can say is that."

She exhales a sigh. "Too bad." Her lips curl down at the corners.

"Leave Bram alone to geek out with his buddies, Karie. Worse now with that HB."

"I thought he worked at your mom's company—some whiz-kid programmer?"

"Think that's going to stop him from playing virtual reality games all night?"

"Say, what's with that HB anyway? You tried one yet?"

"Yeah, with Joey. Told you already."

"Yeah, right, sorry, must be the scotch." She laughs, takes another swig. She gets that mischievous gleam in her eye. "Why not crash their party." Wink, wink. Hopeful interest, wild speculation.

"Better yet. We can wait until they're done and use the extra pair."

Karie's eyebrow lifts. "They're expensive. How'd they get hold of them?"

"Bram's been given some as test models from where he works."

"Oh. Lucky Bram."

"Maybe not. Last time I saw them they were dancing around in a circle, half naked, holding hands."

"Haha, whatever yanks your crank."

I give her a playful shove. "You're a junkie, just like them, Karie, admit it?"

She flashes me a roguish wink, ties back her hair in a ponytail.

We run out of things to do and pad down the hall. I knock once. Hear muffled groans, exclamations. "Go away." I purse my lips, peer sideways at Karie who only nods, twirling her hair again. There's no other way to play this.

I burst through the door.

We stand there, self-consciously, both me and Karie, sidling from foot to foot.

"What now?" Bram's at his desk, fiddling with connecting the haloband to his computer. Carl and Rabin are hovering over his shoulder, eyeing his progress. Their impatience to get their halobands on again is palpable.

"We were just wondering—"

Rabin's interested, his keen green eyes flashing, sizing Karie up.

"Hey, you guys want in for some role playing?" he asks, twirling his unit in a relaxed fist.

I nod. "Karie hasn't tried it yet."

"We have extras. Starcom gave us demo models to play around with."

"I heard," says Karie.

"To upload extensions," Bram explains. "I've augmented this one with edgier scenarios, and a few other features."

"Awesome." Karie's all aglow.

I recall Joey's lustful hands all over me and wrinkle my nose. "I don't know." That last experience is still etched vividly on my mind.

Karie grabs my arm. "Come on, it'll be whack. I haven't tried one of these things yet."

"Okay, but you two take the augmented ones," I say. "I've done it before and it's already weird enough."

Carl and Rabin trade grins and nods.

I acquiesce, though a part of me is telling me to walk away.

The visor goes over my head. I see Karie putting on hers and her pink mouth, chock full of lipstick, rounding in a tiny, pinched 'o'.

One minute we're standing there looking awkwardly at each other then comes the hypnotic music, the soundtrack from a psychedelic orchestra, and we dissolve in a wash of color and cloud.

Karie and I are on a dark lake dotted with small ice floes pumping our legs in a yellow paddleboat shaped like a bathtub. We're dodging ice chunks as we chug along. Carl and Rabin are paddling ahead of us toward the end of the lake where there's some commotion. Either they're seeing something interesting or are trying to get away from us. Where's Bram? I'm searching for him, but there's no other boat in sight. Odd, but my mind just blanks out, as if I forgot what I was concerned about.

"Well, this scene is nice," I say.

Karie peddles with her feet at furious speed. "Can't this stupid thing go faster?"

"What's up with you?"

"Rabin's hot."

"Yeah, hot," I snort. "While I'm stuck with Carl who's certainly not a ten on the dreamboat scale."

I'm caught up in the scene even though I don't want to be. Why do I have the feeling this pairing's her fantasy, not mine?

A dull, distant roar drifts to our ears.

"What's that?" Karie turns to face me full on.

I shrug.

We're not fifty yards from the boys when I gape in frozen dismay. The lake ends in a massive waterfall. Too late, Carl and Rabin are slashing paddles at the water, trying to save themselves but the current is way too strong. Their boat is getting sucked closer, closer to doom. We're all screaming, peddling as fast as we can in the opposite direction but we go tumbling over the edge down tumultuous chutes two-hundred feet high. Falling in free fall, heart in mouth, tongue-swallowing terror.

Cold spray bites my skin, fills my lungs. How does it feel to die? Worse than falling off a sheer cliff. Below, a seething maelstrom of pure white foam meets us…deadly water and rocks.

We're jerked to a halt in midair, floating, suspended like dandelion fluff, the water spilling off us like silver streamers of liquid crystal glass. With magical slowness the water disappears and the deathly roar with it.

Yet I can't stop all the body reactions, the vicarious thrill that terror brings with it, a kind of adrenalin that the body feeds off.

I can almost put my finger on it, this haloband technology. But then the moment of insight almost slips away and I'm back in the dreamscape VR, living the mirage, part of me consumed by it, feeling strangely buzzed at the same time and secretly lusting after more.

Bram is back with us, no worse for wear. We are creeping single file along an overgrown path in the jungle searching for something. A lost civilization. Bram and his buddies' fantasy, certainly not Karie's. We are wary of each other, our primal fear of the wilds, every parrot call, hoot of monkey, feral footpad or animal rustling that may pose a threat. Something predatory, something dangerous is stalking us. Its roar is near, and yet far, like some kind of growl, a trick of the tangled jungle foliage. Bram breaks out in a run, spooked by something ahead. He lets out a cry as his leg is scooped up in a snare and he is whisked up in a tree to dangle upside down from a high branch. A thick vine entwines his leg. I stifle a cry, knowing that it is impossible to get him down without scaling that monster tree. My hand covers my mouth in a silent scream. Tiny gnome-like figures with mud-caked skin and bones and feathers knit together in their hair and noses dance around the base of the tree. Others lift darts to mouth and blow feathered projectiles up at Bram and now at us. One hits me in the shoulder. My hand reaches for it, I feel a small prick as another hits my leg. My vision starts to blur. I fall limp.

Just before I blink out, I glimpse fang-toothed lizards break through the screen of trees. Three of them, shoulder high, monstrous beasts loping on hind legs, all teeth, claws and iridescent, reptilian skin, gleaming like slick ooze.

The scenes fades, our bodies disintegrate in speckles. We are whisked off to another scene. Each of us minus Bram is separated in our own transparent bubble floating over a vast, rust-colored desert below. We can't claw our way out of our bubbles nor can we communicate with each other.

Half of my numbed body is aware I'm still wearing the haloband and half is aware of its powers. Are we on individual quests tailored to our moods, desires and fears? Has it profiled us that accurately?

Carl north, Karie west, Rabin East, me south. Bram, I don't know…Did the gnomes get him. Did the reptiles scale the tree?

My pondering is cut short. I'm whisking toward a mountain on the horizon at fantastic speed.

It's all dun-and blood-red-capped, smooth and worn from the throes of time. I glide over the summit. The bubble bursts and I drop onto its weathered limestone. I pick myself up and enter a cave tunneled in the side of the rock. Inside, a massive figure of stone adorned with gold crouches against a far wall. His gaze is calm, omniscient, but dispassionate. As if drawn by a magnetic force, I inch forward toward the tall shadow and kneel at its feet. Why I do this, I do not know. Like a pilgrim in some primitive rite from ages past. Despite my fascination, I know I'm in a dream and the haloband is far away. Time hangs in limbo. Words rumble in low gutturals from the statue's gaping mouth, words I cannot understand, yet I can guess at their substance—a strong suggestion: *Search deep within your heart. Go fearlessly where destiny allows it, draw upon your untried resources though challenges come your way.*

Before I can get too invested, the next scene is upon me, and the next. This time, a dirt road winding off into maroon twilight. An endless series of engagements, one after the other in swift succession, the five of us plunged into more and more fantastical adventures: scaling impossibly sheer cliffs, immersed in piranha-infested swamps, scrabbling for scarce resources in arid deserts. How long have we been in this altered world? Minutes? Hours?

Each scene is stranger than the last, but having some significance. Of that I am certain.

Suddenly I've had it. I snap out of this reverie, tear off my visor. I'm bathed in sweat. My chest is heaving like the last time, my knees weak as I try to rise. But I sprawl back on the couch. Karie and Rabin are beside me, clasped in some unexpected, sensual embrace. Rabin's leg is draped over her hip, her arm around his shoulder, her nose nuzzled in his throat. Bram's slumped in his chair before his terminal, his mouth hanging open like a fish. His visor is near stripped off, hanging at neck level. He slowly takes off his ear pads and peers over at us. "Whoa, that was a trip."

Carl is not around. I hear him rustling around in the back. He steps out of Bram's closet, garbed in one of Bram's loud orange parkas and a goofy winter hat, mumbling incoherent sounds. His haloband is still strapped to his brow.

Okay, this is getting too bizarre. It's like this haloband thing trips us into dreamland, taps into our subconscious or something and preys on our deepest yearnings, inhibitions and darkest desires.

The grey light of Bram's pad is kind of a letdown, almost too heavy with reality. Sterile of the thrills, buzzes, peril and adventure in that other realm. A place where there's a sense of one's body being invulnerable. Coming out of it proves it. I am alive, though I might have died a thousand deaths.

I rip off Karie's goggles.

She blinks, gasps. "Wow!" She shakes her head and shoves herself away from Rabin, frowning and giggling at the same time. She manages a croak. "I was floating on a misty bank, some cloud city of the future and this guy—" she extends a hand to Rabin "—was some kind of angel."

Rabin's just coming out of his haloband session, rubbing his eyes, the spell broken.

"Doesn't look like any kind of angel to me," I murmur. A bit of drool oozes from the corner of his lip.

Karie tosses her visor aside and giggles as they stare at one another meaningfully. Her eyes glaze. He wipes his cheeks. She very gently embraces him.

Say what? She's known the guy for all but an hour and is now all lovey-dovey? He seems no less smitten and runs his palms along the line of her black dress from shoulder to hip, grips her hand and folds his fingers over hers. I roll my eyes.

I think the programmers of this thing are having a field day today.

Or maybe it's this new 'extension' Bram has uploaded. Who the hell knows? Why in blazes would the company even allow such hacks as Bram to tamper with their hardware, insert his own code and experiment on others?

Bram's eyes are red, as if he's been crying. "I was stoned to death in the dungeons of Morlock."

Chapter 11

As the days pass, I notice increased presence of the haloband. I'm jogging down Dunlee and see a revolving ad in an appliance store window on a glowing 3D holo screen. *"The latest and the greatest, Haloband. Go where you can be part of the cast, be part of the movie! Why wait?"*

Yeah, right, I scoff. A real blast.

More and more people of all ages are wearing the units in the streets, on the trams, at parties, walking around in a daze. Zombies. Some have them around their necks, dangling from their belt or purse, wanting to snatch a spare moment of oblivion. A crawling unease still rakes my gut. One girl sitting on a park bench with visor over her eyes, fingers hiked in the air as if having a conversation with another invisible figure.

The more I think of it there's something seductive about these halobands. The technology seems to extend our world, to complete it by feeding our unrealized fantasies…almost as if it can push past the conscious barriers of the mind into the dreamworlds we all crave. Sinister, too, as far as fads go. By baring our deepest hopes, fears, challenges, it offers something more than a fad. It's arguably a brilliant piece of tech however scary it may be. Where before our world was static, fixed in time and space, this new world of the haloband offers some wild alternative, pulling dark emotions from the depths of our solar plexus and making our bodies react.

Praise to the designers. It is starting to make sense to me. They make us voyeurs of the sensual, explorers of the forbidden and unattainable. They push us to the edge. Just when the drama gets dangerous enough to kill, the scene transitions and whisks us off to another dimension, in the same way a dreamer wakes from a nightmare or a sleepwalker is steered out of harm's way by an anxious family member.

I'm home, ready to go to practice at the club then out with Karie and Leta. Dad's rustling around in the study for his backup holodisk.

"Hey, I'm heading out to the office, honey," he calls up the stairs. "Got a backlog of work to catch up."

Mom comes out of the bathroom in her housecoat, brushing her hair. "What work?"

"Oh, back orders. Stuff. Clara's on overtime until we get the Newbell contract sorted out. By the way, congrats on the haloband sales, Viv. Heard they're up to five million units. Awesome. A new record."

She nods. "Sure, thanks." Her eyes go cold. "What's this with Clara? You and her have lunch together today?"

My father smiles, rubs his jaw. "Why do you ask that?"

"Heading out too, Mom. Kickboxing's tonight." I break the uncomfortable space.

"Three times a week? Really?" Her hazel eyes narrow, a tired sigh escaping her lips, replacing the cold look with a query.

"Tournament's coming up, remember?"

"Well, don't stay out too late, Elly. Exams in five weeks." She wags a finger at me. "I want you back by eleven."

"Sure." *Yeah, like that's going to happen too soon.* My mom, the Aries.

* * *

April's finally upon us. Tonight's the night of the twenty-and-under city championships. Down at the regional center on Jasmine Blvd. There are five octagonal rings center-stage in the low-domed arena with tiers of seats rising on all sides and there's quite a turnout, upwards of a few thousand. All matches are single round, sudden death. Up to the quarter finals. Cuts down the numbers quickly. Each pair of opponents has two minutes to prove themselves. The matches are decided by former and seasoned trainers and kickboxers themselves.

All the regulars are here, groupies, MMA enthusiasts, business people, blue-collar workers, office workers, parents, friends of the contenders. No less than seven fight club schools attending. It's big and Angelos's club, respected as it is, has drawn well in the matchings.

They like to pair the girls with the girls in the first rounds, then it's fair game: mixed, everything goes—age, weight, sex. It's brutal. One of the harsh sports of our time. And me, the slender matchstick frame in my tight black shorts and black and green sports-bra pitted against some rough-necked middle and heavyweights.

Angelos tells us to put that out of our minds. Most of the battle is mental. Most.

I duck a left swing. Drop in a semi-crouch, my bare feet warm against the canvas-covered stage, lay a hook kick around the back of her knees, eliciting a grunt. I've won my first match, against a girl from the *Golden Fists*

Club on the west side. And am on to my second, against another girl from the gang neighborhoods. She's looking mean with her dark pinecone tangle and thick thighs, compared to my slender physique. She bangs her gloves together, stares me down with a ghoulish grin enhanced by her monster mouthguard. We bunt gloves and await the ref's signal. Immediately my intuition's going off in my head to keep a healthy distance from her legs and don't let this brash bitch get any momentum on me. Rack's still in, so is Conn. I get a glimpse on either side of me. Angelos can't be at two matches at once, but he decides to watch mine and offer support. Just his presence and encouragement means the world. It boosts my spirits and I lift my chin a peg higher. I can see Mom out there too. Though she hates fighting and kickboxing, I know she's secretly proud of me. With her hand over her mouth or her throat at every hit.

Rack loses his match. I hear him swearing and kicking at the cage. Not a knockout but plenty of bruises on the left side of his face and a nearly-closed eye. I'm stunned. So too does Conn lose his first round. Max and Joey were edged out early on so looks as if I'm the only one left from our club who's still in the tournament.

Torv with the shaggy brown curls, leather jacket and patched-over jeans, is there, sitting in the audience, third row, watching me with a hawk's gaze, though with less of a delinquent's smirk than usual. I look away, catch the smile eating at the corner of his lips.

Focus on the match, Ellan.

My opponent sees I'm distracted and slow on the start signal, smacks me hard on the side of the head. I feel the blood roar in my left ear. She gets a solid whack to my right thigh with her strong leg and almost trips me. Shit, I'm off balance, losing my rhythm. I stumble away from her iron feet, avoiding more damage. Too many mistakes, Ellan. Too many unguarded hits. It'll cost you.

She wants to end it quickly. I can see it in her wolfish, copper-colored eyes, the slant of her head, the way she leads with her punches in a slug-kill way. I play it dumb, like a scared kid, hoping to draw her into a mistake, and while I see her eager satisfaction as she makes little rabbit steps into my zone, I twist and duck a cut. Leaning back, I spring up, spin with all my weight thrust into a classic reverse roundhouse kick that smacks her right shoulder. She's staggering back. I lean in, lay a strong right in her midriff. She lets out a woof of air and I let her have it full on. A barrage of cuts.

Lightning fast. She's stumbling, shaking the sweat out of her eyes, hoarse of breath, and now on the defensive. I've won this, I've got enough points. Just have to keep her at bay. We dance around, circling like a couple of wranglers at the corral and poke and jab at each other with windy breaths. Now a boring strategic fight. She figures out my play at the last instant and gets desperate but now I jigger sideways out of reach of those legs, stronger than mine.

Sure enough, the bell rings and the judges call it. 10-9, 9-7, 11-8, hit for hit, in my favor. I lift a gloved hand in the air and do my victory salute and walk around the cage's perimeter as is expected. The cheers rise.

A little close, but a win.

The cheers rise from the spectators around the cage. Here at Jasmine Blvd's Regional Center the rings are packed close together and kind of surreal with the bright lights shining down. Almost enough to mesmerize.

We're not quite into the second hour and we're already at quarter finals.

I've made it this far, and I still can't believe it. My heart's thudding like a jackhammer. The lights are too bright. The buzz of background noise saws at my brain.

Joey belts out something from the sidelines. I see him pump a fist and he's sweating a lot with a coppery puffiness around his mouth. Angelos gives me the thumbs up.

The unsmiling ref escorts me to the next ring, closer to the center, and as I walk on and gaze at my opponent, my heart quails. He's like tall, 6' 1" with short-cropped army cut, blue-tinted beard and snaky, dragon tats on his shoulders. He looks fresh and eager, is fresh and eager, because I've seen him in the middle ring where he knocked his opponent out cold. Absolutely ruthless.

He takes one look at me and almost bellies over in laughter. He does a mincy little chicken walk that gets the crowd's attention, like as if to say, *What? You want me to fight a skinny girl? Puh-lease.* The crowd is going wild with hoots and cat-calls.

But I know this guy has weaknesses, all fighters do, even if every cell in my body knows he is going to win. Funny how an affirmation can become prophecy. Is my lack of confidence my biggest weakness? Angelos keeps telling me so. He's telling me that now with his eyes, his fingers, hands, all his body language. He's sitting front row center, nodding his head and lifting a fist. He's dressed in white with a red sash around his waist and a matching headband. He looks like the instructor I've always aspired to be, and he looks serious, not in any pretentious way, but with a fierce gaze that says this is the real thing, Ellan. Make it your best.

It gives me new determination to fight hard—and win.

I come jabbing in and blocking, showing him I'm not a gutless waif. Matters little. I feel the kick grind into my ribs, as I'm knocked sideways, pushed to the cage. These are octagonal rings versus square like we have at Angelos's. Doesn't let you get holed up in a corner. No ropes, but a hard-metal black mesh like chickenwire that encloses the ring as if we are chickens in a coop. Nothing funny about it. No, sirree Bob. The air is squeezed out of my lungs. I'm gasping, falling back, stumbling away from his predictable follow up kick. My mind slows to a dream cadence, like in the haloband. Oddly it comforts me. For a flash I'm back in the scene in the bathtub race just before the waterfall. Facing oblivion. When I'm in a tournament, it's no different. Yet in haloband, you go on to the next scene without the aches and bruises.

Somehow the insight fires me to new determination.

So I stick it to him.

He comes at me, smacking his gloves together like he's joe-schmo slugger or something—the crowd's voices are slowed down, underwater monotones, like some monster's death gurgle. My ears are buzzing. A wash of angry clown faces peer up at me from the audience, with horse-toothed sneers and duck bills. I dodge his hard left, sneak an uppercut under his left armpit, sweat rolling off my bare arms, shutting out the foul reek of him, hammer a left-right combo into his naked ribs. He jerks back in surprise, covering up but flailing. I slam-kick him left and right to his slab-sided flanks. He backpedals, blocks one of my kicks, but one gets through. He's now staggering slow-mo into the mesh like an awkward ragdoll. The crowd goes crazy. Roars, hoots of laughter. That pisses him off royally. Now he's crazy mad, cussing and swearing—and spitting at me like a spoiled kid who didn't get his way. I made him look foolish, a mere girl half his size, pushing him back into the cage. Angelos's always taught us if we can get under an opponent's skin...

He's raising a fist with a face lit up like a Xmas tree.

I lean in to pummel him badly while he's off balance. Another mistake.

Never underestimate your opponent. Angelos's first lesson.

Stupido, you just underestimated this schmo. He's blocked every fist you've put to him in the last five seconds. Now his upper body is flexing as he catches me a strong right with his superior reach and height. He's back on his feet, bobbing like a jackrabbit, as if none of my hits has fazed him and now I know I'm screwed. I should have drawn him out again, feinted before laying into him versus getting too greedy.

Last thing I see is Angelos's eyes closing and his face-palming while the crunch of a glove, a hard right to my left cheek has me spinning sideways. Down I sag, blocking his left hook but the damage has been done.

Luckily the bell rings. The match is over, to be decided by the judges.

I smooth out my mouth, throbbing now, feeling the shock of battle, the tingle even through my chin pads, not surprised to see the judges' rulings in favor of Buzz Cut. 15-7, 14-7, 15-8.

Well, good show, Ellan, but you're out.

Feeling proud of my accomplishment all the same. I hobble out of the cage in a half circle on rubbery legs. I'm aching all over but feel lightheaded and stupid and sore, and yet with a sense of pride.

A series of bright lights and muffled, congratulatory voices, catcalls and slaps on the back greet me. Then there're towels around my neck, rubbing the sweat off my shoulders. A giant water bottle is shoved into my hand and I tilt it back and guzzle half of it. Angelos is at my side, talking about how I did good and other things a mile a minute. I nod. I can't keep up with everything he's saying. "That bum didn't deserve that win. You had him, Ellan, you just flubbed it at the end."

Joey's giving me a bear hug which hurts my tender ribs. "Another perfect reason why I never want to be in the ring with you, slugger."

I'm savoring a space of peace as the matches go on to the semifinals. I slump on the benches, blinking away the haze.

I run a furry tongue over my puffed up lip, my mind distant. Kojak Teegar, with the buzzcut, our skinhead, is moving well in his next fight. Running around his opponent, fast jabbing him, keeping himself away from those powerful legs and meat-chopper fists: a short bulky Oriental fellow who grunts a lot and uses a lot of hard muscle. Those thighs look dangerous too and I wouldn't want to have either of them blocking me.

Ouch. A right slug to Kojak's head. He staggers. The Asian has deked him out. Kojak comes back and rabbit punches him in the kidney. Shouts erupt from the audience. Boos. Hisses. The ref blows the whistle. There's a big outcry. Foul. Kojak is protesting, making a big drama out of it, as if he's

Mr. Innocent. He's just stalling for time, sabotaging the Asian's sense of rhythm. The strategy gives him a chance to regroup. He isn't winning any friends in the meantime, but the ref orders the two back in the fight. The kid gloves are off and they slug it out. Some blood now streams from Kojak's eye, despite his blue-padded headgear. It's riveting stuff, the watershed moment of close-contested kickboxing matches.

The bell rings. It's over before it begins. It's close, but my previous opponent's out.

Now it's the Asian against an up and comer from a club out of town in Westmont, a Jerry Wald. The final. Wald's almost as tall as Kojak, but reminds me a bit of Torv. This newbie shows no emotion. Technically he's good. I can tell as he jabs and covers up, never getting anything but a mild sting on his arms as the pair circle like cats, but he seems robotic, like a machine compared to the Asian who I see is Lin Keung.

What's his weakness? Even in my after-match lull, my kickboxer's mind stretches to find it.

The others from my club are engrossed, including Angelos. Rocking back on their heels, they growl in contempt as easily as yelling vindication as blows and kicks are ladled out with fury.

A familiar voice breaks out of the shadows. That of a dark figure in patchy jeans. "Bravo. You did good. I'm impressed."

I shrug. "What do you care, Torv?" I turn back to the match.

His lips purse in a freakish smile. "Oh, but I do."

"Yeah, well, I got lucky."

"No luck from where I'm standing. You're just good." He shifts closer and touches my shoulder. He rocks from foot to foot. "Listen, about the rave. Vin—well, he's a jerkoff and we'd been smoking this bad stuff that messed up my brain." He holds up a hand. "No, I know, it's no excuse, I was an a-hole, but just needed to get it off my chest, say my piece. That's all."

"Yeah, well you said it." I shrug again. "Now, get lost." I regret the brush-off the moment it's out because I realize he's sincere and it took a lot for him to say that. More than I probably could ever know, if I knew half the past of Torv Drego.

He's not leaving too soon, yet I can sense more words need to be said and that last comment stung.

"Quit looking so glum and feeling sorry for yourself. You always such a hardass on yourself?"

"Yeah, well, I deserved to lose that fight."

He gives his head an exasperated shake. "Crapola. You should've clocked him, jabbed him in that magic moment during that second last punch when wonko went ballistic. He's the one got lucky. He was stumbling, tired, thrown off his game."

"That's what I'm telling her," says Rack. "That's what Angelos has been saying too."

I open my mouth to object when I realize what he says is true. I knew it at the time, just couldn't piece it together. The after match buzz is calming my nerves, letting me isolate the critical moment.

"We should spar sometime," Torv suggests. "We both could learn something from each other, never know."

My heart jerks one way then another. He looks like a bronze god looking at me like that. Am I softening to this guy? Why should I trust him? But there's something about his energy, in his clear-eyed, penitent expression that tells me he's not the mean bastard he is. There's a lot more to Torv Drego than meets the eye.

"Sure." I find myself saying, nodding like a grade three kid.

Joey catches wind of our conversation and hustles forward to brush Torv a cold glare. "Beat it. You're not welcome here."

He's only trying to shield me from street toughs like Torv, and perhaps my own overly trusting nature.

I shrug, nurse my swollen lip. There'll be a few ugly bruises under my arms, on my hips and thighs. I look around, but Torv is gone. He's melted into the shadows.

Wild cheers from the audience. The scores are in. Lin Keung, has defeated the newcomer.

As the crowd disperses, Joey offers to drive me home. We break out of the milling throng. I can't find my mom anywhere. Funny, how that last expression on Torv's face is imprinted in my mind. Solemn but kind of brazen, as if there's more to play out between us. Weird or what?

Joey's drawing all kinds of hints about us hooking up again. At least he's not tactless enough to push for anything tonight. I find myself daydreaming of joining him again in that virtual reality shop. Really? I snap out of that startling thought. Do I really like him that much? Joey was okay, in a kind of kid-like, brotherly way, but not sure I was that serious about him.

Funny, how my mind is still on Torv.

Chapter 12

The soccer witches have not let up on their persecution of me and Karie. Karie is seeing Rabin Gorm. They are getting along very well, so I've heard. I am invited to more parties, at Nord's and others, even at Ben Gilsen's. I've completely lost interest in him. Funny how I had such a stupid crush on that loser. Someone who's so not up to my standard. Joey's always there for me, eager to spend time with me and play chauffeur to the raves.

I play along with him for now, but when we're on the floor, me in my tight black jeans, I'm a free spirit, weaving in and out of the group like I always do—I push him away when he tries to get too cozy. Though a part of me is always on the alert for Torv making another surprise entrance. Wanting it, but dreading the outcome.

Peters's reassigning this project has really got my back up. *Your erstwhile attempt, Miss Weis, is insufficient.* I can still hear his stodgy lecturer's voice worrying at my ear. What bull. Thing is, do I dare dig up more scandals from the darkweb? A rebellious part of me has my lips puckering in a smirk. You only live once, girl. I can always plead insanity.

I brush off the consequences with a dry laugh.

I click up on the darkweb page and find I'm locked out again. I brandish a fist at the touchscreen and chew my lip, ready to belt someone. Dammit, this project has to get finished or Peters'll flunk me out of science class.

I ping Bram. "This shit isn't working. Can you come up?"

A groan vibrates from the receiver.

He enters my room, bare-chested and wearing his traditional brown cargo pants. He pushes me out of the way. Taps the virtual keypad and pulls up a dark window with super small white text, some shell program monitor, he says. Bram seems distracted, irritated, his matt of black hair in disarray. The top banner has the same queer icon of a blindfolded wizard sitting on a golden throne. He invokes some protocols and a bunch of other stuff. Numbers, figures, widgets, hex codes appear, which I guess must be passwords.

His face crinkles in a frown. "Whoa, what's this? Backdoor to a backdoor—?"

I peer on, glassy-eyed. "What do you mean? Sounds like some bad movie."

He ignores me. His face turns pale. "I bet even Starcom doesn't know about this. Just our bad luck."

"What's that supposed to—"

"All yours, kiddo. Not my problem." He gets up to go. Frowns. Then trips back, looks it over. "Something's wrong." Claws at his chin as if there's going to be hell to pay. Then leaves with a thoughtful look pasted on his stubbled cheeks, looking tired and resentful.

"You need some sleep, Bro."

"Yeah. Have fun digging the darkweb for info...I have to check this out more. You'll get more articles. Way more."

I shake my head in puzzled wonder. "Wait, how can Starcom leave something like this open?"

Bram sighs. "They can't control everything. These companies have access to things you can't imagine, Ellan. That's why I'm still working for them." He snorts out a laugh, one lacking all humor.

"No, it's because Mom got you a job, otherwise you'd be circlejerking with your pals daytimes too."

"Shut up." Bram's face goes red. "I still had to pass the interview."

"You did, but how many other guys would have gotten the job if they weren't Vivian Weis's son?"

He goes quiet, sits down to tap more entries in my antique laptop, frowning, in a thoughtful mood.

"Oh, by the way, dad's screwing around."

"It's old news."

"Having to live with her, I don't blame him." I shrug.

"You're always down on Mom."

"Just because I'm not an ass-kisser like you—"

"Hey, you want me to wipe that screen?" He reaches over to pull down the darkweb window.

"No, no, no, no." I swat his hands away. "Relax, just a joke."

Bram leaves. So, another night of browsing forbidden information. Like a gremlin I'm drawn to this ghoulish pastime, greedily soaking up as many facts as possible, my mind an endless magnet for collecting iron filings of truth.

The big centers, like NY, Chicago, LA seem to have been hit the hardest after what appears to be a viral purge—turned into ghost towns under the new norm of the no man's lands of the dispossessed. Without power or infrastructure, especially through the winters, they've been reduced to skeletons, stripped of life.

I learn, even Levenbrook, our city, had a different name prior to the Cataclysm. Though I can't find which city it used to be.

My searches lead down different avenues. Tonight it's all about greenhouse gases, melting icecaps, tornadoes, floods. How big oil doesn't want innovative technologies to take over, meaning, usurp their energy monopoly on the world and keep milking the planet for every drop of oil, fracking and offshore drilling everywhere, poisoning this earth for a fat payoff. That, and GMOs and antibiotics, and more 5G and viruses. No wonder this earth went to shit and most of the human race died.

I start to see a pattern here in the articles' content, and a wealth of other leading facts and grim truths that Ignatia brought to the public.

Big banks force world's governments to bail them out. Market economies fail. Big 5 rule the globe.

Bankrupt cities, states, nations continue to decline. World famine. Intelligence agencies linked to cybercrime and fomenting us-vs-them militarism.

It was a wonder Ignatia didn't get herself killed earlier. I see reports of other whistleblowers before her: Edward Snowden, Chelsea Manning, Julian Assange, Richard Bowen, all reporting on corrupt governments and corporations. I wonder how corrupt our government is. I wonder if even the whistleblowers weren't just government agents themselves. Everything seems to be run by Starcom and Agra. How much can they be trusted? After seeing Rane speak at the rollout, with his greasy smile and oily acclaims of haloband, I don't trust him farther than I can spit. Now I resent my mom working for that company.

Another thought crosses my mind. Who's hosting this information? Whenever I try to invoke a tracer on 'therighttoknow.truth' or 'donjonnews.gate' or a host of others, I get 'Node unknown. IP untraceable'. Shit, I should have asked Bram... Maybe not tonight. He's pissed. And worried, really anxious about something.

As if under a time deadline or curfew, I frantically pore over as much information as I can. It's overwhelming. A ton of data. I upload images, vids, copy-paste pages of text to my wristlet. Part of me is wondering if that's such a good idea, but I don't know where else to put it. Even if I transfer it to an external holodisk, it has to go through the network, and is thus, theoretically traceable. I'm no hacker but even I know the risk.

As I lie on my bed, I fall asleep to the glow of the darkweb, my wristlet in full screen mode, hundreds of images, damning headlines, like firefly ghosts from a distant past…

I wake to the crash of breaking glass and angry shouts. My parents arguing again. I groan. What time is it? 2AM? I sigh, wipe the sleep out of my eyes. I bury my head under the pillow, but it's no use. I heave a curse and get up and patter down the hall. I'm feeling dirty and heavy in my street clothes. I take a crouching pose by the bannister.

"I heard you on the wristphone, Lars. Talking with Clare, again."

"That was just a business call."

"Don't lie to me. How does, 'next time I'll get more coverage with you around, baby' sound, you bastard?"

"Viv, I…"

"If you're going to do it, Lars, just be honest. For god's sake, not as if I'm that dense."

"I know, I should have broken it off earlier, or at least told you about it…It was—a moment of weakness."

"Weakness. Yes, I know about weakness. You're the epitome of it."

My dad's voice suddenly goes up a few pitches. "So, if you're not angry, does this mean we can—"

"Absolutely not." She snorts an ugly husky sound from the bottom of her throat. "I think you should sleep in the spare room. Until we can work things out. If that's at all possible."

Work things out? What kind of joke is that? I crouch lower, my stomach in knots. *Dad, you're up shit creek now.*

"But I'll not tear Bram and Ellan apart."

"Good luck with that. Even Ellan's been asking weird questions, looking at me in weird ways, as if I'm some monster or alien from another planet."

"Only got yourself to blame for that. You hardly spend time with her, and when you do, it's all about you and never about her. And what's this other one I heard you talking to… Gabrielle's her name?"

"How did—"

"Your son's a computer hacker, remember? What do you think?"

"That bloody fink. I'll wring his neck."

"Touch him and I'll garrote you. For the record, he did it reluctantly."

"Or what, the battle witch'll throw him in chains?" Dad's teeth flash in a sarcastic grunt. "Rat out his own father? Kid needs to get laid more."

"You brought it on yourself, Lars. Don't blame it on anyone else."

But dad had already stopped listening. He'd thrown down his stuff and stomped into the study and slammed the door.

I slink back to my bed. Great. Nice family. I have a miserable night getting to sleep, tossing and turning, wondering what worse can happen.

Chapter 13

The darkweb revelations are haunting me. The more I look around, the more this place, this city, doesn't make sense. It doesn't seem real to me. The abandoned buildings, the lack of birds, the hum of the 6G booster transmitters planted everywhere with their ugly rabbit ears. A fabricated place, a city haunted with a secret past.

I'm drawn to the darkweb like a zombie to fresh meat—it scares me, yet at the same time, thrills me.

More and more I hit the streets jogging to clear my brain. This time, a long one, down by the Jackson River and the beginning of the greenbelt, what little is left. I'm just working up a sweat down the canal service road that runs abreast Tydon Park, starting to feel my chest loosen, a white baseball cap shading my eyes, when a small engine purrs up in my vicinity.

A black and silver VX60 motorbike with dull grey handlebars and chromium rear panels pulls in beside me.

The rider keeps steady with my pace. I glance over. Black-booted feet set far forward. Gloved hands high on handlebars wide apart like one of the classic choppers. Not surprised it's Torv. Stalker. Despite the reputation of criminality he has buzzing about him, I'm impressed with his ride. He's dressed in jeans and a lighter-colored suede jacket than last time I saw him.

"You're a jogger. Nice."

"Whatever gave you that idea?" I chirp back, not slowing my pace.

He nods, smiles. "You up for a ride?"

My eyes wander from his chest to the full length of his upper thighs fitted in tight jeans to his confident posture on the bike. Everything from black riding gloves to the ripple in his leather and brazen, devil-may-care gaze has a way of raising a heat in my body. "With you?"

"No, with the candyman."

I chuckle. "Where to?"

"Where you want to go?"

I think about it. Picking up my pace, eyes straight ahead, I make a decision. "How about out of this city? Somewhere in the country. Always wanted to see the Caledon Woods."

"Sure, then let's go." He rumbles out a playful chuckle, half-turns and pats the area of seat behind him.

I hop on, my hesitant hands grip his substantial shoulders.

He pulls out and does a U-turn in the street, catching me off guard, making me latch onto him tighter.

The air feels invigorating on my skin, whooshes my hair back. The engine purrs, a fine-tuned electric. He revs it. We fly with the wind. Not much traffic. Only a few transports and semis carrying supplies from Westmount and further.

The skies are clear, a light blue, hazed with yellow smog and high cirrus at the zenith. We see the greenbelt, leave the last of the traffic monitors behind. GMO cornfields, twenty feet high, flip by, their monster corn cobs a blur.

"Don't go too fast."

"Relax. They don't have speed detectors on this stretch," he calls back. "I know this stretch of road—no cameras."

"Whatever. You're driving."

We turn off on some feeder roads where there are gnarled oaks and rolling fields.

We come to a bridge over a river. The water is black, as if it's come from some deep mine upriver or underwater shaft. I know there is one up there somewhere from what I've heard. We're leaving the city district and heading into Caledon County.

I see a patch of woods which straddles the road on either side. A small opening in the trees hints of an animal path. I point it out and Torv slows. He nods, acknowledges my desire with a raised arm. He loops back to the trail and parks the bike a decent distance up the path so we are hidden from the road. I just want to be in nature. I kneel down beside a set of hoof prints in the damp soil. Deer? In secret glee, I follow the trail to a small clearing of stately pines. Some giant oaks hulk deeper within the forest, crowding the pines. Sure enough there's a mother doe grazing. She's rooting among pine cones, nudging the choice ones over to her twin fawns. Torv watches me, my silent rapture, looks up to the whispering pines rustling in the breeze, reaches down puts a grass blade between his teeth. He takes his time, exhales a slow breath, studies me.

The deer catch sight of us and leap off into the cover of foliage, legs kicking high and white tails wagging, as if annoyed at our intrusion.

There are actual birds here. Robins, jays, though they seem skittish, distrustful of our presence. I don't blame them. I'd be too, considering what humans have done to their habitat, if half of anything on the darkweb is true.

"You know, tree trunks never were supposed to grow that big around."

Torv nods. "According to folklore, they used to grow for centuries. You learn all this nature stuff from your darkweb?"

"So many paradoxes, so many unanswered questions. I wish I could pull this woman Ignatia out of time and talk to her about what really went on."

"Ignatia?"

"Some reporter. A rebel whistleblower who was killed. Remember my presentation?"

"Yeah, I remember."

Torv's gaze is distant, faraway. On one hand he looks like a dangerous ex-con with his muscles and facial scar and tattoos across his wrists and at the base of his throat. On the other hand, he's a very handsome man. A figure of mystery.

"If I had my way, I'd create my own movement," I murmur as I twirl my hair. "No radio towers, no 6G+, no Starcom networks or people walking around in a daze wearing stupid visors. Plus a free web that exposes everything for all who are curious."

He shrugs. "Maybe you will."

"At least then if we have to do class projects, we'd have proper sources."

He gives me a vague thumbs up, as if he's only half listening.

"Oh, and school'd be different—way less math and more stuff about plants and animals."

He steps close and caresses my cheek with a finger. It's a gentle, intimate gesture. Harmless, in fact.

But I look away as my face heats up, not sure what I'm feeling. Torv looks even more rugged and captivating, his lean profile and the prickly stubble on his chin imbuing him with a savage look. Too many mixed emotions bubble to the surface, ones that muddy the chaos of the past even more.

I learn a funny thing about myself in that moment. I'd always been closing myself off to guys. That one gentle touch from this badboy by reputation exposed that truth. I pull away, not ready for the Ellan of old to explore unfamiliar feelings.

"Why're you so mean? I mean to the other kids at school. They're all scared shitless of you."

He laughs, a sad little chuckle. "I'm not mean. It's just an act."

I shrug. "Makes no sense to me."

He reacts to my incomprehension with a brisk chopping motion. "Let me tell you a story. Once upon a time, there was a little boy, nine years old. Call him 'Me', and then there's Biffy, Vin's bro. These little shits had just lifted some stuff at the local K-10 convenience store. Nothing major. Some smokes, candy, the donation change jar. They were getting back to their hideout. Ran into some of the Spikes.

"One of them yells out, 'Streets are dangerous, boys, join us. You want protection? Give us some of your stash.' Me, the little boy, shakes his head and keeps moving, gripping our share of the spoils, not looking for any trouble. I take Biffy by the shoulder, shuttle him on. Too scared of the gangs, not willing to pay their protection fee. Too proud of our own neighborhood and too leery of the gangs we look down upon. They could have taken that stuff from us as easy as rats snagging cheese. They could have roughed us up for fun, but had no time to waste on a couple of punk kids. I was relieved to get away from them. The biggest heist I'd done in my young career. Biffy was just as scared as I was. And as proud.

"So I refuse the gang's offer. What do I get? Another rival gang, *The Smokers*, blown up on some crack drug, creeping out of the rat-black shadows as we're hustling down the back alley, some stupid short cut.

"We run. Biffy's not as fast as me. They trip him, take him down. I crouch in the back alley under some garbage bags, hardly daring to breathe. Too chicken to come out and defend him. Then I come when I hear his pleading. By that time he was real messed up. They were high and used him as a punching bag.

"They used me too, but a regular patrol car was shining its lights further up the alley and they somehow got spooked by the flashing reds and left us there in the filth and the dark. Biffy's all bashed and bruised and not moving, and I'm crawling, blood dripping from my nose and one arm and two fingers broken.

"When I finally get home and croak out a story, my old man cuffs my head and nearly sends me across the room when he hears what I did. Biffy'd died of a concussion. My old man says from now on you run with the Spikes. They would have protected you, you moron. They're your new street family. Go, do it! He wallops me, despite my aching arm, and from that day on, that very evening, I humble myself before *The Spikes*, become one of them."

I pass my dry tongue over my teeth, my voice hoarse. "You were just a kid. I didn't know."

"Nobody does. Now you do."

I stare at the trees in silence, lost in a daze. I'm trying to imagine what I would have done with a father like that. Many words come to my lips. I wonder how that would have scarred a young kid the age of Torv, seeing his best friend killed, and thinking he'd been the cause. But I know the last thing Torv wants is sympathy.

"So where'd you learn to fight?"

He inches forward and inclines his head. "Vin's cousin. Ever since I joined that gang, he used to take me out behind the old packing warehouses on Solar Drive and beat the crap out of me. Until I got faster and could defend myself. Let's just say I learned the ropes in a hell of a hurry...only so many black eyes and bruises a kid can take."

I look at him in horror.

He chuckles, a raw, dark laugh. "Don't worry, it's nothing. They used to spring stuff like that on all of the newbies. Like this old game The Spikes'd play. They'd blindfold me and any new recruits they were vetting for the club with duct tape so you'd pull half your eyebrows and hair off if you tried to claw the tape off and put you in a circle and take pot shots at you until you learned to listen and anticipate their moves. And I mean like any moves. Shuffle of boot, a breath of air, whiff of sweat."

I stare aghast. Angelos's training seems like small fry compared to this.

"Learn to move fast, Ellan, like a viper. Take hits, recover or else get clubbed."

A knowing exclamation hisses between my teeth. "Sounds like Angelos—our instructor. *Anticipate or die. Never underestimate your opponent. Never give up.*"

The ghost of a smile touches his lips. "Like to meet this Angelos guy."

"He was there at the tournament, but I never thought to introduce you. Nor did you stay long enough to talk to him." I flash on an idea. "Why don't you join our club? You could—"

"Nah." His shoulders lift in indifference. "Too many rules. Gotta pay too. I like to play by my own rules."

"Too bad. You'd like Angelos."

"Maybe. Look, all this is just theory. Hours upon hours of sparring is the only way to make any of it hit home."

I see it's not catching him, my suggestion re the club. "Still doesn't explain why you bully those other kids."

"Aw, get off it," he groans. "Most of those kids need to learn to stand up for themselves. I'm the one to rub their noses in the dirt, though they may hate me for it. I'm the blunt edge of reality. Half of them are too mouthy or cocky to begin with."

"Like the pot calling the kettle black." I turn at a clacking of claws from behind us. A long brown furry animal, scrabbles up the trunk of a withered oak. A tree weasel? Beady eyes glare down from a midway branch, tail flicking, black nose twitching, as if pissed at us for invading its territory.

Torv's lips curl in a smile. "Feisty bugger. You want to walk some? Maybe we'll come across some more terrors deeper in the woods." He seems as captivated as me.

We leave the bike farther behind and head up the trail. I consider all that has been said as the silence deepens between us.

"So what'd they do to the scum who killed Biffy?"

His eyes grow hard, a cold, dangerous look. A shadow of the same Torv I remember from the rave comes drifting back. "The Spikes found the ones who perpetrated it. They staked them out, beat the crap out of them with pipes, cut their nuts off and stuffed them in dumpsters."

I swallow hard. I can't help but feel a shiver prickle up my spine.

"All to say, Biffy was avenged."

I struggle to meet his gaze. I can just imagine the gang wars that escalated as a result.

"Enough morbid talk," he says. "We're supposed to be enjoying a nature walk here, right?"

"Right." I give a nervous laugh.

"Look, I can show you some tricks. Here's one, when you have the guy thinking he's got you at an advantage—like that doofus at the tournament—drop down, scoop out his legs from underneath him… Like this—" He falls on his back, spins, scissor-locks my shins and has me falling flat on my ass.

I yowl, struggle like a fish, but he's tightening his lean-muscled thighs around my waist and grappling me in a classic wrestler's pose and I can feel the wind go out of me. "Okay, enough. Got it." Then his muscles go slack and I'm gasping while he's laughing.

"You think that's funny?"

"Where're your kickboxing techniques now?" He scrambles to his feet and extends a hand.

I grab it and spring up on my feet. But I twist his index finger and thumb back and have him bending at the knees to avoid snapping his fingers. I give him a shove, lips curling in mockery. He grimaces as he's knocked back, shaking the sting out of his hand. His fists are up and he's crouched in fighter stance.

With a vindictive cry, I launch myself at him, going full out with a series of kicks and punches. It's different fighting without gloves. There are more kicks, more jabs to fleshy parts as bone on bone only breaks knuckles. He moves back and forward with me, taking every one of my hits with a placid grin, blocking many, but a few get through. I can feel his body prepared for the strikes, rock-hard, conditioned. He does a little head roll, cracks his neck. His eyes are steady, watching my brow, taking in every detail, as unnerving as it is.

My foot lashes out, a thunking switch kick to his ribs. He grabs my left leg, lifts it up. I teeter backward, cry out, fall back on my butt again.

"You're a slow learner, Elly. *Balance*. You already showed me your weakness."

I spring up, back arched, land on my feet with fists protecting my head.

"Nice!" He claps. "Word of advice: "You're too predictable. You need to look like you're going to strike in one place, then mix it up and move the other way."

"Says you."

"Says me."

A scowl forms between my lips. "Angelos's been telling me that for a year. What gives it away?"

"Your eyes. The tilt of your knuckles."

I think about that for a while.

This time I duck and fake him out, I'm kneeing him in the waist. I bump him back with another kick, trip him, fling him down on the grass and rise overtop him but he pulls me down with him and wraps his long arms around me. I'm struggling. Knees and elbows. Our faces are inches apart. I can feel his hot breath on my cheek. I can make out every detail of the pale scar from cheek to nostril. I feel his warm breath on my lips. Our lips touch.

I relax into his embrace, lean into his powerful chest. It's strong and reassuring with the smell of sweat and engine oil—and something else, pine needles and after shave. My skin breaks out in pleasurable tingles. He looks down at me under his knitted brows. I close my eyes and let my muscles go lax. All my tension slips away for a brief moment. He does not try to go further—and I appreciate that.

If only life were like this. Away from the city. In nature, able to disappear into the trees and forget the woes of the world, school projects, and thoughts of the future. Here with a guy, albeit unpredictable and living on the fringe of society, who makes me sweat, awakens a visceral thrill in my gut and somehow 'gets' me. But I know dreams are just illusion.

I can feel his hand circling my waist and the fingers of his other hand more insistent as they trace butterfly patterns on my back. His tongue probes my own and my breath catches. A husky note resonates in my throat. My breath quickens.

I push my fists between our heaving chests. "Not now. Hold up."

He stops. An instant's hesitation flashes in his eyes followed by a perplexed glint. Then vanishes as quickly as it came.

"Sure, whatever you say, Elly." He rolls over, staring up at the trees as they sway and rustle in the wind. A deep sigh resonates from his chest.

I lie beside him, letting my blood cool, collecting my raging emotions. We lie like that for some time. Just the scent of him in my nostrils, the birdcalls, the rustling leaves, sounds we rarely hear in the city, a muted thrum. The aroma of earth and pine envelops us in a warm embrace.

A rumble of thunder sounds from afar. Storm clouds are gathering and the temperature dropping. The first gusts of wind whip at our hair.

A rain drop hits my face. Then another. I look up into the slate-grey sky getting darker by the minute. "We'd better go."

He grunts his agreement. We leg it back to the bike. Torv mounts and fires it up. I hop in behind and we bounce down the trail in the direction of town. On the long ride back we do our best to outrun the storm. There's no talk about hooking up later, but I'm thinking it (and sense he is too), as the ominous clouds brew. So much for paradise. No one'd believe tough guy Torv would open up like that. Maybe there'll be more to come.

Chapter 14

The tender, heated moments with Torv linger in my cells. Into the evening. Into the next day. Hours pass in a blur.

I'm home after school, ready to hit the club, and pause at the murmur of voices. Dad's husky laugh rings out from the patio. The door's open a crack. He must be talking on his wristlet.

Curious, I pad softly into the study that leads out onto the double doors where a small garden and barbecue lie. I glance sidewise, notice he's got a haloband tucked in his briefcase on the table.

Odd. Since when's he into that? Maybe he's going to try it out on Lois, or Clare? A kinky eve at the office?

Not funny, Ellan.

Their muffled voices echo louder. The name of a new woman— *Gabrielle*. More of dad's husky laughter.

He gets off the call, turns, sees me, and knows I heard everything, or the few words that matter. "Oh, Elly, hi. Hey, way to go, heard you made it to the quarter finals at the tournament." He drifts in from the patio.

I nod, as if it's old news, hardly important to me. "Thanks…" I scratch my elbow, rubbing at a sore spot, suddenly feeling sorer. I flash him a pained look. "Why, Dad?" It's all I can say in my sad, hoarse voice.

He slumps at the desk, looks away. His knuckly fingers grab tufts of his thinning salt-and-pepper hair.

"Wait until it's your turn, Ellan. Wait until you have to make your own way. You'll see. It's not all roses. All downhill from high school."

"Something to look forward to then."

I try to imagine kissing and making it with Joey while I'm also dating Gilsen and Torv. There was an odd thrill about it, sure. Primal. But yet another part not so nice. Sleazy. Like the old paradox. Part felt good, like being wildly free and sensual and in-the-moment, but part as if I were a supreme slut. So which was it? Maybe things aren't so black and white. A lot to pore over as I turn to go. Maybe I shouldn't judge dad too harshly.

Dad seems to sense my churning and my about turn. His shoulders straighten, his face breaks out in a wary grin. "Good. I see you're thinking. Not taking the boots to the old man—yet. I'm knackered. Gotta go to bed."

"Sweet dreams," I say.

He manages a laconic laugh.

* * *

I want to explore more of the darkweb. But I'm afraid of what I might see.

That's a joke. What more could I see that could unnerve me at this point?

I let my fingers dance over the keypad. I can hardly type the web searches fast enough. Shocking articles appear:

Human immune system weaker than ever. Smog levels reach max count in the 100 most-populated cities. Soil nutrients depleted. Pesticides blamed. Acid rain and E. coli levels rise higher than ever.

Scientists believe killer plague is a product of mutations spawned by man-made toxins. 5G+ linked to increasing—

Then the window disappears. A blinking red message pops up in a bold font:

"SECURITY VIOLATION"

My heart misses a beat. No, it flutters, it pounds. What the hell does that mean?

What do you think, dumbo? Your session was flagged. You're in big trouble.

What now? In a panic I tap to close the window. But it won't close. Shit, now I'm done for? Whoever's found me out, they must be tracking me.

I lurch out into the hallway and call for Bram. "Bram!" Actually 'yell' is a better word.

His door shudders open and he stumbles out of his room as if he's been on a haloband holiday. I shuttle him into my room and close the door. He's still clutching his visor, winged out, his face hazed in a groggy pallor which turns to a scowl when he sees the blinking text. "Don't touch it," he rasps in a quiet monotone. He looks more annoyed than anything but there is a warble of anxiety in his voice, which is uncharacteristic of him. I swallow.

"I'll have to rework the portal." He scrunches his face into another feral scowl. "Find out what they know. What they can trace."

"I'm sorry to get you in this mess, Bram."

"Not your fault, kiddo. Should've been more careful." He shuffles away. "Whatever you do, don't touch that terminal. I can block it from my end and make it a dead node. I hope."

That last addition doesn't give me much confidence.

I lie in my bed cocooned and shivering under the sheets, bathed in a cold sweat. What have you done, Ellan?

* * *

I awake to a voice hissing in my ear.

"Ellan, wake up."

"Wha—"

"We've got a problem. A snag."

My eyes focus on a blurry face illumined by dim light from the hall. "What the hell you mean, Bram, we've got a problem? What are you doing in my room?"

"Listen—" He's rattling his haloband in a loose-limbed fist. "The extension I uploaded's in a loop with a test bot. I need to go in and shake the damn thing up. Bastard. Maybe if I try VR-ing into the scene…I can fix it, jiggle the bot unstuck."

"What the crap—get out of here. Are you nutso?" Memory dawns and I remember the breach, and my heart does a swan dive.

He rubs his chin, lost in thought. "Thing is, I need you to watch me. Don't want to go in alone."

This is too weird. I'm shaking, blinking, swinging my leaden legs to the floor. It's all Greek to me. "Get Carl or Rabin to do it. Why bug me?"

"I can't. Rabin's taking Karie out, and Carl, well, he's Carl—he has issues."

I massage my temples, lance him a blank stare.

"Look. I've got to get this extension ironed out. If they come—I mean, Starcom—because of this stupid breach, and they find I've been messing with it, it could go bad for all of us."

"You mean you're applying these extension hacks without authorization? I thought you said—"

"Forget what I said, Elly. Listen to me, I can only do it from the inside, and with you."

"How's that? This makes no sense."

"For crap sake," he growls, "it's complicated. I don't have time to explain it to you."

He sees me paralyzed and with a gape-mouthed grimace.

"Look, think of it as payback for me going out on a limb with you on darkweb. I didn't need to give you the links but I did."

"Okay, but this time only, Bram, no more. I hate that bloody haloband."

"Okay, I know. Just bear with me." He gives me a dog-eared grin. "No kinky guy's fantasy."

I roll my eyes. "Whatever."

We assemble in Bram's crib by his desk. I'm still half asleep, and trying not to get too worried.

"Here, I have to upload this last update." He flips on the holodisk, a two-inch cube of glossy transparent blue with enough terabytes to light the world. He enters a password. I assume it wirelessly feeds the hack extension to his visor. All this only fuels my unease.

"Ready to go." He grins while I can only grimace. "Here's yours." He thrusts a blue and white visor into my tense fingers.

I clutch his arm. "How do you know you can get back to this place in the VR land? Where you put the bot?"

He nods. "Don't worry, I know. I installed a glaring marker along the way, a colored prism, a way for me to fast track to the test scene, as soon as I slip into VR."

"Sure, it's your skull on the line." I shrug.

We don our headgear. The hour is late, 1 AM maybe? We take seats in chairs opposite each other, him in front of his super terminal. I feel the familiar wash of white light as the cinematic music assails my ears and hazy figures start to emerge in sync with the music.

We're in our own worlds, but they're interwoven. I see bits of Bram's world, and I'm guessing he sees bits of mine. His is either a forest of elves and faeries and sword-slinging mercenaries, or a vast grid of computer games with virtual tanks and helicopters and bazookas where the subjects morph with their vehicle and are traveling at high speeds to some other secret high stakes destination. Mine is more ocean and sea, and I'm in a merman fantasy, a giant cruise ship with wings and the edges of our worlds are about to interconnect. Why always boats? But then something misfires and our worlds collide head on and I'm thrust into his reality.

In this reality, I'm a grime-smeared marine crouched in a muddy ditch with three other soldiers bearing high-powered dart guns. We peer past a line of sandbags upon a grim, weird scene.

I see Bram creeping up on a stationary armored truck, stuck in the sand. I see the prism he was talking about, glowing a baleful orange, strapped to the side by a wire cord. He nods, makes an A-OK sign with thumb and forefinger back at us as he scuttles forward on hands and knees like a crab. An AK47 machine gun with strange tubes and extensions to either side is clutched and trained in front of him. He's sighting on an enemy sergeant with an ox's head, unloading a crate of explosives from the back of the van. I gape. The animal figure seems caught in a loop. No sooner does he unload it, than he picks the crate up again and puts it back in the van. Those weird horns gleaming with a strange yellow life dip into the box of grenades, infusing them with bursts of luminescence.

The bot.

Bram looses a volley of shots. *Rat-a-tat-tat.* The sergeant-enemy-hybrid falls, blood kicking up from his shattered neck, as half his head and horns are blown away. The prism lights up a lurid red color. Bram scrambles to his feet and rushes over to retrieve it.

As soon as he grabs it, his world explodes. Mine too.

There's a brilliant flash of light. My throat erupts in a wild cry. My heart pounds like a hammer. I clutch at my haloglasses, fling them off but they're still stuck to my ears. I peer over at Bram sprawled in his chair. He jerks like a marionette.

His goggles short. A blue band of fire arcs from ear to ear. The visor smokes. He convulses in his chair then slumps and rolls to the floor.

I stifle a cry of horror as my own visor pulses with a surge of current.

An indescribable blurry sensation washes over me, as if my mind is now vibrating on a wide open circuit. My forehead buzzes. I'm still seeing speckled images in front of my eyes from the haloband trip: the van, prism, camoed soldiers lying dead in the sand. I'm groping in the air.

I run over to Bram's side, flinging my hated haloband off. "Bram!" He's out cold. No response. I rip off his goggles. His eyes stare wide open. Shallow breaths rasp from his lungs. His glistening lips tremble with spittle.

"Bram! Mom! Dad!"

I hear a rush in my ears. My brain is still tracking but spins with recurrent images from the HB.

Doors open and close. Footsteps in the hall.

Some time later, the door bursts open. Mom comes hurrying over to my side.

"What the hell happened? Oh my god! Tell me."

I gaze helplessly. "I don't know. The glasses just shorted out. Next thing I know, Bram's on the floor. "

"Jesus." Mom's face is flushed. She pats him on the cheeks. "Bram! Bram!"

No response. She slaps him again.

Dad strides in, shrugging his bathrobe tighter around his shoulders. "What the hell?"

"Lars! We've got to get him to a hospital," Mom pleads.

Dad dials emergency. Within minutes, an ambulance arrives. Two paramedics check Bram's pulse. They strap him on a stretcher and carry him down the stairs with an oxygen mask strapped over his face. With an angry grimace, Mom crouches to snatch up the haloband. We all pile into the ambulance and head to the Starcom clinic. But the medics don't allow us to see him.

I keep seeing flashbacks from the haloband as we wait in the lobby. It's starting to worry me now. The disturbing images, the ox's head splattered, Bram charging in, accompanied by *feelings, of doom.*

They take me in a back ER to have me examined. A nurse checks my blood pressure, tests reflexes, shines a light in my eyes, poking and prodding here and there, asking how I am feeling. But I assure her I am fine and that Bram is the priority. She seems to accept that.

We're back out in the waiting room again. Fluorescent lights are too bright for my eyes. My head starts to spin again. My throat and nose are dry from an antiseptic smell thick in the air. Mom's sitting beside me, wringing her wrists. Her eyes are rimmed red. With one hand she keeps pulling at her dress in nervous exhaustion. Dad looks five years older. I hate to see him like that with his long, haggard face.

I try to look away; instead I watch the doctors and nurses come and go with their air of efficient gravitas. What a terrible place to work. I could never survive here.

It seems hours before a doctor comes to speak with us, before we can see Bram. He quizzes us about the haloband. I talk about the flash of light. His eyes seem to widen and his lips purse.

A specialist in neurology joins the group, and Mom and Dad are getting more worried.

"They're defective!" Mom yells.

"There's not enough evidence to prove that, ma'am. It may have contributed to his condition."

"What condition? Tell me you have a treatment."

"It's more complex than that, Mrs. Weis. Your son has a record of ADD and sleepwalking. All giving high probability for his current catatonic state."

"Catatonic state?" My mom's shrinking, sagging like a ragdoll, shaking her head, her eyes welling up with tears.

She stumbles out in the hall.

She's been on her wristlet for a long time. I get a rotten, sick feeling in the pit of my stomach that she is poised to do something drastic. But what can I do? When I think of her and how likely she is to take on Starcom and rake them over the coals, my gut tenses. The feeling's overpowering enough to have me jumping up to search her out. Dad's trailing after me in a semi-daze, in stiff, jerky hops, as if knowing something's not right. Mom's leaning, pale and withdrawn, against the wall, her hand trembling. Dad comes to join her, puts his arm around her shoulder. I'm at his side, my own arm tucked around her waist.

"Surely we use the damaged goggles as evidence?" she asks.

Dad exhales a weary sigh. "The reality is, Viv, no way they're going to get engineers to admit their mistakes, or anything like it. I'm guessing it'd be a month, maybe a year, before we'd get any expert opinion on what actually went wrong."

Mom shakes her head. "It's soul-crushing. So what's that mean, Lars, that we're screwed? Bram's screwed?"

"For all our sakes, I hope not."

My heart sinks. I turn away as guilt eats at me.

C. TURNER, L. LASERRE

Chapter 15

Finally, they let us see Bram.

Two orderlies in grey gowns usher us into a small private room at the back of the facility. We see him propped on his bed, staring straight ahead with unblinking eyes as if unaware of our presence. Dad's choked with grief. A lost look pools in his eyes and strangled gurgle comes from his throat. My heart crumbles. For the first time, I see how alike they are.

A dozen memories flood back: of my brother, Bram the geek, playing in the snow, or splashing mud puddles at me in the rain, annoying as only a big brother can be.

Three soft grey-upholstered chairs range to the side and I can see Mom staggering over to one. Long bands of fluorescent lights line the ceiling. Wires are attached to Bram's temples and wrists, hooked to monitors with lots of lights and levers. An IV unit feeds liquid into his right vein.

As broken up as I am to see him here, something about the scene seems too contrived. Bram here, Starcom offering to treat him free of charge when word came through that the haloband's circuitry was at the root of his injury. Everybody knows medical attention is prohibitively expensive everywhere in the nation, and those gathered can guess it was the haloband that got him into this mess.

A nurse in a white coat motions us to the chairs at the side.

"Mr. and Mrs. Weis? Glad you're here. Please sit down. Your son has a very serious condition. One called Myscopia Syndrome."

"What's that?" my mom croaks.

"Myscopia…It means his occipital lobe, part of the cerebral cortex, has shut down and has gone into a wait mode, a similar state to, let's say, a daydream. The haloband was created to induce a similar state in participants to make the 4D experience more vivid. It seems your son is 'stuck' there. He appears to be susceptible to visual and auditory stimuli and was brought to a threshold by the unit." She adds hastily, "—as would anybody of his high sensitivity although he is a very unusual case, maybe one in a hundred thousand."

"This is just not possible," my mom says in a hoarse voice. "Please fix it."

"We can't fix it, ma'am. It's important to realize that Bram would have developed this syndrome in the next one to five years with or without application of the haloband's stimuli."

"Bullshit. It was a direct effect of that moronic haloband that got him into this state."

"That has not been proven."

"Mom, take it easy." I pull her away from the nurse, whom she looks ready to slug.

Mom ignores me. "I can prove it." She rips out the damming haloband from her purse and dangles it before the nurse's face. I clasp her arm in a warning embrace. Dad's beside me, holding her back. Remembering the security personnel who had greeted us at the Starcom clinic doors, with tasers, guns, and vests, it does not seem wise to antagonize them.

"Just treat him."

"Yes, we are. We have cyclopentazine. A brain stimulator." She holds up a pill bottle and gives a supercilious smile.

Mom slaps the pills away. "I don't want your stupid pills. Nor does Bram. I want him symptom free, back to the way I knew him."

The nurse lifts a palm gently. "I'm afraid that's all we have, Mrs. Weis. As I said, it's Myscopia. Not a side effect of the haloband."

"We're going to see about this. I'm going to sue."

"That's certainly your right."

"Damn right it is. Please leave now. Leave us alone with our son."

The nurse nods. The woman, whom I see is actually a doctor, bows her head and with a resigned sigh, leaves.

Bram just sits there like a zombie. I stare horrified at him, wrestling with these disclosures, unable to accept that the Bram I've known all these years is the one who looks drugged up on some debilitating drug, gazing listlessly off into space like a vegetable.

My mom touches his arm but he doesn't register it. *Wait, his pupil narrowed.* The lids flutter ever so gently. Didn't they? Maybe there is hope.

But we don't get any more reactions from him.

After a long time, we head home. There's nothing we can do for Bram by waiting around. I'm exhausted.

It's like 6 AM by the time we roll in through the front door. A somber mood surrounds the household. I mope about my room, wanting to relieve my frustrations by diving into the darkweb to research brain traumas. But I know, even if I had a password, that is fraught with disaster. I finally give up and doze off in my low couch-futon bed, only to give myself over to restless, harrowing dreams.

* * *

I awake to a tug on my shoulder. The blurry face of my mother.

"Hey, Elly, wake up. I'm heading over to see Bram again. You want to come?"

Mom is on her knees, whispering in my ear. It's touching to see her crouching near. She smells of perfume—honey and lilies. Yet dark circles surround her usually bright eyes.

"Huh? What time is it?"

"Noon."

"Oh, that late? Yeah, sure." I rub my own eyes and heave a deep yawn, laden with the weight of memory that comes crashing back.

We take the car to Meadowvale. We see Bram in the same comatose state as before. His neck, head and shoulders are propped up on pale yellow pillows. The IV is removed. No longer are any wires attached to his head. His eyes stare ahead, but his cheeks have more pink color, though that is relative, considering the troglodyte nature of his pastimes: hacking, playing serpents and dragons and halobanding. I bend and crouch near his ear. "Hey Bram," I whisper, "you goofus, we're all waiting for you to wake up. Have the decency to at least give us a high sign."

Mom's lips pale. Several moments pass. We just stand there like zombies. Trading awkward stares. Filled with hollow thoughts.

But as if he registers my silent will to come out of his coma, I see him blink, hear him swallow and groan.

"Ugh. What time is it?" He shakes his head. "Where am I?"

Mom leaps over to the bedside in a frenzied fit of elation. "Here at Meadowdale. Bram, oh Bram, you're awake!" She rocks from foot to foot, locks her fingers in his. "You've been sick, Bram." I rush over with no less amazement and grip his arm. I can only gasp relief.

He stares in confusion. "What's with you? I don't get it? Why am I in a hospital gown?"

"It's a long story," Mom says. "You had an accident."

"Ah...I remember. Zoning in to the urban web, a pseudo dungeon crawl, then bam, great big blank space."

"Yes, that's about it." I can't believe he's talking, and remembering.

A green light is blinking on one of the monitors and a doctor comes running. "Bram, you're back."

Before Mom or I can get a word in edgewise, another doctor bursts through the door and they shoo us out of the room.

* * *

We break back in after some time when the orderly is not guarding the door. A white-coated doctor is bent over him peering into his eyes. I blink twice in shock to see Bram with a blue visor like the haloband over his eyes.

"What the bloody hell? Take that thing off him," Mom cries and we scramble in, in unison.

The doctor turns and frowns. "You're not supposed to be in here, Mrs. Weis. Nurse!" His eyes search for the head nurse. I reach to snatch the haloband off Bram's brow but the doctor grabs my wrist. I break out of that hold in two seconds, daring him with a fierce stare to try more. "Wait," he cries, flustered. "We're seeing if he responds to the HB. Nurse! Get over here, please."

"What? Burning more of his brain cells with that fool thing that fried him in the first place?" Mom pushes in inches from his face.

"We don't—"

"I don't care what you're doing. Take that thing off. It's not a stethoscope, it's a menace."

"We don't know that for certain."

"Well, I sure as hell do." Mom rips off the visor, throws it to the floor while I distract the flustered doctor by stepping into his personal space. He bares his teeth, reaching for the emergency security line.

"Calm down, Mrs. Weis. I can assure you—"

"Don't tell me to calm down!" Mom lifts a clenched fist, trembling in rage. I agree. I hate it when she is like this, but a deep, dark rage is pumping in my veins. The same rage when my cat got run over by the city garbage truck when it came barreling by outside our house. I reacted just like my mom.

Bram stirs groggily from his haloband holiday.

"Come on, Bram. We're getting out of here." Mom grabs his wrist and pulls him out of bed. I reach into the locker to get his clothes. I help him put on his shoes.

"I'm okay, Mom."

"No, you're not okay."

The nurse has returned with others. She flinches. "That's not advisable, ma'am. Bram's likely to have a relapse. He will need to be treated. Studied by our doctors. His condition is fragile. He's under observation, officially classified."

"Not anymore. Save your funny farm for another stooge. I'd like to strap CEO Rane into that bed and feed him cyclopentazone, or whatever it is you're feeding my son."

"Cyclopentazine. And we administer it by syringe, at least in the later stages."

"Good for you, now buzz off."

We guide Bram down the hall, Mom and I on either side of him. Bram is back in the land of the living. We sign a waiver for his release at the front desk. The two stubble-chinned security guards dressed in grey-blue uniforms and with tasers at their hips cast us dark looks as we pass through the mesh but have no authority to detain us—yet. They let us pass.

We get Bram home and settled in his room. Starcom is calling Mom, demanding to know why we've taken Bram from their world-class clinic. Mom doesn't want to talk to them, but she negotiates a lengthy leave of absence for him. At dinner, he's somewhat groggy and lethargic, though he says he's fine. Something's not quite right. Bram's slower on the draw. He takes his time answering questions. He does a lot of staring into space— *daydreaming* as the doctors called it. Understandable, given his ordeal and that he was catatonic. They probably fed him a bathtub of drugs. Is he going to slip back into a trance like the doctor says? Will he really bounce back and be the regular, sharp-tongued, insolent Bram I've always known and loved? I shake my head as a protracted pang of doubt prickles up my back. Life is never that simple.

Dad's in high spirits as he returns from work to have Bram back at home. Bram is able to hold a conversation but his mind is still a blank regarding the particulars of his zapout during the haloband episode. Mom is not happy. She's pacing the living room like a caged tiger. I'm afraid she and Dad are going to erupt in an argument any second.

They do, and it's not pretty.

"Someone's got to pay, Lars. Those smug doctors over at Starcom are like a bunch of predatory weasels. All their quack science and patronizing airs. They've filed a writ to bring him in. They'll force us to comply."

"I know Viv, you already gone over that, but calm down. Bram's in the middle of a sensitive time and he's in need of support. Let's not upset the apple cart. If they need to run more tests on him—"

"Screw the tests! Are you not hearing me, Lars? You didn't see him with that haloband over his head. They're monsters. To think I worked for that company for so many years."

I put my hands over my head to stop the words ringing in my ears. "Mom, take it easy. Chill."

She pauses, her mouth cinched.

"You two are not the enemy." I move closer and place a soothing hand on her shoulder. "Bram's back. He's safe here at home, isn't he? Starcom is just another big company, they don't give a damn about us or him, and they'll see him drown, all of us, if necessary. When I was hauled down to Hent's office, she pretended to be my friend, to protect my interests, but I could see she was only covering her ass and was scared about repercussions. Imagine what Starcom'll do, if they think you know more than you should and build a case against them. They'll crucify you."

"I agree. Elly's right," Dad says. He bows his head.

Mom's mouth trembles, but she grows quieter still as she takes it all in. I can tell she's going ahead with whatever sly scheme she's cooked up. Too much of the rebellious streak in her. Like me.

The sinking feeling in my gut about her safety resurges.

Dad makes a wise retreat and doesn't rile her.

Though I know she will stop at nothing to make Starcom pay, she remains strangely quiet. Every time I think of her and the company I feel nauseous. I see the grotesque skull and crossbones hovering over a pool of red hot lava, the same I experienced when I got zapped by the haloband.

Mom breathes a tired sigh. She goes off to the minibar to fix herself a drink.

I turn to Bram, a whisper in my throat. "What do you feel when you go into these states?"

He furls his brow. "Just an obliviousness. Blankness, as if I'm floating in a cloud and nothing can hurt me." He laughs, a humorless sigh. "Not unlike a haloband scene."

"Can you hear what we're saying when you've checked out?"

"Kind of. It's like I'm underwater and whirling around me are fuzzy shapes, all grey and yellow, like faces and forms."

I shake my head. A small shiver ripples up my spine. "Sounds real messed up, Bram."

"Yeah, it is." He scowls. "I feel as if a few minutes pass then I come out of it. Only to hear you guys tell me I've been out for two hours or longer." He shakes his head. "All that time I feel as if I couldn't give a shit about anyone or anything."

"Weird. You look haggard. Your skin's all puffy and cheeks droopy. Your eyes super red. It can't be good for you."

"No, it's probably not." He shrugs. "But what can I do?"

"You don't seem too uptight about it."

He gives a harsh laugh. "As I said, I couldn't care less."

The admission upsets me. A side effect of haloband, defective manufacture, or is there some dark motive behind Starcom putting people in a coma? I feel as if a sliver of glass is shoved in my chest.

I pull on Bram's arm. "What do you remember? Anything about the blackout?"

He gives a shaky cough. "No. Only that the scene is cleansed. The prism is gone too. Whenever I go anywhere near that parked armored car, the bot has been removed."

"Are you crazy?" I stare at him only in amazement. "You actually put that visor back on?"

"Sure, why not? Only way I could find out."

"Your life, your brain, Bram."

"Starcom must have gone in and mopped up the evidence," he muses, as if part of him is absent. "Can't say I blame them. That's what I'd do. Cover my ass."

He darts his eyes nervously back and forth. Mom is still at the minibar, staring into space, swirling a white stick in her drink. She looks as if she's going to wander back into the family room any moment when she snaps out of her reverie. The front door shuts. Dad's gone.

Bram's voice takes on an edgy rasp. "This haloband thing is whacked out evil, Elly. If you only knew what it's capable of…" He bites his lip.

"In some respects I do."

He continues as if he hadn't heard me. "I've hacked into stuff that even the highest level programmers aren't aware of."

"Like what?" Suddenly I'm interested.

"Secret documents…code snippets." His voice goes to a lower pitch. "Ever wonder why it offers all those choices?"

"That's easy, bro. To give you variety of entertainment scenarios, a quick distraction."

"No." He gives his head a vigorous shake. "It's another way to start messing with your mind. Each choice comes with rewards and punishments."

I start to object but then I close my mouth. I suddenly remember on that bizarro trip with Joey, how I was 'punished' by losing my mermaid privileges when I chose the cruise ship over the palace.

"This feedback loop from the wristlet. They use our body signals to read the subconscious, create some invasive profile of us…use it to feed us data anchors, psych anchors, datagrams, whatever the hell they want and—" He swallows what seems a lump in his throat.

"What?"

"Nothing." He shakes his head again. His pale lips quiver and I know he wants to say more. I let him. "After I hacked into company records, I started to piece it together, Ellan, but I was already too deep into the haloband—to save myself."

My heart beats faster. I feel my skin prickle in a hot flush.

"They've accessed everything, Ellan. Quantum computers linked with supercomputers run the device. They've cross-referenced billions of recorded dreams and archetypal symbols. Scanned every movie, book, story in human history and use it as reference to create these 'fabulous' VR soap operas we become part of."

"It just means they embellish them, up their game to movie quality—"

"No! To mess up your mind. Remember—we're talking about the subconscious here. Dreams. Archetypes. Weirdness. Ever notice how dreams make no sense? But you still wake up feeling really bad or guilty or sometimes feeling really up as if you're on top of the world? Haloband's like that. Their plan—"

What was he talking about? Archetypes? I have no clue what that means.

"Their plan, I don't know—maybe keep us locked in some VR land, prisoners of the mind. With bars nobody can crack. Not sure what it is but once they've hooked everybody, we're doomed."

"So why did you keep the thing on 24-7 when—"

"I couldn't help it, Elly. This thing sucks you in." His face is pained. "The more you use it, the more you crave it. You can't escape it…"

He would know. Crave it like a junkie his bayludes. I've barely dabbled in the thing and still hate it. I don't plan on using it ever again.

He peers at me. "What's up with mom? She's taking forever to mix her drink. Look at her. She's wound as high as a crazy clock."

"I was going to ask you. Wish I knew what she's been doing over at Starcom. She's been acting on edge for the last few days."

"She's changed all her passwords," said Bram. "I can't monitor her movements at work."

"Since when are a few passwords a problem for you?"

"Since I was in a coma."

"Okay, sorry." I sigh. "Be careful, Bram. I worry about you." My fingers reach for his hunched shoulders. "I don't like this at all. Especially the stuff about archetypes. I don't get them. I shudder every time I think about that monster Starcom."

He gives my wrist a squeeze. "Me too, sis. Watch your back. There's—"

He halts in mid-sentence. His tongue lolls. I see his eyes glaze over, then as he slips back into one of those blank, quasi-catatonic states, I beat my fists against his arm. The Bram I know has suddenly blinked out.

Chapter 16

I'm back at school this week, though my heart is not into anything. Except maybe gym.

Soccer's amping up...the rivalry, the roughness, but that's not surprising. Something's going to blow. Another sinking feeling hollows out my stomach. A lot of that these days, ever since Bram and I got zapped by that haloband. Fragmented images. Grainy, speckled ones. Of fights, balls hurled, kicked shins, harsh words, a trapped figure in an abandoned lot. That last one makes no sense to me.

I shove my anxiety down. No one's going to believe me, or care. I feel something's off, even after I lied to the doctors, but I don't know what.

It's Thursday morning. We're out in the soccer field taking up our practice positions. Zandra's team against ours. There's a big end of season match coming up, so there's a concerted drive to look sharp. Ms. Gates's pointing and giving us pep talks on how to drive the ball deep into enemy territory, right to the opponent's net. A silly, comical thought flashes in my head. Brenda Gates and Nelly as a tag team. It would make an interesting study. No Nellies in the playing field here. The school board would if it could, but the holographic signal can't reach that far, or so I think.

The ball's in our end. The other team's handling it very well. For some bizarre reason our defense sucks today. I'm playing center. I have sprinted back to help out. Karie and Leta are at my wings, waiting for me to intercept then chip the ball back to them. Zandra's controlling the ball with a vindictive persistence. I'm running alongside her, trying to wrest the ball out from under her strong legs, but she's quick, like a greyhound, and deking me out. I grunt and force my way in. She gets an idea, makes a fancy move, an unexpected right angle twist, suddenly... Boom. Her heavyweight Bess barrels straight into my midsection and knocks me head over heels to the ground. Not before Zandra has an open sight on the net and kicks the ball hard into the corner.

3-2. Wow, they're all cheering. What, no whistle blown for a foul? They're only one behind now. Zandra's pumping her fist in the air. Her teammates are crowding around, slapping her on the back, congratulating her.

Karie helps me up, in a grim, *what-the-hell* kind of way. I'm nursing my bruised elbow and my grass-stained knees, every cell in my body is wanting to go over and pound that bitch into the ground. I resist the urge, remembering what Angelos told us. No unwarranted aggression. *Kickboxing's not meant as a weapon against people. Only to be used in self-defense.*

Good one, Angelos, tell that to bimbos like Zandra.

Some goofus on our team, in a knee-jerk reaction, kicks the ball over the wall.

"Hey, that was dumb," I cry out. "Now we've no ball to finish the game."

"Exactly." She glares at me in defiance.

"Relax, I'll get it," Karie offers.

I look at the north wall and the crumbled area where a single person might—and I say, might—scale it. Maybe fifty yards down. The weather-blasted brick's deteriorated more than ever, leaving a glaring enough gap for an agile person to squeeze through. We scoot over and peer through the jagged opening. The windowless remains of crumbled warehouse blocks rise in profusion. Whole walls have disintegrated, leaving only skeletal girders and plaster-rubbled floors in grey ruin. A dark blur rises in my brain. I remember the earlier premonition I had; again, the flash of blood and broken bones, multiple fracture wounds jumps out like a lightning strike. My heart falters. Whoever was going into that place was not coming out.

I grab Karie's arm. "Don't go."

"What's wrong with you?" She flings off my hand. "You an overprotective mother or what?"

I gaze back at her. The crumbling gap is more ominous than ever. Like the serrated jaws of a hostile reptile. Of course it isn't. It's only my imagination, the hyperjinx of an unwanted premonition. My fingers twitch and I shake my head. "Karie, can't explain… An accident in waiting."

"What are you dawdling about for?" Zandra comes trotting over like a mare in heat, a sneer on her flushed face. "Chickens. We need that ball. Someone's going over to get it."

"Why don't you, you bitch?" says the girl who kicked it over in the first place.

"Sure I'll go," Zandra challenges. "You wimps are nothing but cowards."

"I wouldn't go in there," I warn her.

"Says who? You trying to stall the game? Because you're one point ahead and we're on a roll?" Her derisive snort speckles us with nasal spray.

Other members of Zandra's team are gathering. They grumble in agreement.

I can see I'm outnumbered. Okay, let the witch do it. I'm glad it's her hide at stake, not Karie's, but still, I don't want to see anybody hurt, even Zandra. These visions—I don't know whether to trust them—or discard them. The gym teacher's calling out some of the other girls on their passing shots and footwork way down at the other end of the field.

Zandra squeezes past the broken section while I poke my head through and stare after her.

We mill around, friends and foes, trading uncomfortable jokes and grumbles. It's been a long time since Zandra's been gone and I'm getting fidgety. "Where the hell is she?"

Suddenly a muffled scream breaks the silence.

The hairs rise on the small of my back. We're all paralyzed. For the space of a moment we gather round the hole. All of us are afraid to advance.

I see the instructor hurrying over on heavy feet. "What's going on here?"

One of us admits that Zandra went through the gap. Gates heaves a frustrated sigh and then ducks toward the crumbling crack, craning her neck, but can see nothing, except the bleak view we could see earlier: dilapidated ruins. She struggles to push her bulk through but can hardly wedge her shin and thick thigh in.

She pulls back with disgust. "Stay put," she hisses at us. "All of you." She speaks into her wristlet and dogtrots back for reinforcements.

I gaze through the hole and feel my stomach lurch. A voice within tells me it's too late already.

I gather courage at Ms. Gates's retreating form and catch Karie's solemn gaze. We trade uneasy frowns and she clamps her jaw. Ignoring the mutters of distress around us, I sneak through the jagged crack. Karie follows my lead.

Our sneakers crunch on the broken, weed-ridden stone. There's a ravaged warehouse in front of us, four stories high, stripped of windows and doors. Only a skeleton of a ruin remains, gutted by vandals and age.

I can hear a muted whimpering in the air, *Aaagh*, punctuated by anguished gasps. Karie and I hump it up and thread our way through the crumbled brick closer to the agonized sounds. More buildings range up ahead, each in states of worsening repair. The cement is like the playing field, damp from a recent rain. Wafts of old rotting timbers reach our nostrils.

The ball must have rolled somewhere here into the first floor of the building. Karie and I edge our way in. We peek around the corner of a corroded cement pillar. There, we catch a glimpse of a pale limb sticking out from behind a small mound of rubble. A figure is trapped under some detritus and a tilted cross beam. It's just like in my vision—rubble, a trapped figure, broken bones—and I freeze, my blood running cold.

Zandra's breathing and still conscious but her eyes are half-closed, clouded in pain and a haze of terror. Both her hip and shoulders are pinned by the notched beam. I can see a dark wound at her side and some massing blood.

Karie and I try to heave the crosspiece off her but it's no use. The thing's far too heavy and it's stuck at one end. We reel back on our haunches and suck air between our teeth.

I scrabble over to clasp Zandra's fingers, cold and dry and pasty. I tell her it will be okay.

But I know it won't. I can barely imagine the pain she must be suffering. To my left, I spy the white-and-black-checkered soccer ball, a guilty culprit straddled in the shadows of must and mildewed cement. Strange that our fiery rivalry has come to this.

The banshee scream of an ambulance echoes somewhere beyond the wall. *Good.* I look up. A flash of hope surges in my chest. The vehicle must have ridden right up onto the playing field. There might be time to save her.

A crunch of boots soon echoes our way, on the heels of the tumult of desperate voices drifting in the molder. Karie scrambles out to wave her hand. She tilts up on her toes. "Over here! Over here!" I stay crouched, still clasping Zandra's cold, nerveless fingers.

Before long paramedics arrive where I crouch. A team of auxiliaries has smashed the wall back with sledgehammers. I stand back, my arms wrapped around my middle. A white stretcher comes through. They nudge me away. Gingerly they raise the beam and lift Zandra from the pebbly crater. She looks pretty banged up. That loose dangerous crosspiece must have fallen on her when she approached. The ball—it must have smacked the beam, destabilized it that fractional inch to make it a living time bomb when she'd tried to dig the ball out. She's still alive because the paramedics braced her neck, attached an oxygen mask and wrapped her in a cotton blanket before rushing her out. Ms. Gates tells us all to go home.

In the glare of flashing red lights and shouts and radio chatter my sick dismay does not abate. Accompanied now by a flash of shameful regret...that I did not try harder to hold her back.

I hear the whispers in our group, arms hugging chests. *Ellan, the witch. She said 'accident in waiting'.*

Karie steps up. "No, stupid, she's the one who told Zandra not to go in, remember?"

"Bull." Bess, Zandra's best friend, glares at me. "You never liked her. What are you, some hexer?"

They all back away from me. "Did you wish it on her?"

"No!" I cry. "What are you talking about?" I shield my body from their abuse, the fearful stares and negative waves of energy. My fists ball, wanting to smack them for accusing me of witchcraft. But I shake my head, feeling fear and dismay overshadow that sick feeling brimming in my gut.

Why this newfound visionary power? I sense bad things coming, but no good things. In a macabre way, I seem to have become psychic.

Ms. Hent, our principal, has bustled out onto the field like a sergeant major and excuses us from classes for the day. I take the tram home, my spirits low, but try to send positive energy Zandra's way.

Chapter 17

Vivian Weis slaps shut her compact. Her hiss is one of outrage. She's a very unhappy camper.

She catches a glimpse of her reflection in the ladies' room at Starcom Labs and scowls.

Dang, woman, scowl anymore and you're going to need *Purofane* to smooth out those wrinkles. Yet something is still bothering her. The access codes should still be working. There was a no expiry limit on them— granted to all A6 level personnel.

She drifts out of the rest room, tugging at her long, frizzy bangs in a distracted mood. She runs the high clearance password through the terminal in her office.

ACCESS DENIED

Vivian passes her tongue over her front teeth. She taps the password into the logon screen.

USER not authorized for that access. CLASSIFIED.

Why the hell is it classified? she rages. *Damn.* She knits her brow as her frustration mounts. The clinical tests of haloband should be public knowledge. A flutter of unease stirs in her throat. The lockout sounds fishy to even her most trusting ear. As more time passes, warning bells go off in Vivian Weis's brain.

She plunges head in hands, at the edge of panic, thinking of Bram and his propensity for slipping back into catatonic states. Desperation creeps over her like the obstinate ache of a chronic back problem. There is no way she can let this go…she has to protect her family.

* * *

It's late at night in the West Wing of Starcom Labs when she hears the shuffle of feet. She jerks back from the terminal and closes the window. All her digging into various company databases has yielded only the most minimal of useful information. She puts on her best face and forces a smile as a broad-shouldered man in casual wear and white T-shirt with a light mop of sandy hair walks by the row of holo-terminals on the raised deck.

"Viv?"

"Hey, Hal, fancy meeting you. Working late?"

He looks up, his eyes brightening.

"Yeah, rollout's been tough. Deborah has us all working overtime."

"I bet she has, if I know Deb. This haloband is hot stuff."

"Tell me about it. Say, what are you doing here? Pretty late."

"Ah, you know the drill, same old. Say, think you can get me an A3-level clearance? For some reason the system's locked me out."

The big man hesitates, his bushy brows arching. "Well, I don't know. What do you need it for?"

"Well, just need some numbers on our HB pretrial successes and failures. Internal surface details only. You know the thing. Nothing to get worked up about."

He scratches his high cheekbones. He bites his lip. "Mmm...dunno, Viv."

She brushes up to him, lean hip against warm leg, presses closer against his chest, making sure to allow for some breast contact.

Hal's licks his lips. "You're a married woman, Viv. Shouldn't be doing that—tempting innocent men."

"Oh, you're hardly innocent, Hal," Viv teases. "Think you can handle it." She gives an airy chuckle, one that turns husky, a bit more sensual than necessary.

Hal shakes his head, the edge of a broad grin creasing his chiseled face. "I shouldn't be doing this, Viv. It could land me in trouble."

"As I said, don't worry, Hal. I just need the insider scoop on the pretrials. A ballpark figure, nothing more, the pros and cons. Only minor stats."

His hands reach for and circle round Viv's shoulders. Small grey eyes struggle to resist but stray suggestively to the swell of her chest then to the lean, tapered line of her thighs and ribs and tight blouse. "You're a fine-looking woman, Viv. Heard you and Lars aren't getting along so well these days."

"You heard right."

Hal sighs. "Okay, Viv. But you owe me one—A big one—this is like old times, and I don't mean just a dinner or a coffee somewhere."

"Whatever, Hal, if it works for you. This is important."

No guilt. No shame. After what sleazy activities Lars has been up to, she has license for some payback, even if it is a harmless flirtation or two. The business world can be a cruel arena. Besides this foray was nothing. She'd dated Hal long before when she and Lars had taken a 'timeout' several years ago when the marriage was going sour. Hal had no new surprises or tricks to teach her. Just a replay of some old, nostalgic memories, nothing more, then she'd break it off.

Viv convinces herself she'll keep more tidy promises. Anything to get to the bottom of Bram's mysterious mental lapses. It was because of a side effect of the haloband—she knew it and there'd be hell to pay. Then she thinks of him, his recent lapses of staring into space like a zombie, sitting half comatose at his computer desk staring into a blank screen with drool trickling out the corner of his mouth. She swallows hard and stifles the whimper in her throat as Hal moves to one of the big holo screens and searches for a temporary guest password. As the images of Bram keep flooding back to her, wet tears spring to her eyes.

She wipes them away quickly as Hal rises and his lips stretch in an oily grin as he invites her to browse the terminal.

Viv scans with satisfaction.

"Here you go. Don't say I didn't do anything for you, or tell who gave you access to A3." He sweeps his arm toward the display.

Viv flashes him a conspiratorial grin. No sooner has Hal moved on to the digital processing lab than Viv is deadpan, tapping icons furiously on the page and zeroing in on the relevant data that details the latest pretrial document. Viv stops, exhales, her lips parted, eyes slits of rebellious fire. The document is dated one week ago and it is not pretty.

Report on HB, as compiled by Nathan E. Soames, Phd, Varicore Enterprises, Senior Science Consultant.

Conclusions: Device extremely addictive.

Recommendation: This product should not be brought to market, until significant and/or serious alterations are made.

Side effects: Listlessness, mood swings, brain fog, an intense desire to recapture the thrill of endless sensual stimuli.

Other risks: seizures, amnesia, increased heart rate, high blood pressure, mild to moderate catatonic behavior.

It is the last part that makes her eyes widen in despair and her breath catch in rage.

Symptoms: Confusion of reality with fact, distorted spatial reality and dissociation of the senses. Fragmented reality. Real life becomes a series of movie-like dream sequences. Haloband becomes reality.

Continual use of HB has made test subjects 20-40% more susceptible to subliminal suggestions. These can be corporate suggestions, ads or slogans.

Mind control: +22%

Surveillance potential: +51%

Consumer habit monitoring: +79%

(*Note: Pool of test subjects includes 1000 random volunteers, some outfitted with placebos in the form of a dummy device resembling haloband.)

Recap: Severely addictive, overpowering to the senses. Product cannot guarantee that users will not overreact or overextend themselves with continued use.

The on-board VR technology uses an extended database of test-subject dream experiences coupled with neural net and linguistic learning heuristics that can produce disturbing effects on the human psyche.

Bottom line: high risk of neurotransmitter overload, misfire, even trauma and breakdowns.

The last line makes Viv's blood run cold.

Bastards. So they lied. They tried to push HB through without proper field testing and quality control. Now Bram's messed up and nothing can save him.

With a shaky hand, Viv taps a message to Lars and tells him she will be staying late tonight. On a whim she hits speed-dial. She gets voicemail; he's probably out himself, 'entertaining'. She grits her teeth and digs in her feet, compiling her case, word by word against Starcom. How timely this controversial school project of Ellan's is with the machinations of Starcom.

Viv continues her snooping, poking and prodding, coming across more shocking details, like the fact that Starcom has contracted other secret, psychological research and AI groups around the nation, ranked high in C-

Sec clearance. She doesn't realize that Hal has unwittingly given her a passcode access to West Wing C, otherwise unknown and off limits.

Heart-pounding, she debates whether to go further. She has enough data. Yet she's come this far. She straightens her spine and rises from her seat. Nobody ever told her that curiosity killed the cat.

* * *

Viv steps into an alcove she's never seen before. It looks like a vast techno-matrix of rack-mounted servers. Literally, endless rows of them, going as far down in the inky darkness as the eye can see. A dull hum permeates the sterile surroundings. The air, chill for her tastes, has her wrapping her arms about her chest and stamping her feet. A cloud of anxiety settles over her brain as she moves forward. A cloud storage room? Not quite. Long glass tubes, like glasshouse aquariums, stretch the length of the server cabinets, fastened at waist height. But what on earth are the fibrous ovoids with the ropy exteriors floating in what looks like liquid jelly in the tubes? They are melon-sized and light brown in color. Could they be some kind of bio-luminescent medium for lighting? No, that's impractical. Why not just use fluorescent bulbs? These were…bio-fusion tech?

Goose pimples crawl over Viv's skin. A shiver crawls up her spine. A new wave of AI? She'd heard of new advances in AI research, merging the electronic with organic, but thought it all just fiction. Yet before her eyes, in Starcom labs, is an experimental aberration.

Vivian gulps and backs away. This was something beyond her understanding. She could get seriously slammed for being here. How had she even managed to get past the security barrier? Hal's passcode? A glitch?

Focus on the end result. To get info on Bram's haloband fiasco and collect evidence.

But what more evidence than this? She crouches to snap photos of the artificial brains, or whatever the macabre assembly was, with her wristlet.

And yet, her imagination wanders upon the possibility that this lab could be the engine that drives the haloband's AI. She'd heard reports of the fantastic scenarios haloband had spun. Each scene, one more different, more highly-personal sequence after the next that moved the participant in some distinct and peculiar way. How else could a central server service millions of users 4D-VR simultaneously? Silicon AI was dead, stupid, just sterile machine learning. How could haloband perform its wonders, without some real biological influence?

A Wizard of Oz?

Viv shakes her head in doubt. These fibroids, like living organisms, look alive, floating in the slightly stained water, an odd yellowish tint. Grotesque. She doesn't know what to make of it. Her finger rises to tap the glass.

"Ma'am, these halls are off limits to staff." The voice jumps out at her from the shadows, like a highwayman's challenge.

A bulky man approaches with a flashlight, boots echoing on the hard-tiled floor. He motions her to the side. He has tasers and Kevlar vest with the black and grey Starcom trademark on it.

"Oh, sorry, I must have taken a wrong turn."

He looks at her crosswise, suspicion flowering in his expression. "ID please?"

She holds up her wristlet which he swipes with his own.

An image with orange level security appears on his visual monitor. "How'd you get in here? Gate D should have locked you out back there."

Viv stammers, shakes her head. "Dunno, sir. The door slid open, and I needed to go to the bathroom and I was lost—consulting with my colleague Hal Menzes, on a matter of reports."

"Please go back to Floor B and do not return to this section—ever again. Is that clear?"

"Sorry, sir. An honest mistake. It won't happen again."

"I urge you to keep quiet about the ah, decorative light fixtures. What goes on in West Wing D is highly experimental."

Viv lifts two fingers in a peace sign. "Mums the word."

Decorative light fixtures, my ass.

* * *

Viv Weis has managed to squeeze out of a tight situation. Even she is not so naïve to deny that her luck may be running out. Yet she is on a mission. And an Aries on a mission is a dangerous thing. The next morning, bleary-eyed, she stands outside Stan Rane's office, gripping a sheaf of documents with anger brewing in her heart. She catches him in the thick-carpeted hallway as he's heading for an early meeting. Blue suit, tanned and fit, clean-shaven, respectable, a most eligible bachelor by all standards.

"Stan, a moment of your time."

He turns and flashes her a quick glance. "Viv, just the person I wanted to see. Did you get the reports to our sponsors?"

"It's precisely that I wanted to talk to you about."

"Oh?" Rane's grey-flecked brows arch in surprise. "Didn't Nadine forward the files from our tech consultants?"

"Nadine did, but it wasn't enough—" Viv pauses. "I had to do some more digging of my own."

"Digging? Meaning?"

"Just that." She slaps a printed copy of the Varicore Enterprises Report in his hands.

His eyes do a little cross. "That's classified," he hisses. "What the hell are you doing with it?" Crimson bands of color suffuse his neck. He crooks his fingers like claws, flipping through the pages.

"It's my job, isn't it, Stan? To have some idea of how and why we promote our products on the market. Or what do you hire us dumb blonds for?"

"Settle down." He looks from side to side, his coal-fire eyes darting every which way, as if wondering who may have overheard.

"Isn't me the one who's cussing, Stan."

"Vivian, this is a world ruled by—how shall I put it—powerful people who run powerful companies that do not want progress hindered by technicalities. A place where the early bird gets the worm and the dog with the loudest bark, sharpest teeth and claws rules the pack. You get my meaning?"

"Loud and clear, Stan."

"Listen, Mobile Links were on top of this haloband idea. Any lag in rollout could have meant they would scoop it out from under us. We can work out the bugs in the hardware later."

"Is that what you call them? Bugs? My son's in the hospital because of those *bugs* and this piece of crap."

"I'm sorry you see it that way, Viv—sorry for your son, but there are bound to be some casualties along the way—sensitive types who OD on air time and suffer negative experiences."

"Suffer negative experiences… That your idea of a sick euphemism? It's major money and mind control, not to mention surveillance, mega profit for Starcom. Let's all go out and create a new wave of robots for society. No pesky protests. The soma of the new age."

"Careful, Viv. Those sentiments can get you fired or put away."

"I'm not going to shut up, Stan. You guys lied. I thought this device was intended to entertain and open people's minds in a creative way. Not the reverse, to make them into zombies and damage their brains."

"You're overreacting, Viv. Bram's misfortune was an accident. My sources inform me your son was hacking into the unit and uploading new extensions. That's grounds for dismissal in any court of law. No wonder he got fried."

"It was supposed to be safe. Why would you allow that feature if there was the slightest hint of danger?"

"A can opener cuts off a customer's finger because said customer adds a sharp new homemade part to it. Is the company that builds the can opener culpable for the injury?"

She shakes her head in frustration, not daring to believe that it was Bram's fault.

"I built this company from an early age when the world was recovering from crisis. We have research labs all over the globe. Asia, Europe, Africa."

"One of the good guys. All these so-called funds you donated to research and charities—all a sham."

"I think you don't know what you're getting yourself into, if you persist in taking this further."

"I think I do."

"What are your intentions?" He rocks back on his heels, arms crossed on his chest.

"Hold accountable a pack of shysters. Kick their butts."

His feral mask of mockery only remotely resembles a grin. Rane's true nature is showing now through his veneer of gentility. "Very noble of you. My advice—stay out of the dog pits, Viv, and keep your pointy nose out of places where it doesn't belong. You might find more than your son in the hospital."

"A threat?"

"I don't make threats, Viv. I make dreams come true." He shafts her a malicious smile then turns on his heel.

"I pegged you wrong Mr. Rane," Viv calls after. "I thought you were one of the good guys. Guess I was mistaken."

"Security, please escort Mrs. Weis back to her office. Give her one hour, no more, to clean out her belongings." He turns toward her, points a pistol finger. "Take more care with whom you flirt in the science lab."

Viv blanches.

The big-boned security guy, Mike, who appears on the scene, shifts from foot to foot, as if little liking his duty. "Miss. Ma'am…let's go."

Viv shrugs off his arm. "I can walk, thank you. Don't touch me."

Viv's underlip quivers. Her world is slowly crumbling apart. *It has always been like this. Why did you think any different?* She's just been fooling herself, taking this job, entertaining high expectations and ideals about accountability and safety-checked products.

Weakness gives way to anger. Viv clenches her fists. *You're a fighter, suck it up!*

She knows what she must do. The worst case scenario she has anticipated and now congratulates herself that she has downloaded a heap of data already and stored it in a safe place. She doesn't need on-site access to build her case against Starcom.

Chapter 18

"Archetype: A typical character, action, or situation that seems to represent universal patterns of human nature…"

I stare at the words on my wristlet, reading down further, struggling to make sense of it.

"The root of an archetype exists in the 'collective unconscious' of humankind. 'Collective unconscious' refers to experiences shared by a race or culture. Such experiences include such things as love, religion, death, birth, life, struggle, and survival. Ex: The Hero. He or she is a character who predominantly exhibits goodness, and struggles against evil. These experiences exist in the subconscious of every individual, and are re-created in literature, or in other forms of art…"

Well, certainly a mouthful. Sounds like great fodder for haloband as it spins through its bazillion stories and scenarios. Still don't think I get it completely.

I close my wristlet and swing away from my desk, bleary-eyed. Bram's still not improving. He has relapses, a few each day. He just stops whatever he's doing, stares into space with a wide-eyed look, bordering on the sublime. When we wave a hand or touch him or shake him he doesn't respond, as if he's locked in his haloband world. Maybe he is.

Mom is getting frantic. I know she's found something incriminating, but won't tell, hidden it deep down in some titanium vault.

She sits on the couch, face fixed in a fierce look, while Dad stands at the table, clearing the dishes. Bram's up in his room, content to disappear into his cyberworld whenever he's conscious.

I remain silent witness to the arguments.

"You forget, I got him into that company, Lars. Now he's a half vegetable, at least part of the time." A dam bursts in her. "Those bastards hushed up the truth. Made a mockery of safety protocols. Played with human lives. Tampered with safety standards, doctoring the numbers."

"Can you prove it?"

"Yes, I have the veri-sealed documents."

Dad pauses. He snatches at his chin, rubs the back of his neck, lips peeled back in a stunned grimace. "We're in trouble. I'm as incensed as you, but you're putting the kids—all of us, in danger."

"They're covering it up, Lars. The trials, the lab results. The health risks, havoc to the body. I tried to approach Stan Rane, so he'd do the right thing, but he threatened and fired me."

"Maybe there is some rational explanation for this. Wait—what? You got fired?"

"That's what I said."

Dad stares slack-jawed. "Let's think this through." He looks ready to implode. He reaches for her arm, but with a grip too tight. Mom wrenches her arm away. "Don't touch me!"

I see my father recoil. He goes white with shock. My mom remains frigid and bitter, as if she's not being heard. As if she sees an adversary in Dad, in everyone. "Well, they won't get far, Lars. Rane denied everything, blamed Bram for his own misfortune even when I confronted him. Those responsible are not going to get away with this."

"What did you do?" He steps back from her in horror.

"I'm on top of it. All of them will pay."

"How?"

There's a banging on the door. Startled eyes turn. I leap from the couch. "Mom, I'm afraid." I clench my fists, suck in a hissing breath. She curls an arm around my shoulders.

"Who the hell's that?" my father growls. "At this hour?" He goes to check. He opens the door a crack. Four security personnel from Starcom stand there with a stiff-necked C-Sec officer holding up a slip of paper looking like a warrant.

"Shit!" Mom scrambles down the hall. My knees feel suddenly weak. What's happening?

I knew they were bad people the moment I glimpsed them. The look of their hard eyes, militant expressions and ramrod posture, so matter-of-fact, but underneath, cold as reptiles.

"Vivian Weis?" one rasps. The door rattles on its hinges. The chain lock keeps them from coming in.

My dad's voice carries over my frozen stupor. "She's just here. I'll get her for you."

"If you please, Mr. Weis, hurry up. Your wife is wanted for questioning regarding unlawful access to company files."

"I—I'm sorry, there must be a mistake."

"No mistake, Mr. Weis. Open up. We can search by force, if necessary."

He nods. "Okay."

As Dad tries to stall, they snap the chain lock and move in, with black automatics and assault gear at their hips, the whole enchilada. One pushes past me and orders me to stay on the couch. Lars glares at another, white-fisted. They all have Starcom or C-Sec symbols on their vests, the latter, a U-shaped shield, golden with red bands.

They search the house but they don't find her. Of course, she has slipped out the patio doors and made for the back street. I'm grateful for that and relief flows in my veins, but where will Mom go? Who are these guys to waltz in and make offensive accusations? What has she done?

All answers which I know, but my teenage brain, numbed and confused, refuses to accept it.

They haul Bram downstairs and question him but he is only half there. Still there's defiance in his clipped answers and he tells one of the warrant officers to screw himself. That ends with the butt of a taser stuck in his face. Dad moves to interfere but one of the Starcom officers pushes him against the wall and restrains him, wrenching his arm behind his back.

What is it with these guys? I jerk to my feet in fighter's stance, knees bent, fists raised just above chin level. My muscles tense, ready to pommel this oaf and it's all I can do to stop myself from kicking him in the groin. But a wiser voice cautions me to stand down.

I feel powerless in my own home—so does Dad. His ashen face says it all. I can't help but flash on Ignatia and the trials she experienced with angry mobs, stormtroopers, guns. Can the same ugly show of force be at our doorstep?

No, I thrust the impossible down. This is not the same level of horror, is it?

Their search is not pretty. Furniture tossed, closets ransacked, clothes flung helter-skelter. Their last words to Dad as they troop out the open doorway, "You'd do well to call Starcom as soon as she makes an appearance. We strongly urge you to tell her to come in peaceably."

My dad nods glumly, mouth set in a thin line. I glare back with hatred. Bram is sprawled on the couch, blank-faced.

Dad calls Mom on her wristlet but there's no answer. She must be blocking her calls.

I pace back and forth. "Can't they track her with her wristlet?"

Bram lifts himself weakly from the couch and wipes his sweaty brow. "Theoretically they can. But Mom's too smart for that."

"So what do we do?" I ask.

"We wait." Dad slumps at the table.

"Well, I'm not going to sit around here doing nothing."

"Ellan—" Dad reaches out a hand.

But I'm already out the door.

* * *

Vivian Weis is a wreck. She has a cigarette in her hand, drawing in a breath, and has chain-smoked half a pack already, something she hasn't done since her twenties when she stepped into the business world. Dark circles ring her eyes. She's afraid. Afraid to send a message to Lars or Ellan or Bram, to warn them what terrible danger they're in. Fearful of what may be bugged or monitored and what may not. She's just purchased a trendy beige hat to conceal her hair. She's hidden out in the clothing department store, pretending to try on clothes, shop for makeup, flipping on dark glasses. Even picked up a set of scissors to cut her bangs. She's about to administer brown dye to her hair in the washroom when an attendant, suspicious of her lengthy stay, escorts her out, warning her that the facilities are not public salons.

The only other place she can think to go is the library. She needs web access, but doesn't want to chance the main branch. A risk yes, but what isn't, now that Starcom is out for blood and has decided to play dirty.

Was it her breach of West Wing, or maybe it was the hint she'd given Rane about how she would expose the haloband scandal and that she had the documents to prove it? Likely both.

Vivian rounds up the courage to go to the subsidiary branch ten blocks away, not the main one. The scanner may recognize her. She walks through the parallel plates as innocently as possible. No alarm buzz. A relief washes over her.

Vivian takes the stairs two at a time and plops herself down at one of the terminals on the second floor. She pretends to do book searches, on 'post-Cataclysmic interest rates', but accesses the company website instead.

She pulls up a remote info-drive account at Starcom under her secretary's ID, whose password she knows. There, she transfers the most damning, pertinent data to a secure file folder protected by another password. Now time is critical, for that act will certainly be tracked. Breathless, she taps with furious speed at the terminal. Only moments before they will be on to her so she's got to get out of here and find a new place of hiding. What's that? She closes the window at the sound of footfall. Fumbling with her wristpad, she pulls up the quick memo to her daughter she's drafted up earlier. She adds the folder access code and password and sends it, careful to delete the contents right after and shred all evidence it ever existed.

The library security team snatches at her wrist. A barrel-chested, uniformed attendant taps the screen where she was entering data, trying to call up her last activity.

"Not showing much here." He levels her a nasty glare. "Sending secret love notes out, are we, Ms. Weis? I think you'd better come with us."

"Get your hands off me, apes." They grab her hands, twist her arms behind her back. Her purse and all its contents clatter to the floor. "Ow, not so rough!" Her eyes snap shut, only to widen in horror as she sees the Starcom logo below their name lapels.

She kicks and cries out. To no avail. None too gently they haul her off the premises, immune to the looks of shock on people's faces, and her looking the fool in public.

* * *

Viv is taken to the D Ward of Starcom Labs, a secure section reserved for only the most special cases. Amidst periods of waking and dreaming, she finds herself sitting in a chair. A padded one on whose arms her own are strapped down with extra-resilient velcro. Groggily, she registers a technician looming over her, a young female, clad in grey trousers and matching sleeveless shirt, tapping a long hypodermic needle which she plunges into Viv's left bicep. New levels of tingling ecstasy assault Viv's nerve centers, and she grins, a clown's grin, as deeper euphoria and clouds of yesteryear fill her horizon. A familiar visor, blue with white ear pads, is strapped on her head, a device she has rarely tried—yet. She is in the haloband universe. The images that stream past her mind's eye are astounding: fairy castles, crystal trees, magical figures laden with gossamer and snow, fields of endless, mile-high corn stalks and windblown wheat plants whose golden grains and kernels sing music, but somehow her mind is overloaded with all these impossible collages. She's falling...into a yawning abyss, an endless plummet down into a dark sea. Her mouth opens wide as a sea cave, but her breath sticks to her lungs, try as she might to suck air in and out. It's as if she takes the whole world into her belly and spews it back out. A silent scream explodes in her throat, fills the void of emptiness, of peril, fear, and wonder, but as with all silent screams, nothing comes out.

Chapter 19

Mom's been gone for 24 hours. I'm worried sick. Dad's a mental case. We've gone to the police but they say they can't do much until three days have elapsed—in which case they'll be able to file a missing persons report. Wife in a failing marriage. High-profile, stressful job. Left under duress, yeah, they've seen it before. But maybe not a recent warrant issued by a supposed C-Sec officer who doesn't show up on police records.

I need to do something with my restless energy. Channel it. I go to the *Iron Kick Club*, start smashing punching bags. No use. The sinking feeling and dismal hollow emptiness refuse to go away. Luckily Angelos isn't there. He'd crucify me for technique—sloppy and full of rage. The few students who are there kind of look at me weirdly, as if I'm having a miserable day. *Yeah. Slightly.*

I'm out in the car with Joey, not good company, unable to think straight with my mother gone. How I miss her! Dad's continually drunk, and Bram, I don't know what's up with him. Sometimes he's out like a drug addict, other times he's lucid and hacking surveillance cameras to look for Mom. I'm doing anything I can, dancing, toking up, looking for Mom in coffee shops, movie houses, food stores, but the sad truth, is that I know I won't find her. She's trapped somewhere like a fly in a web. A sudden thought hits me. I pull up my wristlet. "*Stop the car.*"

Joey looks at me in confusion.

I tap on the inbox to my alternate email. Empty. But when was the last time I'd checked my spam folder? I see words appear beside the folder's avatar, a horned devil with a sinister grin. From Bumblebee to Sagefly. That's the alias I'd given my mother in case any of us gets in trouble. My heart chills.

I read the message. It's got a delayed timestamp. Shit, why tagged as spam? How long has it been sitting there?

"*Send this to editor of KCX news right away. Delete this message, Sagefly. Memorize access file: th9432 @ vinecom, pw 34#GH. Get it to Damien Hurse, editor at the network. Fast! They've blocked all outside contact except through this portal of B's. They're playing slimy hardball. By the time you read this I'm probably in custody. I fear they're coming after you too. Trust nobody. I can only send this out through B's encrypted channel. Sorry to get you involved in this. Love you. Forgive me."*

I panic. Eyes pinched shut, I visualize the words and numbers, ready to tap the delete button.

"Pull over, Joey."

"Say what?"

"Stop the bloody car!"

"Okay, take it easy. What's wrong with you?" He rubs the back of his neck.

My fingers are steepled like claws on my temples. "I need to think."

We're parked at the side of the road between Steb and Jabeson, far from the corner and a glaring sodium arc lampost. Residential houses huddle on either side, low bungalows from a reconstructed section of the old quarter. The city lights are just coming on. I lean over and show Joey the message. His eyes bulge. He gives me a look and a low whistle. "That's your mom?" he says.

I nod, eyes filling with tears. A new terrible feeling hits me when I think of her, because I know the worst has happened to her and that there's nothing I can do.

Joey runs his fingers through his wavy hair. "Damn, this is serious shit."

"We've got to go to the police."

"You kidding? You can't trust anyone," he scoffs. "You heard what she said."

I bite my lip. Grief assails me. *Where is she? What are they doing to her?*

I look up the email of the editor, Damien Hurse, and am ready to send the message like my mom said but either the network is down or they've blocked my outgoing messages. I can't even delete the message. "Jesus!"

What's more, I'm getting this cold, bloodless feeling that Bram and Dad are in trouble. In my mind's eye, he's all bloodied up and Bram is lying sprawled on the floor, bruised and bewildered.

I have to get to them!

Joey's in a funk, his dark, flushed face confused as all hell at my erratic behavior.

"Drive!" I order him.

"Where?"

"Home!"

"Okay, whatever you like."

It's early evening and a dull smog haze creates a misty afterglow over the city. We pass random pedestrians, shops with neon signs, crumbled street corners, traffic lights with 6G+ aerials, the usual stuff, but it's all veiled in an unreal dream in my mind. There's a stiff silence between me and Joey. He's angry because I won't let him into my world, tell him what's going on. Rightfully so, but who am I to put him in danger? What must he be thinking: mom in custody, me in imminent danger?

We pull up on our street with the tiny row houses and small lawns out front and he parks on the opposite curb. Joey lets me out. The house looks as it should. A faint glow spills from the curtained, living room window. The garage door is down and Dad's car is parked in the driveway. We see a figure perched on the other side of the street. Joey squints. "Is that who I think it is? That gang scum. What the hell is he doing here?"

Torv's sitting on his parked bike taking a long drag on a cigarette, as if waiting for me. I'm as surprised as Joey, but a part of me is feeling more fear and uncertainty than ever. Also, I don't like the way my pulse races when I'm around Torv. I'm moved that my friends are there and give a care enough to look out for me, but not if I'm jeopardizing their safety.

Joey makes to get out with me but I know—that sixth sense is tingling—that if he comes with me, something bad's going to happen.

"Go back home! Don't come in, Joey. Promise me." I grip his arm tight, pleading with my eyes.

"Okay." But I can see beyond the sullen droop of lips, the doubt and defiance in his face.

I scuttle out of the car, glancing away from Torv who is staring with an air of strained puzzlement. I scramble up the walk and burst through the front door.

The house seems normal. A mellow glow of the living room light bathes the family room in soft tones.

Dad's in the living room pacing around the coffee table. His anxious face tells me he's worried out of his mind at my mother's prolonged absence. Bram has brought his computer down to the coffee table. A silver cube six inches square. A quad Vestex Terra-Ionium cube driving multiple thirty-inch holo screens. Probably to track any communications from Mom, or hack any surveillance systems that show her whereabouts. He's just sitting there looking spaced-out.

I bolt the door behind me and kick off my shoes and glance about. I'm starting to doubt my earlier premonition about the two of them in danger when Dad staggers around the back of the living room couch. "Any news?" He looks terrible, dark circles pooling under his eyes, his breath reeking of whiskey.

"No—I mean, yes." I back away from his rankness, not wanting to alarm either of them. Bram seems to stir, his lips mouthing silent words as if he's in VR-HB land.

My father makes a careless gesture. "Karie was here a while ago, looking for you, wondering where you were."

I mutter under my breath. Was I supposed to meet up with her earlier? My mind's a blank. "Mom sent a message a while back. Joey just dropped me off."

"Wha—?" Dad stumbles closer, a hopeful, eager, haunted look in his eyes. I'm appalled at how haggard and ravaged his face is.

Fingers grab my wristlet and turn the screen his way before I can try deleting the message again. He reads the note, eyes red circles. The bit about the bumblebee and apologies and love you and all, seem to make him scowl which turns into an expression of immense pain and hurt. "Why didn't she send it to me?" His face looks bewildered, red, hollowed-out.

I tap several times on the trash icon. The message finally blinks out. "She probably tried, Dad. She was running for her life, under duress. She was trying to conceal it by sending it as bumblebee to me."

He nods robotically, bitterly, as if not believing it or not wanting to believe it. "We have no clue where she is," he says, lifting a hand in a futile gesture. "Successive calls to the police station and her office at Starcom have yielded nothing. No information, no assurances.

Bram makes the unfortunate decision to reach for the visor tucked under the table. In a dreamlike daze, as if he's absorbed little of the conversation, he fastens it around his head. Dad finally blows, knocks over the Sheckley bottle of whiskey.

"Take that stupid thing off. What are you thinking, Bram? I should burn that piece of crud." Dad's in a funk, pissed, in a foul, drunken mood.

Bram just stares at him, used to the inebriated outbursts.

In this case, I must agree with my father.

"Relax, Dad." Bram calmly takes off his visor, rubs his eyes with the heels of his hands, as if coming out of a deep sleep. Maybe the crash of the bottle made him alert. "I'm trying to go back in time to find out what happened to me. Maybe I can get some clues as to what messed me up."

Dad shakes his head. "Sounds stupid and dangerous. Why not devote more efforts to finding your mother? If those doctors couldn't figure out how to fix you, how can you?"

"Only so much I can do to find Mom. Got spy bots looking everywhere. Wherever she is or whoever's got her has covered his tracks well."

"We're wasting time." I raise a clenched fist. "We have to get Mom's message out. I haven't been able to get it through. Network's down."

Bram grunts. "No, it isn't. Lemme see your wristlet." He holds out a hand.

He frowns. "Blocked? Or micro-monitored? You've been hacked. Good thing you trashed the message."

"Great."

"What did she send you?"

"A password and account." I tap my head. "In here."

"Read them back to me then." His fingers dance over the viewpad as I mouth the information back at him from memory.

He's labeled the message 'High priority' with a hacker's finesse. "Okay, it's sequenced. The node exists. Wouldn't have believed it. Let me upload a copy before it's quarantined."

He taps his main holo screen. "Come on, hurry up," he grumbles at the unit. The endless seconds are maddening. "Only got a partial. I'll send it on anyway."

I hear a soft ping and peer over his shoulder at the incoming message. *"Hi Bram, Can you resend? Message corrupted. Damien."*

Bram sighs in frustration. "Damn. The packet's not loading. Starcom must have put a blocker on it."

He flips to the other screen and brings up some graphs and conversion charts. "Network is buggered. Thrashing. Why?" He taps his holo screen furiously. "Have to try something else."

An acrid taste clogs my throat. Doom is coming. Question is when?

Several loud raps shake the door. I roll my eyes. Here we go again. Bram swears, frantically trying to delete traces of the email conversation. He reaches for his haloband visor.

Dad steps over to the door with a frown. He opens the door a crack.

"What do you want? More goons from Starcom? Get lost. We don't need or want you." This time there're two bulky men wearing black, unmarked vests. They put shoulders to the door and burst through, splintering wood. Chain and lock fall to the floor.

I gaze in horror mixed with awe.

"Hey, who are you? You can't just barge in here as if you own the place—" Dad's face reddens as the man shoves him back.

"Try me, buddy."

My father lashes out at the man's arm, his other arm springing back to clock him in the face.

"Dad, no!"

But it's too late. The officer jams the butt of his taser up into my dad's face.

Dad sags. Blood spurts from his mashed nose and upper lip.

Hands go to my mouth. I scream. My fists knot and I'm on the move. My father, doubling over, groaning, lips working, croaks, *"Run!"*

Muscled, ape-like arms are reaching for me. I duck a groping hand and make for the patio.

"Get back here, kid!" the second officer roars. His taser is lifting up to my face. It grazes my shoulder. My left side flames in sudden agony. The shoulder bone feels as if it has been hit with a metal sledge. My lips quiver, trying to frame words.

"Aghh!...Ow, you bastards. Are you people insane?"

"Shut up. What did your mother tell you? Did she ping you anything, write anything down, give you any documents?"

"No! Are you people for real? What do you want from us?" The pain has faded to near numbness. I gasp and stagger over to help my father, even as the background pins and needles in my shoulder almost make me puke. They'd given me a low stun dosage, otherwise I'd be on the floor, crawling like a worm.

The officer's lizard eyes bore into my skin. If they've done this to us, what had they done to Mom? I shudder as nausea rises from my churning stomach.

"Check their wrist coms," the other orders.

The second, more wiry officer grabs my arm, twists, causing me to cry out in pain. He pulls up the 'recently accessed' panel on my wristlet. His eyes beetle over the text, but he doesn't find anything because I deleted everything. Bram's is next. He's oblivious, or feigning oblivion, jacked into 6G VR. The haloband's on his head.

"You hear me, kid? Give me that." The guard cuffs Bram, knocks off the blue visor. Bram sprawls on the floor. He immediately goes into a funk, like a kid without a favorite toy. He bares his teeth.

The guard bullies him back on the couch. "Worth fighting for, eh, kid?"

"Yeah, check it out," the other says. "Maybe the kid's hiding something in that gizmo."

"You serious?"

"You saw how he put it on so suddenly when we came in."

"Okay, let's see what this VR shit is all about." He snatches the visor up and straps it to his own head. He makes a point of elbowing Bram in the head.

"Let up, Roy. I didn't mean literally. We're on a job here. Not to jack off on video games."

"Shut up. Watch those two delinquents. Pops here doesn't look like he's going to be fighting too much anymore." He kicks him in the gut and my father moans as he tries to crawl to his feet.

This is where I go batshit. I spring to my feet like a tigress. Two strides and I'm spinning in midair. The pain has dwindled enough for me to lob every ounce of strength of my upper body into a bone-crunching heel whip. My right foot swings high, smashes into the first shithead's groin. Sags him. His protective garb takes most of the force but my knee is moving into his jaw. He goes down on his kneecaps, falling forward.

"Bastards," I hiss. "Take that!" I stomp on his wrist, snatch the taser from his slack grip and veer away from his groping fingers.

Bram jumps to his feet before the couch. The other guard howls, rips off the visor, as I drive the taser up into his throat. His knees buckle and he falls like a freshly-killed animal.

Bram peers into his eyes, feels his pulse. "He looks dead."

"Good."

"No, not good, Ellan. That's like assault. We have to get out of here." The other guard is groaning, coming to.

I kneel before my father and I clutch his hand.

"Go!" His croaking voice spits out blood.

"Dad!"

He lifts his head feebly. "I'll be okay. Go! Run."

My heart lurches in dismay as tires screech in the driveway. An unmarked van veers up on our front lawn. The headlights point into our window.

Bram and I burst through the door. There're three of them coming out of the van's sliding doors. We try to deke around them. But it is an ambitious plan. In the back of my mind I'm thinking, why no sirens? Why unmarked vans?

The lead goon, a towering, broad-shouldered man with bullet head and massive fists, motions to his two henchmen. One with thick, bottle glasses and a hefty stride cuts off our exit to the street. The other grim-faced with a badger beard, blocks escape via the side of the house.

They are fast and efficient and my left side is still numbed from the taser. Badger-beard grabs me with ham hands while the other drags Bram toward the back of the van.

"Watch it!" I cry.

The lead thug's fingers dig into my arm.

I fling off his grip, but Badger-beard tightens his hold. The two of them bump me along to the unmarked van parked close by where Bram is being controlled.

Joey scrambles up the walkway, his face pale and crinkled in a grimace. "Hey, who the hell are you? "You're not even C-Sec. By whose authority—"

"Shut up, kid. Buzz off, if you know what's good for you."

A chill of foreboding crawls up my spine. *Joey, why? I told you to go home.*

"Hear me, kid? Go home and play your video games."

"Very funny." Joey advances to block their way. He's bouncing on the balls of his feet in kickboxing stance.

It only amuses them. Bottle-glasses's taser flashes in a hairy, mallet fist and shocks him in the ribs. Joey falls to the cement with a groan, gyrating on the paves.

"Joey!" I struggle to reach him.

Easier to try containing a wild cat. With a surge of adrenalin, I rock left and right in Badger-beard's grip, struggling to jam my elbow in his teeth, but he's twisted my arm so hard that I feel as if my wrist'll snap.

Lead goon beckons another of his henchman out of the van to check for any other lurkers. The man's not even two strides out of the vehicle when another figure comes leaping over the hood with a length of pipe. He smacks the lackey hard in the hip. With a rebel yell, he lays into the back of Badger-beard who's got me in a choke hold. The man sags to his knees. I break his arm with a savage kick and hustle to close with the one holding Bram.

Torv roundhouse kicks the taser out of Bottle-glasses's hand. Bram drops in a heap and crab-scuttles for the safety of the hedge, but the driver comes out to snatch him up in a head lock, dragging him back to the idling vehicle.

The lead thug produces a dart gun in his right hand and fires point blank.

Thunk. "OW". I feel an icy spasm in my left shoulder. I slump, look down, see a star-petalled dart sticking out. I pull it out and chuck it to the sidewalk. Too late. I'm wincing as if bitten by a poisonous spider.

My head is spinning. I see Joey writhing on the ground, Torv lashing out, Bram kicking and swearing. "Leave her alone, you bastards." Bram is going berserk. Dizziness tips my world as a greyness touches my eyes and forms haze over. I wobble and slump to my knees.

Torv dives as a dart wings off the front fender of the van, missing his ribs by an inch.

The leader waves his gun somewhere in the shadows where Torv's taken cover. "Back off, punk. Stay crouched there like the rat scum you are. You didn't see anything here. Now beat it."

The remaining two hustle Bram and me to the van. The leader returns to drag his two henchmen lying in agonized heaps toward the rear doors. From the hedges come Torv's muffled curses but he's not bold or stupid enough to take on the man wielding the gun.

They thrust us all in the back and speed off. My last glimpse through the tinted back window is of Torv kneeling down to tend to Joey. Before we're gagged and blindfolded.

Chapter 20

Footsteps sound from the hall. Latches turn in the locked door of the small, cinderblock room in which I've been confined. Bright lights make me squint, as three men enter and move forward after having flicked some invisible switch. I rise groggily to a half crouch, my back against the wall. How long have I been here? An hour, a day?

A familiar voice speaks. The distinguished owner wears a brown tweed suit and bears a kindly, sympathetic face as a father would have. "Ellan, I'm glad you're here." CEO Rane reaches out and touches my arm. There's something reptilian about that touch. I spring away, fists naturally coiled, my body tense.

"Where's my mother?" I demand in a hostile breath. The man repulses me, in everything he stands for and is about, everything Starcom does. I wipe at my arm where the slimy snake's hand has soiled me.

"We're taking you to her," Rane assures. He nods at his closest aide, a burly, buck-toothed man standing at his side, armed and dangerous. "She's been worried sick about you."

"I'll bet she has."

White walls line the halls. I shake off the cobwebs in my brain as the security men prod me down the corridor. There are two of them who accompany me, the first, the lead thug from earlier at my parent's house. I scowl, trying to piece events of the past together. Only a blank space resides in my mind—nothing from the time I was hauled into the van and brought here.

"Where's Bram?"

"Your brother's safe. Just answering a few of our questions."

"What questions?"

But Rane is through answering for now.

We enter a room marked 'Section D. Special patients. Unauthorized entry prohibited'. More white walls, this time tinged with green, dazzlingly bright overhead fluorescent lights, a bed and two chairs, one empty and one occupied. The small room is already claustrophobic and my mother is slumped in the nearest padded chair like in a movie theater, the tip of her tongue touching the top of her bottom lip. The bed is placed over to the side and arranged with an IV unit and vital signs monitor. It makes me feel sick to my stomach. The sterile, creepy quality to the whole arrangement reminds me of something out of a loony ward, or a surreal haloband stage.

"Your mother is very sick, Ellan. In her distraught condition, she suffered what must have been a 'nervous breakdown'."

I stumble over to her side, feeling the ache in my spine from the blows, tasers, the trank gun. I listen in a half-stupor to my mom's rasping breath and Rane's monotonous narrative. My eyes stare at the zombieish look in my mom's dilated pupils. I whisper, "What have they done to you?" I turn grief-stricken eyes to Rane. "What did you do to her?"

"Nothing. See for yourself." He sweeps a long arm in plush suede. "In an impulsive attempt to discover the triggers that sent Bram over the edge, she broke into secure company labs, rifled through classified records, and scanned Bram's last VR events. She put on an experimental HB, with intent to visit those same events. We have it all on holo camera. I'm thinking she was desperate enough to don the experimental glasses herself, with extra sensory locators. Why, we're not sure." Rane lifts an upturned palm. I listen in an open-mouthed daze as he discusses my mother as casually as someone would a sick pet. "The trauma of the past days, reliving those events spurred her to tragic action. We have her on morphine and hydroxenol."

"That's a lie!" I rasp in a hollow voice. "She'd never do that."

"Oh, yes she would, and did. Yesterday she was admitted, violent and desperate to a Starcom clinic, escorted by security officers after she blitzed out in a public library and became unstable. Our men had to forcibly escort her kicking and screaming to our clinic. We've attempted several therapies, including dopamine injections and electric shocks, none completely successful.

"She has been delusional and spouting all sorts of crazy notions of conspiracy theories about haloband and uttering vague threats. Did she tell you anything? Send you any documents or data? If so, we must know now, to protect you and avoid any legal complications in the near future. It is in everyone's best interests."

My mom, once beautiful, looks twenty years older, ragged and unkempt, her grey-green hospital gown rank with sweat and urine.

"Mom, is this true?"

Her eyes glaze over. Her lips work as if trying to tell me something. My head spins. Her voice is like a dying snake's hiss. *"Take it off…take the visor off."* Those words a gibbering pleading. *"Don't tell them,"* she croaks.

My throat is choked with grief. My instinct is right. They've messed with her. They screwed her up. Maybe permanently. I feel like wailing and striking fists and feet at all of these monsters.

"Take it off," my mom pleads.

I stare, dumbfounded. What's she talking about?

"You see, she's delirious."

I shake my head, squinting back tears.

"Tell us what you know."

"Don't tell them," whispers Mom.

"You evil cretinous bastard." I rise in a flurry and catch Rane a grazing blow on the face. His closest aide darts in and grabs my wrists and pulls me into his chest while the other tapes my wrists together. Rane's head dips as he massages the puffiness already forming on his chin, lips puckered in a twisted grin.

Now Rane studies me with amusement. "I hear you are quite the fighter. No more clawing out people's eyes or kneeing men in the groin here."

Mom's eyes glimmer as she tries to stand. Her voice ringing clearer, rasps, "No, don't you see? They just want to—"

"Silence," interrupts Rane. "Give that woman her medicine."

An orderly enters and force feeds her some green pills. I can't tell how many and neither can I stifle the gobbling whimper coming up in my throat.

"Don't worry, Ellan. You'll be fine. You see, we've had to sedate her. She has been hysterical."

"Monsters! All of you." I tear at my bonds. "Release me. Let me out of here."

"No, no, no. You're not going anywhere until we get to the bottom of this—and until we get the truth out of you. Take the mother back to Section D2."

"You can't keep us here. It's against the law."

He gives a raucous laugh. "We are the law. Where's the file?"

"I don't know anything about a bloody file."

"Oh, I think you do. The one your mom sent you from the library at 23:37 two nights ago."

I shake my head. Though a flash of icicle fear trickles through my veins. My palms sweat ice.

The CEO sighs. "Well, if that's the way it's going to be, we can arrange some special accident for you. 'Tragedy strikes the Weis family'. His face crinkles in a twisted mask of fake pity. "How can we spin it?" CEO Rane muses. "'Sister was taken with such grief over the brother that she tries to retrace the path of VR sensations leading up to his breakdown.'" Maybe we can spur more emotional impact from the story by having her go the way of the mother, as repetitive as it is."

The lead security guard arches brows in interest. "It could work."

I turn on him ready to claw his eyes out, smack his teeth in, with hate in my eyes. "Haloband's no different than 6G+ or your crazy 6G transmitters. Spewing radiation and killing us all, damaging human cells—only HB works on the brain directly."

Rane spreads his arms. "6G, 5G, what's the difference?... We've been doing it for decades. Why stop now? Who will care at this late date?"

"You've known about the health risks since the beginning of its rollout and covered them up, faked reports, doctored tests, fooled the people and convinced corrupted governments to let it pass. Life spans have decreased to 60-65 years average. There are more birth defects and chronic disease than ever in the history of humankind."

"Welcome to the new age, kid. I advise you to get used to it. Science proves the human body adapts."

"It will never adapt." My rant was going nowhere. Rane was as ruthless as a serial killer.

He motions. "Have Mr. Malcolm question her. He never fails."

"Yes, sir." The lead guard bumps me along, his iron grip digging into my raw wrists.

I struggle to chop, punch, take him out but a white cloth clamps over my nose and chloroform takes me out.

* * *

Torv nurses the ache in his hip where the four-eyed bastard clubbed him. He stoops to check on Joey who's moaning on the paves. "You okay?"

"Had better days. Yeah, fine."

Torv doesn't think Joey looks fine, the way he is wincing and massaging his ribs where they tasered him. He helps him up and gets him over to his bike. "Where they taking them?" Torv asks.

"Starcom, where else?" Joey leans unsteadily against the seat.

"So, let's go then crash the party—or have you had about enough kickboxing for one day?" He chuckles, his scarred face and crooked grin making for an eerie sight to Joey under the dim city lights.

Joey winces. "Let's get Angelos first." He rubs at his left side.

"Why?"

"Angelos can help. He's strong. A good fighter. Plus he's a friend."

"Where? Your club?"

"Yeah, you know him?"

"No." Torv kicks the bike into gear. Joey hops on stiffly behind, gnawing on his lip.

"But gonna find out how good a fighter he is."

* * *

My eyes flutter open.

I'm in an old board room, stark, disused, with smells of carpet, antiseptic, dust and disuse. Faces come into focus. Two men in a dimly-lit room.

There's a bare table in the center. I'm sitting in one chair, my back pressed against it, wrists bound. The interrogator is on the other side, smiling at me with a goblin grin. He's got all the prerequisites for an amiable, cherubic sort with roly-poly nose, good-natured smile, receding hairline and medium build.

"Hello, Ellan," he says cheerily. He motions to the heavyset guard who'd passed acrid smelling salts in front of my nose. "Glad you've joined us today, and are back to the land of the living."

He cocks his head in curiosity. "You can't be as dangerous as they say you are—now can you?"

My singular glare tells him otherwise.

He frowns, flips through a dossier, as if amused. "Well, well, a relatively non-violent but long record of insubordination over the years—speaking out in class, swearing at teachers, a few punches, rallying your peers into causes, like this discussion group, 'Voice of the Past'. Oh my, in the second grade you lit your classmate's hair on fire, Zandra. Apparently she had pushed your friend into a mud puddle. Naughty, naughty. A real bleeding-heart vigilante. But nothing like this last bout, dipping into the darkweb, using hacked passwords, exposing sensitive documents to unfriendly eyes.

Tsk, tsk, tsk. You and your mother and brother…a whole family of whistleblowers." He trills out a cynical chuckle that ends in a hyena's cackle.

My lip curls.

"Here, don't be offended, dear girl. I'll take the restraints off you. Would you like that?"

I give him an alley-cat stare. He snips the wrist tape.

"There, how about a hot drink?"

I muster a shrug. *Okay, good cop-bad cop routine.* It's predictable enough to be insulting. I flex my fingers, massage my raw wrists. Passing a tongue over my dry lips, I turn my head far enough to catch a glimpse of the guard out of my peripheral vision by the door. I assess his position, vulnerability, his suspicion factor, alertness, meanwhile wondering what else this bozo in front of me's going to promise next. He signals his bully boy to pour some hot liquid out of a thermos they have stashed under the table.

All sweet-talk lies to get what they want out of me. *Information.*

Sleaze-bag interrogator sighs. "You should be honored at having this conversation with me. Most problem cases don't make it this far. Make no mistake, you will tell me what we need to know, and you will follow my instructions afterward. My track record is 100%."

His animated grey eyes glint the coldest of ice, and I know he is a man who does not bluff.

"Such a pretty girl." He leans over and strokes my arm and draws a finger down my cheek. "Listen, Ellan, things can go a lot easier for you, if you comply."

"What do you want?"

"The file."

I stare back unruffled.

"You have a boyfriend?"

I shrug.

"How about Joey? The Italian." His soft grey eyes narrow on me, gauging my reaction.

I remain stone-faced.

He waggles his eyebrows. "No? How about Gilsen?"

I start. How'd they know about him? What game's this louse playing with me?

"Or this wild one, Torv?" He laughs and draws another finger down my cheek. "Listen, I can make things go a lot smoother for you."

My heart pounds. It repulses me his hand touching my cheek—they must know it is the one thing I hate the most—at the same time the possibility thrills me, for I see an opportunity.

I let some crocodile tears wet my eyes. It's not easy, but these are not easy times. "Why don't you let me go?"

"We will, Elly, after you tell us about the file. Where is it? Who did you send it to?"

I shake my head.

"We will release you once we've secured the documents."

Fat chance. If they could lie about the past, cover up history, fake haloband safety tests, they could lie about anything.

I let my eyes drift, cup the glass in my hands, take a tentative sip. As I'm tipping the cup to my lips, just as he's turning his gaze aside, I upend it in his face.

He stumbles backward over his chair, cursing, clutching at his eyes seared with hot tea.

I'm up and moving before the other guy can react. Interrogator must be blinded, because he's groping with both hands, stumbling over chairs. Never offer a sweet-looking girl a hot drink, loser.

I smash the other guy in the groin with a spinning twist kick, and he's doubling over, but not subdued. Another kick to the Adam's Apple breaks his windpipe and as he claws at his throat, his face purpling, I feel a range of emotions. Dismay. Vindication. Horror. Triumph. So this is what it's like when one reverts to cave man instincts. There is a second of startled silence before the man falls forward on his knees, holding this throat, as he chokes to death.

Shit, I just killed somebody. I stare in horror.

Only for a second. I snatch up the taser and I knee my interrogator in the gut as he slumps over his buddy friend. I apply my knuckles to an acupuncture point. Angelos has taught a select few of us some vulnerable points. Interrogator's down for the count. The tip of his tongue protrudes from the corner of his mouth.

I lock them both in the room. The hall's straight and narrow, softly lit at this hour and several doors range to the left on the same side as my cubicle. My heart's beating like a triphammer. It's not going to be long before other goons know their team is down and I've escaped. They'll be after me without mercy, and there'll be no liberties like free hands. I don't have much time. Find Mom, Bram. Get the hell out of here.

Chapter 21

The hall is empty. It is wide with translucent ceiling panels. In either direction tiled flooring stretches fifty yards. My ears prick to the gentle whoosh of air being circulated from somewhere above. A hidden vent? Also a very low hum of machinery, unnoticeable to the casual ear. Lights are not intolerably bright like the room where they'd kept Mom, but still not dim enough for my tastes. Where am I, in another clinic? During off hours?

Every instinct is telling me to run from this freakish place and get as far away as possible, but I can't leave Bram and Mom behind. They wouldn't abandon me. They need help.

A fire like no other burns in my gut, my alert mind blossoming with the dark gift of premonition. Do I have what it takes to save my family? Fear lurks at the edges of the fire. Joey could *try* it, but he'd end up dead pretty quickly. A guy like Torv can do it, but I am not Torv. I am your basic good girl, trained not to spit in the street, to be polite to friends, neighbors and strangers. But these are not polite times. This is war.

On the wall opposite, I see a placard labeled, *'Learning Research Labs'* with a white arrow that points back the way I came. No way I'm going back there. I frown. Strange for a clinic. Ahead, more overhead lights shine on the wall with another arrow and a neat sign writ in tiny white letters, *'Wing 8. Conference room, Data mapping, Exits.'* Okay, better, but weird nevertheless. Never heard of this clinic before. Unless…

I peer behind me—an echoing step. If someone walks down the hall behind me, I'd be hard pressed to explain my presence without an ID card or visitor's pass.

Settle down, Ellan. Forget it. Focus on your mission, not what you don't have.

I hustle down the hall, feeling naked and vulnerable. I realize I'm still wearing the grubby hooded sweatshirt I'd worn when I was driving with Joey…but now it smells like a used dish rag. What I fear most is one of the trank guns catching me by surprise. If I'm caught wandering these eerie halls and I'm hit, it's game over. I shudder at what they'd do to me.

Section D2.

Where is it? I had to get my family the hell out of here.

First Bram.

I make it down about seventy yards of hallway. Only a small room of terminals to my right. There's a T-junction ahead. Voices to the left. I crouch on the balls of my feet, weighing my options. I peek around the corner. A figure in grey uniform patrols a locked steel door like my recent prison. His voice leaps out, as if he's on to me, but it's only him talking on his wrist communicator.

"Yeah, Wilson and I have a bet going that we can crack our boy before Malcolm gets it out of that karate kid in E7."

A pause.

"Don't worry, Craig. Tell Rane we'll have the IP, and the password of the file before midnight." He clicks off his wristlet and sighs. *"Impatient buggers."*

I slide down to my knees. *Think, Ellan, how can you get past that door?*

Shit, if Bram tells them the password and the location of the original source, we'll never get the incriminating truth to Hurse.

My heart goes into overdrive. I run through the various possibilities, none good.

Rush the guard? No, even with the taser, impossible to take him out with him on high alert.

Lure him over to the corner then club him?

Better, but no, he isn't that incompetent.

Diversion. Create a disturbance and lure him away. But how? There's only that small room of holo-screens down the way. I'd have to find some stuff to wreck, smash it and litter it on the floor, draw him away. Nah, too messy.

Hurry then! Time is running out. How long do you think before they discover your handiwork back in the isolation room?

Just as I am about to commit to a desperate act, the door clicks open. I slide my head around the corner. Another dim figure emerges from Bram's room, male, I think. Bram's interrogator. I crouch, straining my ears.

"Any luck?"

"He's about ready to give us the location. Give him another twenty minutes then we'll tag team. I'm going out for a bite to eat. You want anything?"

"Yeah. Burgers down at the caf. Get me a double cheese with onion rings. Double pickle, onions, relish, catsup, hot sauce, and some bacon—"

"Hold up, fool. I'm not going to remember all that. Why don't you come with me?"

"Naw, supposed to stay at my post."

"Oh, where's our bird going to fly, Charlie? Through a locked door?"

The man grunts. "Okay. Five minutes. I'm going to lock up."

I hear a four digit lock code being tapped. Bing, Bing, Bong, Bong. Two highs and two lows, all different pitches. The pattern is imprinted on my mind. I can remember it.

I hear their boots clop away down the hall. To my fortune, in a direction opposite me.

Thank the gods. Some angel must be shining her beneficent light over me.

I creep down the hall and plant myself before the steel door. Studying the holo keypad, a luminous rectangle above the doorknob, I lift my hand and trace a tentative pattern. There's a swipe card mechanism beside the numerical pad. I bite my lip. This had better work or a swarm of security is going to be on my ass. I hope it doesn't require a swipe card for me to get it in. I enter the digits on the numerical pad as I remember the audio pattern. Two highs and two lows. Thing is, can I get it right before it times out and triggers an alarm? Here goes nothing.

8 7 3 1

A long beep sounds. Nope. The screen flashes. I close my eyes. The second digit is off by a pitch. Okay, how many pitches? One I think.

8 6 3 1

Closer, but no cigar. The long beep again. Okay, last chance. Get it right, Ellan. I close my eyes. Something is off with the last digit. I strain my memory, trying to remember that stupid pattern. You only get three chances, Ellan. It's stuck in my mind but I'm distracted. Hands are shaking, knowing the immensity of the stakes, the face of that dead guy with his purpling face in my brain. I suck in a deep breath as I steady my fingers.

8 6 3 2

Bingo! The door clicks open.

Like a ghost, I slip inside.

Bram is pacing on the other side of a steel table like the one I had in my room. He raises his fists, blinks, ready to protect himself, an angry droop at the corners of his lips. He looks sick and pasty, mentally beaten down.

"Elly." He looks as if he expects some monster to sink jaws in his flesh. His bloodshot eyes dart left to right. "You're alone? How in the hell did you get past them?"

"Later, Bram. We gotta fly!" I snatch at his elbow. He grits his teeth and falters. I steady him. He puts a hand on my shoulder and we both hobble to the door. His brown eyes blaze with pride and amazement.

"You okay?" I grip his arm tighter.

"Yeah, one of those mind lapses. Those guards worked me over but good."

"Yeah, I bet, but we got to hoof it."

I pull him past the door. We're out in the hallway and he's shifting from foot to foot. For safety, I enter the lock code again. Could buy us more time if burger man comes back in five minutes as he says.

Time is our enemy. When they discover the grisly scene back in the interrogation room…

Bram forces his stumbling feet toward the nearest emergency exit where the fire escape signs are marked with glaring red arrows, but I pull him back. "No, Bram, they'll be coming back from that way."

"Why? It's the nearest exit."

"Yes, but—" I click my tongue, give my head an apprehensive shake. "First place they'll intercept us. Down here."

"What, deeper into this hellhole?"

"Where else?" I push on.

I steer him toward the 'Learning Research Labs'. He doesn't like it. But he has no choice. He's moving okay, better than I expected, but I'm appalled at how haggard he looks. Deep lines on his face. Pallid as a ghost. His breath huffing with every step.

We skitter down the halls, like escaped convicts on the run.

"This place seems bigger than one of the Starcom clinics. What's with all these 'Learning Research Labs?'"

"We're in the main branch of Starcom."

I gape at him. "Get out of here. Not in a clinic?" I slow up, slightly bewildered.

"No such luck. We'd be out of here in a flash if that were so. More important than ever for us to get the shit out of here. They're going to throw a dragnet over us soon."

"We have to get Mom."

"How?"

"She's in section D2."

"You saw her?"

"Yeah, your friendly neighborhood boss, CEO Rane took me to see her. She's in bad shape. They've done something to her."

Bram's knuckles whiten and veins pop in his forehead as his fists knot. "I'll kill that shithole bastard if I see him. How can we get to her? That place'll be crawling with security."

"Not when I was there. They had her sequestered in some solitary confinement." I pause, my brows knit. "Unless we can light a fire under their ass."

"How? What are you thinking?"

"Tell you later." I was getting a grim vibe about trying to spring her so soon after locating Bram. So I revised my plans. I'd learned to trust that feeling after the last situation with Joey and Torv, not to mention Zandra. "First we have to get that message to Hurse. Can you send it from here?

"Not from my wristlet, but maybe from one of these terminals."

"Do it. Do it now."

Shit, I should have sent that message the first chance I had.

The first lab we find, we approach and sneak glances through the wide windows. Fortunately it's empty, about twenty vacant terminals staring back at us, after hours. Bram stands by the door and gazes hard at the key code entry. He swipes his wristlet. We hear the door click. A risk but it's a sign they're not onto us yet.

Yet.

He taps the screen of the first terminal. It lights up, showing the Starcom logo, 'SC' painted in bold, dead center with the galaxy background and Saturn tipped on its edge—the same graphics I remember at the rollout so long ago. Bram's fiddling with his wrist com. His mind's functioning better. I was worried about him before. He's typing a password with steady fingers into a remote terminal.

"Wait, won't they know it's you? And come looking for us?"

"No, it's a fake id." Bram grins. "Unless 'Elward Kline' is a person of interest."

I give him a look of wry wonder then chime off the password and node number I've still committed to memory. He works his magic. Fingers tapping holo screen. He digs up the damning document.

"Okay, it's still intact," he says with a sigh of relief. His eyes make a quick scan. "No wonder they were so keen on nuking it before we could send it somewhere. This stuff is whack. It'll bring down headquarters. Well, too late, suckers." He taps the send button.

I grind my teeth with triumph.

He brushes off my expectant look. "No, I didn't wait for a confirmation."

A devil-may-care impulse comes over me as I push Bram aside. I logon to my own wristlet account and use quick touch to access my latest feeds, the ones from the darkweb. 5G Birth defects, GMO and contagion. Mr. Hurse is going to have some interesting reading tonight.

No sooner have I tapped the send button than in my mind's eye I see a battered ship sailing a leaden sea, a black pennant flying with skull and crossbones at half mast. I pause, a quickening in my blood. Doom is waiting. No sea storm or lava-spewing volcano but doom nevertheless as the ship sails on toward a sallow, gloom-heavy horizon. It's bad, but I'm hoping can't be that bad.

Bram looks in horror. "Is that what I think it is? Why'd you send that?"

"I could give a crap at this point, Bram. Look at what Starcom's done to us, to Mom, Dad. We haven't come this far for nothing, have we?"

"No." He shakes his head fiercely. A single act of defiance that might change the world.

Where did it begin and where did it end? I could spend my whole life digging up the secrets of our past, exposing Starcom and the other corrupt companies. For what? To be branded a rebel, persecuted, beaten down, punished for my standing up and truthdigging, for the rest of my days? Was it worth it? Was Ignatia's fate worth it?

One more thing I have to do. I send a quick message to Joey telling him we're okay. I tap out some frantic but brief words under Bram's fake ID: *Bram and I are in Starcom making our way to get Mom.* Then before I close the window, I brush Bram a searching glance. "Can you sabotage the network somehow?"

He croaks out an exasperated grunt. "I'm a hacker, not a miracle worker, Ellan. Get real."

"Okay, Mom is vindicated at least, her desperate gamble will not go to waste. Now we've got to get her out of here."

Bram flaps his hand and gives a hopeless grunt. "Why not make our escape and get the police to handle it?"

"That's a joke. We can't trust them, Bram. Think. Dad's mashed up face? What did C-Sec do to try and locate Mom? All the time these ghouls at Starcom had her."

His lower lip trembles. "You're right."

The darkweb is right. These companies just get more and more ruthless and secretly manipulative as time goes on, until it gets to the point they want to control the world and cut down anything in their path.

Bram, as if reading my mind, stares. "I remember a day where I worshiped tech. Now I hate it."

He rubs the back of his neck. "Never been to this section of the company."

"That makes two of us."

Chapter 22

We come to a checkpoint. Just a barrier of tempered glass with wire mesh. No guards. We have to pass our wristlets through the scanner in order to pass.

Now my heart sags. We'll never get through. I was ready to abandon this hopeless quest. That or just bust through and take my chances.

Bram holds me back. "Wait." He fiddles with his wristlet, a screen of system options, then waves it over the scanner and pushes me through.

I gasp. The green light flashes above the mesh and I hear a small bell-like ping.

Bram adjusts his wristlet again and casually walks through after me. Bram, the wizard. How could I have doubted him?

We hurry down more labyrinthine halls. Endless corridors. Countless tech labs, terminals, fluorescent lights, but fortunately practically no one around. The few employees we've passed have been engineers, geeks like Bram who haven't registered suspicion. At least, not yet. We slow up, keeping our eyes trained ahead of us and walk as normally as we can.

One youngish guy in a lab coat stops and questions us. Bram nods, talks to him in a soothing voice, flashes his wristlet ID, and allays the guy's qualms. For a while I think he's buying it.

"You say you are heading to West Wing?"

"West Wing." Bram points back the way we came. "We kind of got lost. I was visiting Ned Sners out in Visual Kinesthetics, Bay F and thought I'd take the scenic route back."

"That so?" The engineer frowns. "You're a long way from West Wing. How'd you get over here?"

Bram shrugs.

The engineer hesitates. "You look terrible."

"Yeah, well, late night coding. You know how it is."

"Well, never mind." He beckons. "I can take you there."

"Ah, no trouble."

"It's fine. I'm on a coffee break and need to stretch my legs, relax my brain. This code we're working on has my brain spinning." He scratches his peach fuzz head. "Multiple recursion, D-splice tree searches. We're trying to find the fastest and least expensive way to index user profile data at root level."

"Wicked," Bram says.

He beams. "Kind of like the traveling salesperson problem but not nearly as hardcore. What do you do?"

"Our team's trying to automate 3D to 4D, and come up with more visually stimulating ways to embed haloband 4D into a web browser."

"Looking at those raccoon eyes of yours, I'd guess working nose to grindstone. Careful you don't get burned out. And you are?" He flashes me a curious glance.

"Oh, I'm Elly Weis. Bram's my brother." I shove the taser deeper in my sweatshirt's front pouch, hoping he won't notice the telltale bulge. "Just here visiting. Not a geek—I mean computer genius. Quite the opposite." I sweep out an arm. "Quite the place you have here."

His frown deepens. "Yes it is. Odd that they'd allow security access for visitors with no 'A' clearance. There are test wings here that only Level C engineers have access to, even I don't have privileges." He casts Bram an inquisitive gaze.

"Well, as I was saying," Bram picks up. "I have pretty high access."

"Seems so. Follow me." We grudgingly tag at his heels, secretly trading frustrated glances. "I can take you to the next junction."

Bram forces a smile. "Sure, that'd be helpful. Nice of you to take the time." He sucks in a breath and flashes me a quick warning look. It's agony retracing our steps back to the place we came from but better that than arousing this lab rat's suspicion.

"Down there." He lifts a pale hand to a cross corridor. "You'll find Section F. Take a left and two rights. You'll pass the tech auditorium and it's about oh, another hundred yards or couple corridors to the main foyer."

"Easy enough." Bram gives a small wave and pats him on the back. "We're super indebted to you."

We head down the corridor while good Samaritan continues on his march up the main hall.

"Jerk. Asshole. Dumb twit." Bram's growl is a harsh echo in the sterile hall.

"Alright already. I get the message."

After we're out of earshot, I hiss at him, "Damn, that was close. How big is this bloody place?"

"Big. Many acres, Ellan. Mostly underground. It's deceiving. Even I can get lost in the less-secured places sometimes."

"Yeah, no kidding."

"We need to ramp up looking for Mom." I check my wristlet—9:02 PM—and my inner radar, focusing on her and the necessity for haste in getting her out of her room. Still getting a doom signal. Skull and crossbones. My heart sinks. I'm afraid to tell Bram. Window of opportunity closing. "Not yet though." I haven't realized I've spoken aloud.

Bram exhales a frustrated breath. "What's that you say?"

I put a finger to my lips. "Let's keep going. Trust me."

As we stalk the halls, I intuit that being in this building our bodies are being bombarded by much more EMF radiation than outside. Slowly killing us, damaging our cells and disrupting organ function, according to darkweb. Although that hazard seems less of a concern right now.

We're just about to round the corner, head back the way we were going when the echo of thundering boots on tile has us freezing in our tracks. Three security men come bounding down the main hall. We turn about and rush back the way we came. If we had arrived any sooner... Maybe our friendly asshole did us a service.

Bram nods at my silent thought. We leg it down the cross corridor. They're all starting to look the same and my head is spinning.

We pass double elevators which I see go to five floors. The light sticks at G which is where we are now.

Not thirty seconds pass. Again, I hear the clop of heavy footfall down the hall—and something else that sends chills up my spine—the baying of hounds.

Bram pales. "Okay, now we're dead meat. We've wasted too much time screwing around here. They're on to us—they've got tracking dogs."

"I know." We break out in a run. More steel doors to the right. To the left an oval portal is labeled oddly, with a human face, rendered in bug-eyed red. Weird.

"In here." We duck into the first room.

"It's a secure area."

"Swipe your card, do anything."

It's useless in red areas. Unless—" He swipes his wristlet, keys in a code I can't see, and the door clicks open. I blink in amazement. We scramble through. I don't bother asking him how he pulled that off.

This place is creepy. Like super eerie. Half illumined in dull maroon light, full of cryptic, multi-dimensioned schematics of the brain on the walls, electronic charts and chip designs and rows and rows of terminals, giant holo screens, gizmos and sensors, crammed far too closely together for normal purposes. There seem to be samples, or whole instances of brains floating in aquariums with wires connecting them to rack-mounted sensors.

"Jesus, what's this?" Bram's voice is as hollow as a drum.

Lab specimens. Experimental research? Ugh.

We are caught in a hypnotic daze, one that lasts for seconds as we stare frozen-limbed—*we are hunted by evil people.* Bram and I race to the far end of the lab and dive under a table filled with tissue sample monitors while red and green lights flash in our faces.

The door crashes open. I hear harsh commands at the door. Bright cold light is spilling in. "The kid came in here."

"Where the hell is she then?" another growls.

"Dunno. Keep looking. Over there." I hear the rustle of fabric, stiff like Kevlar. "You take the office. I'll take the lab."

I worm lower in my crawlspace behind the workbench, hoping the goons won't see either of us, and that they didn't bring dogs. I catch more dizzying glimpses of devices these people are working on. Some looking chillingly familiar: Headgear, implants, brain scanners, experimental 4D VR displays. I shake my head, wipe the cold sweat out of my eyes. We have to get out of this sinister sideshow.

Boots clop over in our direction.

"Check over here, Louey. Those little bastards may have jumped the security codes. Could be that hacker Weis kid."

Bram and I slither under chairs and benches to a steel double door where the exit is labeled 'AV Sensory Wing'.

The movement has alerted them. They are scrambling after us. We leap up, burst through the door, slamming it tight. Without thinking, I rip out the taser and jam it in the electro-lock keypad. Sparks fly. The mechanism shorts. Fried enough now I hope to keep those bastards at bay.

The hollow thuds of their fists ring on the metal, then shouts echo from behind the door.

We dart away from the jammed door and into an obscure wing which even has Bram confused. We slip through another double door, hardly daring to breathe. This one has no keypad lock but a traditional lock bar.

Only authorized personnel permitted.

"That's us," mouths Bram.

Neither of us is laughing.

We pull the draw bar down.

On tender feet we creep along, our breaths held. This place is no less ill-lit than the last creephole. It looks more like a gigantic movie set. Several movie sets, in fact. In a large hangar. Sprawling ceiling, high sound-baffled walls, cameras, fake forests, life-sized figures, dinosaur models, abandoned factory sets with rusty pipes, space capsules, landing docks, weird backdrops of city scenes. Everything one'd see in a thriller or horror flick with thick, snake-like cables winding over the floor to overhead track lighting and catwalks. I advance on wary feet, taking a quick scan of a long workbench cluttered with a circular saw, hammers, drills and torches.

Must be the film location of all those textural backgrounds in the haloband universe. An infinite number of scenes of infinite variety. How much of haloband was CGI rendered versus artist-created?

My reverie is interrupted by a loud crash. Muffled snarls and barks erupt from somewhere behind us. Then teeth and claws scratch at the metal of the last door through which we passed. My fists jerk up in automatic fighter's stance. I expect jaws to chomp on my neck any second. But they don't. Only jolts of panic spiking up my back. I peer over at Bram. His bloodshot eyes bulge in terror. Good thing we barred that wretched door.

Another sound echoes. A door slamming from the other side of the hangar. A stern command. Then the stealthy tread of purposeful feet and the huff and whine of a dog.

Cornered.

My heart skips a beat. We race deeper into the interior, hoping to lose ourselves in the maze of sets. But what chance do we have against those fang-toothed monsters sniffing us out?

I break for the safety of a fake tree screen. Too late! The deadly skitter of paws is fast on me. Then a black-furred shape charges. Bram blanches in dismay, scrambling for safety. I leap in between him and the menace and wave the taser to ward it off.

But it turns and leaps and I can only see doom before I jam the sparking grey metal in the snapping muzzle. I shriek a curse of rage. Not before it tears at my sleeve and draws blood from my forearm, as my fist clenches in instinctive defense.

The dog spins back on its haunches. It twirls and snaps teeth at an invisible enemy. Amid its yelps and whines, I spring forward and zap it in the ribs. Sparks gush from the weapon as it vibrates in my hand. The Doberman, or Rottweiler—whatever the hell it is—gives a high-pitched yelp and lopes off in a drunken daze, its puny tail tucked between its legs.

I hustle in behind one of the dinosaur models. My lungs heave. This one looks like a raptor with jagged teeth bared and front claws reaching for prey. Bram scurries in behind some rubber bushes. Behind us looms a huge jungle set. Other dinos huddle there which look mechanized. Radio controlled? A skulking guard strides by and as he turns to see my wavering shadow, I leap out and smash him in the back hard. His taser whips up and I feel a familiar tingle brush across my left shin. A ripple of agonizing numbness spreads from ankle to knee. My head drops. What I dread most is being paralyzed to the point of not being able to fight.

I'm not fast enough. He's got me grappled, his rank breath in my ear. His iron grip pins my arms and crushes the air out of me. "Get off me!" I howl. I kick with my heels but it's useless and he lifts me off the ground, calling for backup.

There's a loud crack. He sags. I flop in a heap, turn and see Bram gripping a chair, his chest heaving.

He tosses the broken piece aside. "You alright?"

The throb in my arm from the dog bite is only a background ache. A minor wound, considering the high stakes of the alternative. "I'll live."

Bram signals for the exit. ""Come, on. Time to go."

"Thanks, bro." I rub my chaffed ribs and bleeding forearm. "But first let's start making a mess of this cruddy place."

"What do you mean?"

"I mean burn this shithole." I kick the felled guard in the ribs. "Here, help me torch this place."

"Seriously?"

"Think I'm joking at a time like this, Bram? We've got to help Mom. These creeps are going to keep coming out like maggots on road kill. Only way we can do this is if they're occupied with something else. Like fire. Give them something to keep them occupied."

"And if we fry in the meantime?"

"We're not going to fry. This dino Raptor looks as if she'll go up in flames pretty fast, what with the thick shellac on her. We can use that blowtorch over there to ignite her."

Bram reaches for it on the worktable. He turns back and looks at me queerly. "More to you than meets the eye, Sis."

"Say that when we're out of this mess."

The comment is truer than he thinks. I think back to Ignatia and wonder how she would have reacted in a situation like this. More than anything, she'd light a fire under all their butts. I flash on Dad lying broken on the floor of our house...Joey lying on the pavement, clutching his side...Mom gibbering in a piss-stained hospital gown. I don't feel the least bit guilty about trashing this place.

"Help me haul over some of these wooden chairs, will you? As kindling."

"Good plan."

Sure enough the lacquer on the dino is like lighter fluid. The red flames lick up its torso as Bram torches the feet. Soon it's engulfed in flames along with the chairs. We back away, coughing fumes as grey smoke billows across the whole set.

"Let's make like ghosts and get out of here." Bram's lungs are balking at the smoke. We step over the downed guard, who's coming to.

I can hear the sprinklers starting to kick on. We race for the exit. Out into the bright light of the main hallway we burst, throwing caution to the wind.

Down the first cross corridor we scramble and I pull the first fire alarm. It'll only help the process along the way.

The alarm is tripping out a shrill, monotonous beat. Bram and I run faster than we ever have. "This way to Section D." He seems to know the way to Section D.

I hear the thump thump of employee's footsteps up ahead. The slamming of doors, shouts and anxious murmurs.

The attention is off us. For now.

Bram and I weave our way down a series of narrow halls toward what we believe is the ward. A dry, sterile scent lingers in the air.

A sign, 'Section D', appears on the wall with a characteristic white arrow. Without Bram, I never would have found it. Five doors on the right-hand wall, D2 is the second. Unlike the others, this door is open, automatically unlocking in times of fire.

Mom is sprawled in her chair, with a haloband visor on. With a croak of rage, I leap over and rip it off. No wonder she was raving earlier that time with Rane. These bastards, they've been giving her a healthy dose of it after hours. Some therapy. More like torture.

Mom sputters gibberish. Her eyes flutter.

"Mom, wake up." I slap her cheek gently.

"Get me out of here," she moans. Her back stiffens, her fingers clench my hand. "Out of this fish bowl. Sharks. Stingrays. Piranhas. They're everywhere!"

Bram looks at her aghast. "She's hallucinating. She's delirious."

"No, she's been drugged, Bram, and programmed by these lowlifes."

I get her to her feet. Some color returns to her white-washed face. She instantly recognizes me and gasps.

"I never thought I'd see you again, Ellan."

"You know I'd never abandon you." Tears brim my eyes.

She squeezes Bram's hand. "How'd you get here?" she asks in a child-like voice.

I lash out a foot that lands inches from Bram's chest. "Kickboxing comes in handy."

She shakes her head and makes a feeble but recognizable chuckle. It's good to hear. The first spark of fire I've seen in her since the day she went missing. I grab a grey housecoat hanging from a peg on the nearby wall and drape her in it. Maybe there's hope that she has a chance at recovery.

Bram and I support her on either side, get her out in the hallway, and join the few employees who are scurrying for the exit. Mom's hobbling along, very slowly. Something bad has been done to her. I know it. Something is dangerously wrong with her. As people are making for the checkpoint, Mom bows her head and weeps. I pause, my heart heavy with grief, waiting for the nearest person to get past us.

"What did they do to you?" I croak. Gooseflesh prickles on my skin. "I mean, what did they really do?"

Her trembling fingers reach up to claw at her cheek. I reach up to cover her hand and stroke her gaunt face. She shakes her head, squeezing her eyes shut as if to shut out the fear. "I don't know. I just have dreams, terrible nightmares. Snatches of grey water, swirling voids. They put me in a room, subjected me to disturbing images and creepy music. I think it probes my mind."

My skin crawls. I shudder with suppressed rage. "Those bastards'll pay."

Her eyes become suddenly intense. Fingers grip my arm like claws. "Did you get my message through?"

"Not to worry, Mom. It wasn't all in vain."

Her body slumps in relief. Tears well in her red-rimmed eyes. "I'm sorry—to get you two into this mess. If I wasn't such a hothead."

"Mom, just keep your head up and keep moving. We're going to get out of this."

But somehow I wasn't so sure. Rane and his minions were ready to lock us up and throw away the key. Probably use us as 'experiments' in his therapy ward.

"Let's concentrate on getting out of here," Bram says in a gruff tone. He fiddles with his wrist com. His mind's on full alert. The east gate is up ahead at the end of a high-ceilinged foyer with lots of glass and potted plants and inspirational nature scenes on the walls.

"Dump your taser," he rasps, "—there in that trash bin. It'll only trip the security sensors." I comply. Needless to say, I shove my bloody forearm deeper in my pocket and soldier on.

Chapter 23

Torv and Joey reach the *Iron Kick* Club with a skid of tires and Torv parks the bike up the street two cars past the entrance. The corners of his lips are set in a lopsided grin as Joey limps to the front doors.

"After you," Torv says and sweeps out an arm.

Joey staggers into the bright lights of the gym, flustered and slightly breathless. A few people wave. Angelos, who is busy with two boxers by the bags, ignores him.

Classes are in full swing tonight. A group of juniors range up and down the mats while two spar in the ring. Angelos jumps in with them, coaching, yelling at them now, and grabbing their gloves when they push too hard or expend too much energy.

Torv studies the play with a fixed interest. His dark eyes check out Angelos's moves. Checking to see if this Angelos is who he says he is. While one student comes at Angelos with two left jabs, Angelos steps back, lets the other move in and exhaust himself, then circles around his left heel and gives the junior a love tap on the side of the head. There are mutters of amusement. "You're coming in too strong, Biff. Any of those pokes are easy to block or predict."

Joey makes a squawking sound and flaps his hand. Angelos turns to him. "What?"

"Ellan's in trouble." He limps over to the ropes.

Angelos scowls. "What? Where?"

"Last we saw her she was being hauled in back of a security van, with Bram."

Angelos's breath whistles through his teeth in disbelief. "Who the hell would do that?"

"Starcom."

"What for?"

"Some trumped up charges of conspiracy. I tried to stop them but they tasered me."

Angelos's thin brows arch up in a frown. "Any word from her?"

Joey hangs his head. "No." But then he brightens. "Something just came in a few minutes ago."

He reads the message on his wristlet:

"I'm in Starcom with Bram. They've got my mom but we've escaped."

Angelos hisses at Joey. "Any follow up?"

"No, she's not responding."

Angelos winces. "Damn. We'll have to think this through. We'll have to stake out the front entrance. If she makes it out, she'll need support. We can feign a peaceful demonstration but we'll need signs to make it legit."

Torv tugs at his chin. In his experience nothing with such serious stakes ever resolved peacefully. He watches Joey as he reaches for black markers as others from the club now alerted, raid the storeroom and cut off poster board to size and staple it to wooden stakes. This Joey guy wasn't bad, just a little too hair-triggered and hyper-sensitive—all gangly and jumpy like a nervous spider. Angelos...the guy was a doer. He had a level head about him and an innate sense of how to fight, not like some other pretenders he knew. The few moves he'd witnessed told him that he could rely on a guy like that at his back. Maybe even at his side. He had the grace and speed of a tiger.

"Make the script bold." Angelos flourishes a marker and crouches to demonstrate. "*'Set Ellan and Bram free', 'Weis family detained. Illegal', 'Starcom Guilty of Unlawful Detention', 'Starcom Holds School Girl Captive'.* We'll parade past the gate. Hoist the placards high. Distract them. She'll need support."

The other members grumble agreement. There's a rising outrage palpable in the gym.

Joey bites his lip. "Sure, but—"

"It's important we put the screws to these bozos. You and a couple of other guys get to the north entrance," Angelos instructs. "We'll cover you and run defense." Angelos's hard stare fixes on Joey, his face unreadable as a sphinx. He looks at Torv. "Who's this?"

"A friend," says Joey. "He was staking out her house and stepped up to help."

Angelos's lip firms, as if gauging Torv's character. His Asian eyes take in every nuance, the torn jeans, the steely eyes, the tilt of Torv's head, the don't-screw-with me attitude. "Can you fight?" he asks.

"If I need to."

Angelos nods. "Good. Then Fin, Roy, come." He motions to the green-inked tattoo on Torv's arm and neck. "Any support possible from that gang you're in?"

"I can rally the Spikes, if that's what you mean?" He holds up his wristlet.

"Yes. Just make their presence as invisible as possible. We don't want a full out confrontation here, just some resistance." Angelos claps his hands and rallies the others. "Remember! We're staging a peaceful protest. No violence, just a diversion for Ellan. We scout out the terrain, keep Starcom from doing anything rash and dangerous."

Joey gives a grim nod. "Sure thing, Angelos. We can just—"

"Hush. Let's move." He waves the others out the door.

They pull up in the parking lot outside the main gate of Starcom. Torv on his bike with Joey, Angelos and four others piled in his car. The large, U-shaped parking lot is bounded on two sides by lawn and hedges, a larger and thicker windbreak looms to the east in shadows. There are more vehicles present than is normal for this time of night. A knot of activity buzzes at the south end. Already a crowd of three dozen or more people mill about the glass-paned main entrance. They are kept in check by ten or so armed, vested security guards. Pools of sallow light bathe the interlocked flagstones in a clinical glow, likewise the trim astro turf running beside it. Those gathered are fed up with the effects of haloband. They're brandishing colorful, no-holds-barred signs: *"Get Out of Our Kids' Minds"*, *"Ban Halobands!"*, *"Starcom=A Front For Mind Control!"*, *"Control Minds, Destroy Lives!"* While they're marching back and forth, their chant rises in volume, *"Halobands Have Got to GO, Nothing But a Horror Show"*. Some have stopped in front of the smug security guards taunting them with muttered curses and pleas to 'Get the hell out of our Kids ' lives!"

The guards aren't doing much. Just holding their ground, fingers on dart guns and tasers, staring down the boldest of the protesters, in the hopes they don't get emboldened and jump over the barricade of shields held upright at ground level, or venture up to the glass and spray offensive graffiti all over the windows.

Torv looks over his shoulder. There are small movements in the shrubs. His own guys, hiding in wait. Donnie, Miln, Flitch, others. They've got a good position and are backup—heavyweights—in case this desperate, bold caper goes sour and they need to pull out. Normally Torv wouldn't be doing this, risking his neck over someone he barely knows. But Ellan...well, she is something else, a girl worth the effort.

Torv's lips curve in a grim smile. She has a fire in her that he's seen in few females. A keen light of purpose, something he's missed, ever since…Treina.

Treina. The sad memory pricks at his tough hide, though if he is honest, the dangerously thin veneer of protection he's walled around his heart is wearing thinner. He thrusts the thought away. Not liking the truths it exposes and the way it casts doubt on his mission.

Well, she is gone—taken out after a B&E got out of control and left her lying in a pool of blood on the kitchen floor—and he has to move on. Maybe Ellan can fill some of the hole left by her.

His mind lingers on the recent magical moments of Ellan in his arms under the pine boughs, his lips brushing hers, a moment as sweet as tasting candy for the first time. The light agile strength in her wiry frame as he pulls her against his chest…All that darkweb stuff and having the courage to speak out against accepted norms and stir up old man Peters…it's a testament to her character. He shakes his head in bitter acknowledgment. The thought of her in the clutches of those egghead goons at Starcom makes his blood boil.

A man in a checkered shirt with thin, salt-and-paper hair draws him aside, bringing his musing to an end.

"Who are you?

"Supporters of the cause," he growls. "Who's asking?"

The man tenses and steps back on the defense.

Angelos edges in. "Hold up. I'm Angelos, this is Torv, that's Joey. More are coming."

The man grunts his acknowledgement. "You can join the group and strengthen our numbers. My wife's got more signs."

"We've got our own signs." Angelos points to his students.

"Welcome to the club then."

Torv nods and returns Angelos a crooked grin.

Angelos's supporters take up position in front of the barricade, trading glares with the security men, hoisting signs. All is well, a Mexican standoff, though the Starcom guards are little liking the newcomers and growing numbers of the opposition. Many of their stone-faced lot mill about, packing tasers and what looks like tear gas canisters in loops at their belts. There is some low, garbled chatter into headsets and tapping of earbuds as orders are passed down from above. This standoff looks as if it can erupt into violence at any moment.

A blue, electric zap crackles six feet from Torv's heavy-footed stance. One of the protesters, a stocky, tow-headed man, pitches back with a shriek of agony. He has stepped too close to the invisible line which separates the strong arm of corporate rule from the plaintive squawking of activists. Now he writhes on the paves as fellow allies snarl with bared teeth and erupt in shouts of outrage. Their wounded comrade does not look as if he will be getting up too soon.

Quick as a cat, Angelos springs over to drag the man back to safety. Torv shadows him.

Starcom's goons flag the act as a deliberate provocation. A stubble-bearded guard with a thick jowl slaps Angelos's protective arm away. "Back off, if you know what's good for you."

Torv's hard stare lets him know he will have to fight two not just one. Angelos smiles and holds his ground beside the fallen man. "It's a free world. Take more care when there's an injured man on your doorstep."

"Listen, you cross-eyed bastard. Get the crap away." He sweeps his taser to zap him in the neck. Angelos slips under the menacing movement and kicks the man's elbow, numbing it. With a quick reversal of hands, he pushes the weapon back in the guard's face.

"Agh!" The guard falls, tasered by his own gun.

Angelos coils back on the balls of his feet. "Little kids shouldn't play with little stingers. They could get hurt." He jabs a finger down at him.

The Starcom security people stand momentarily frozen. Their hair-trigger aggression looks bad on them. In a single rush, they come bounding in to take Torv and Angelos down. At the same time, a band of *Spikes* leap out of the bushes, baseball bats and knives in hand. The dozen security men on guard at Gate A are now calling for more backup as they themselves retreat under the new threat. The sign-bearers, fuelled to renewed rage, join in the melee, kicking and slashing out with signs and feet.

Torv grins as he moves in, both fists bared. Joey and the other club members are at his sides. "Well, looks as if they've now got their riot."

Chapter 24

A group of three night-owl employees with 'Veri-server Research Group' on their breasts are clambering through the emergency exit with anxious strides. We tag on their heels, looking as unobtrusive as possible. The security officer on duty waves us through, little concerned with a few stragglers in a time of crisis, though I know Bram is ready to explain how mom and I lost our visitor's passes or something like it. Fortunately it doesn't come to that. We join the growing knot of night employees milling under the east exit sodium arc lamps. Some are making their way toward the parking lot.

C-Sec flashing lights are ahead of us. I pull Bram away from them and the busy lot, though I sense he is eager to put as much distance from Starcom as possible. Instead I steer him along the side of the building toward the northern, main entrance.

Thin wisps rise over the top of the building. I can smell smoke in the air and the distant wail of sirens echoes over the dewed lawn. Soon this area will be cleared out. Yet there is activity of people waving signs and shouting at Starcom security men holding them back with shields and show of force. *"Down with Starcom. Down with haloband!"* I can hear their chanting from a distance. It's like an eerie church litany. Part of my being's gripped in vicious satisfaction.

Tasers, megaphones gripped in hands, and the tried and true method of physical force are their vehicle to quench the rising threat. All is chaos. They won't be able to keep them back for long. A team of eight guards are attempting to secure an exit passage for employees who are bent on escaping the fire at their backs and the mob before them. Good luck with that. At least it diverts attention from us.

I motion to Bram to hustle Mom along. I see an opening in the throng and feel a surge of fresh hope of leaving this hellhole.

"Move along, people!" a sour-faced guard bawls. Security shuttles us through the shielded barricade, oblivious to who we are, flustered by the sudden fire and the mounting threat of massed protesters. We're almost through the line.

"Down with Starcom. Let the Weis family go!" Their chanting sends a pulse of wonder through my body. Word must have leaked out, and that could

only have been through Dad or Joey.

Mom catches a glimpse of a scarecrow figure with a white-bandaged nose. She raises her hand in instant recognition and a garbled voice in a glad cry. "Lars!"

Dad's nose is taped up, fist in the air, as he rallies people to march on Starcom. For one of the first times in my life I am proud of him.

My dad's jaw drops. She starts forward. He runs to meet her half way and they clasp in an all-encompassing embrace.

In my gut I feel a warm sense of familial closeness at this reunion, yet almost at once I'm holding Bram back with a hand on his shoulder. I level him a warning glance. "We can't go there. We're wanted and can only bring more violence down on their heads. We blew the whistle on Starcom and they're out for our blood."

Bram glumly agrees. "Torching their movie studio didn't help either." We edge our way back into the fray, losing ourselves in the crowd and make our way to the main parking lot. I can see the animated figures of Torv and Joey in the throng of protesters, landing blows, even Angelos aiming swinging punches and savage kicks at the advancing guards. Some of the club members are there, Roy and Fin, and Torv's tattooed buddies, poised with knives and bats. Because of their brave and coordinated efforts, I know it has been possible for us to be anonymous enough now to make our escape.

I look back. Over my shoulder I see Torv go down. Angelos drags him to his feet and off to safety. Joey? I don't see his blue jacket anymore. Tears spring into my eyes. I feel a helpless kind of terror, mixed with shame, as it's now Bram dragging me off. In my heart of hearts, I know it's a battle we can't win.

Things are turning ugly. Torv sees me and so does Angelos but they are pushed back as a new wave of C-Sec officers bearing shields descend on them.

For a second I contemplate joining their ranks and taking on the C-Sec and Starcom enforcers whose numbers are growing by the minute. All I can see are pictures of doom in my mind. Blood, handcuffs, tasers and boots to the face; the familiar black-masted ship sailing a roiling sea. Bram being taken down. The rest of our allies beaten by Starcom bullies. Me, taken into some back room, drugged and tortured with no hope of escape. Bram and I with black halobands clipped on our skulls like Mom.

New figures approach. I whirl to face them, my fists up.

It's Karie and Rabin. "Hey, where you going?" They come scrambling after us as Bram and I try to sneak into the shadows past the parking lot and the dogwood hedges. "Trying to sneak off without us?"

"Karie, what the hell you are you doing here?" She's dressed in faded jeans and sweatshirt with a cocky lean to the hip. Rabin's wearing much of the same.

"Same as you, girl. You okay, Ellan? You don't look too good."

"Go back," I hiss at them. My eyes are squeezing shut, trying to pinch out the madness of the day.

"No way, honey. We're here to run interference for you. Bodyguards, if you like. Joey messaged us. You guys are heroes."

"Heroes?" Bram manages a strangled laugh. "No. What we are is screwed. And Rabe, you look like a dumbo dressed in the same getup as your girlfriend. Though can't say as I'd turn down any help right now."

"Bram!" I cry out in defeat.

"Okay." He holds up his palms. "So, what now?" He looks back at the chaos of the barricade lines. "Everywhere's exposed." He heaves a miserable sigh.

"We'll keep moving through the night, maybe hide in the alleys or park." I incline my head toward Karie and Rabin. "If all goes well, we can camp out at Carl's or your place, Rabin."

"Or Karie's," Karie pitches in.

Rabin shrugs. "Sure. We can hide in the tunnels by the reservoir, if need be. It's past the old-town market, you know the place where they sell hand-me-down clothes, tools, and baby strollers. Bram, you're looking fragged. We can throw any heat off our trail down there. Just have to stay away from the west end slums. We'd get knifed before any C-Sec catches up with us."

"Yeah, yeah, tell me something I don't know," Bram mutters.

I don't like any of it nor do I think Rabin's plan would work, but it is better than hanging around here. We'd be closer to Tydon Park which has always been a safe haven for me.

There's some unfriendly activity rustling in the shadows, the click of a dart gun and zap of a taser over the wail of emergency vehicles in the distance. I hush the others and herd them back into the hedgerows. Likely some security people ferreting out more of Torv's crew as they work their way around the perimeter. I hiss another warning and keep them crouched out of sight. As soon as the guards are a safe distance away, I give a brisk signal. We have to keep moving.

Like silent thieves in the night we slink off through the hedgerows and toward the naked glow of the city's streetlamps.

* * *

All is not well with our little plan. We're not a half hour into our pilgrimage when sharp voices ring out and the sounds of pursuing feet. We scurry down an alley, lose ourselves in the gloom. We feel the city breathing down our neck, watching us like a wolf its prey. It seems wherever we run to, flashing lights appear around every corner, like the C-Sec cruiser riding abreast the mouth of the alley where we are crouched to catch a breath. We're just staying ahead by a hair, and only because I've mapped out in my brain the city's best jogging routes. I know the back alleys like the back of my hand. We cut through people's lawns, their back yards, through small parks, across busy streets, down dark, puddled alleys.

We've had to backtrack many times to stay ahead of them. It's only now that we break out in the open. We're at Grise and Main. The moon isn't up and only a few distant stars burn in the black sky. There's unusual activity here. More people are picketing, waving signs, congregating in lively groups. The tram is clacking down the top of the hill to the stop at Jamieson.

The thought of taking the public transit scares us. Bottled up in a cage, easy prey for C-Sec. We remain on foot.

Bram dips down a side street, dim and narrow with old brick buildings. It smells of old cement and cat piss. He halts, to catch his breath, hands on his knees. His face looks grey. "Jesus, this isn't working. I have like zero stamina."

Karie gasps, "Yeah, I agree. Think I've had enough already of this cops and robbers' shit."

"Yeah, well, it was your idea to help them, right, Karie?" Rabin points out.

"Yeah, but—"

"Shh." I'm trying to think. I massage my temples and gauge the distance to the end of the street. Maybe two hundred yards. I'm getting a weird feeling in my third-eye as if something's going awry—like we'll not make it out of this alley. Getting to safety, be it the tunnels or Rabin's house, has never seemed such a faraway dream.

Screeching tires intrude upon my bleak reverie. A low wail echoes off the damp brick. Sirens.

Karie and Rabin take off down the alley. Bram and I follow, but Bram's dragging his feet.

He suddenly just collapses like a ragdoll behind me on the hardtop. I turn back, drop to my knees. "Wait!" I hiss to the others. They stop running. Bram's squatting, staring at the ground, as if he's going to puke. His mouth is quivering, face slack. I shake him. "Bram, snap out of it."

Too late. A Starcom guard races toward us as his partner stays in a nearby cruiser, speaking harsh words into his wristlet. A trank dart spins wide, thunks inches away into the trash cans at my side. I pull Bram down as another whizzes over my head.

The clatter of boots on hardtop echoes closer. Shit. This helmeted, black-bearded bastard's in close now and figures he can take us without the gun, seeing Bram down.

A mistake.

I spring at him. A savage leaping kick thunks into his side. He arches, but his Kevlar absorbs most of the hit. He swings a right, tries to grab me, but I'm faster, and slipperier than an eel. I smash a power fist into his navel. Agony flares up my wrist. He doubles over while my other knee caves in his face. He groans, drops in a noiseless heap. I wrench the trank gun from his nerveless fingers. Sucking air through my teeth, I want to empty the rounds into his body, but I resist as blood pounds in my ears. I shove the gun deep in my back pocket.

There are two more figures coming hard after us and they are smarter.

Thunk, thunk. In my mind's eye a speckled cloud of stardust coalesces into twin trank darts smashing into my ribs.

I seize the trash can top nearest me, whip it up to protect my vitals. *Thump, thump.* Unlike the vision, the darts quiver in the metal and stick there as a shock reverberates up my arm. They are still coming at me. I reach around with my gun arm and fire point blank at the oncoming men. A dart pegs one in the left thigh, the other in the bicep where meat meets the elbow. They stagger and fall.

Can I thank Stan Rane enough for giving me this haloband-induced gift? That spares my neck from the jaws of the wolves?

In a dream trance, I crouch to pull Bram up, slap his face.

His eyes flutter. He shakes his head like a drunken comic.

"What the hell happened to you?"

"Nothing. I'm okay." He stares at the unmoving bodies sprawled on the damp paves. He licks his lips, lifts a weak hand. "Let's get out of here."

I pause. If he has another one of those lapses…I thrust the thought out of my mind.

I try to still the adrenaline rush, but easier to stop an avalanche. Karie and Rabin have been useless. Not that they would have been any use against these camo-suited guys. I'm still mad at them for leaving us here, when they said they'd help us.

He snatches a glance back at the fallen bodies. "Hey, how come those guys have darts in them?"

I show him the gun.

"You did that?" His jaw drops.

I nod.

He looks at me with new respect. He takes the weapon and studies it for a few seconds with a wry grimace. "Standard security model. Same they use in C-Sec. Maybe they have another?"

"Checked." I shake my head. "The other's jammed."

"Well, five rounds left. Use them wisely, sis." He hands the gun back.

Bram's looking paler than ever, on the verge of collapse. Meanwhile my stomach's growling with hunger. I dig in my pocket, find an old, mashed Zero candy bar. I tear off a small piece, give the rest to Bram. He needs it more than I do. His eyes widen and his head dips in gratitude.

We catch up with Rabin and Karie and boot it down the street, under the hum of the streetlamps of Adelaide and their sterile ghostly light.

The 6G+ aerials loom like insect antenna. They look as if they're watching me and I suddenly get a bad feeling.

So does Bram. There's a soft whir of an airborne vehicle, somewhere near, possibly a drone. He looks at our wrists and turns whiter still. "Shit, our wristlets. Got to deactivate them. Stupid or what? They can triangulate our position."

Rabin's pale eyes go wide. "Can't we just turn them off?"

Bram grunts. "It's a myth." He shakes his head in distress. "That's what they'd have us believe. Cops, security. They have special access to networks.

They can track us whether they're up or not. Whole point of the wristlet. Monitor us to death."

"Didn't think of that. Damn." Rabin peers down at his wrist. He and Karie exchange glances and start tapping on their wristlets as if to try to modify the settings and thwart what's already in progress.

"It's not you two guys they're after." Bram's hiss is a harsh rasp. "Only Ellan and me." But I see the desperate look there as he steers his gaze toward me and suddenly I know what we both must do.

The whine of the drone echoes closer. He digs out a small pen from his jeans. It's got a sharp steel ball point. He flexes his left fist before he starts with the raised point.

Karie and Rabe stare aghast as Bram goes about the gory work of carving out of the back of his wrist, the button-sized disc that controls our world. It's only millimeters below the skin, but the gouging's enough to set off a mountain of pain.

Bram gasps for air as he digs out his with the edge of his pen. "Now you." He tosses the pen my way, wiping away the blood dripping down his fingers.

I snatch it out of the air and peer down the street, wondering how much time we have. Without delay, I plunge the sharp tip under the skin. Sharp enough. Do it fast, I tell myself. Don't scream. I clamp my jaw hard and start carving a flap around the perimeter where the small pale disc sits. "OW!" I grit my teeth to ward off the agony.

"Lucky it's not you," says Bram to Karie. "Go on ahead, Rabe, Karie. Need you to scout out the terrain."

Karie nods, licks her lips, as if grateful for the reprieve. The drone is still somewhere above us. Black. Invisible against the night sky.

I peel back a hefty wad of flesh and dig the cursed thing out. A flash of green light flares in the silver steel as it winks out and dies. The whir changes pitch, as if the spybot has veered off, or lost the signal. Nausea threatens to level me as I stoop to throw up, reeling from the pain. Feels as if part of my inner core is being excised. My earliest memories are of me as a young child, staring down in curiosity at that strange yellowish-greenish disc lodged under my skin. I wipe my mouth, swallow the bitter taste in my throat, then twist the hem of my hoodie-sweatshirt tight between fingers to stop the bleeding. The wound's not a nice one. It'll need stitches but that's not likely to happen anytime soon.

Bram has stomached the pain better than I have.

"What powers it?" I stare down at the grisly, blood-slick chip.

He shrugs. "Dunno. Looks as if it has an on-board battery." He peers at the circuitry. "Maybe solar-powered and I'd guess, is regenerated by body heat." He crushes it under his boot heel. Bram's about to reach for mine, but without a second thought, I stomp mine too.

No more triangulation.

We leave the remains in the wet grit of the side street as if they're hot tamales. It's a criminal offense to destroy one's wristlet. We don't think too much of it, considering our predicament and the crimes we've already committed. We catch up to Rabe and Karie and they look at us funny. As if we are aliens from another planet.

"Look, you guys," I say. "You don't have to hang with us. Feel free to take off. I'm not going to bind you to your promise."

Rabin looks away with guilt in his eyes. "No, we'd said we'd help you, and we will."

Karie motions to the lights spilling down the alley from the streetlamps. "If it's not drones it's cameras. They'll be watching us."

"Quick," Bram hisses. "Splash as much mud on your face from these puddles as you can. Wear your hoodies."

"They're still going to see our clothes—that it's four school kids on the run," says Rabin.

"Yeah, well, no reason to make their job easier," Bram points out. "Facial recognition scanners will have less chance of identifying us with mud splatter. Also with protesters on the prowl, they'll stay distracted. I hope."

I dip my fingers in a puddle of oily grit and smear it on my cheeks. I pull down my other sleeve, darken it with goop.

Bram and Rabin look like B-rate bandits, or a couple of cons on the run. I can't help but laugh, but catch myself. There's nothing to laugh about.

Chapter 25

At least we feel more confident than back in the dirty back alleys. We're far away from where we wanted to go, but we remedy that by taking a route directly east toward the tunnels and Tydon Park.

Our small group weaves through the crowds like wraiths. Bram and I nurse our throbbing wrists, Bram with a makeshift bandage of his own. Fortunately there are enough pedestrians on the move to make our furtive movements look less suspicious. We look like thieves, runaways, vandals with grey hoodies and faces half-hidden. All we need is a few spray cans in our hands.

"Now who's the conspiracist?" I say.

Bram grimaces. "We'll have to amp up our pace if we're going to lose these bozos."

"How? Roads are crawling with cops," says Rabin.

True, they're everywhere, like cockroaches. At least most of the police are busy patrolling for protesters.

Speaking of which, a squad car is cruising down the street. Bram swears and gets cold feet. He turns to duck down a crumbled cross alley. A vision pops in my head—of smoke, bright lights, fire and stinging pain—accompanied by a tingling at the base of my spine and the familiar sinking sensation in my navel. Disaster. I hear sirens whining in my mind's ear. C-Sec cars and Starcom vans screeching to a halt, tasers and hand cuffs all over us.

"No, not that way, Bram. This way." My fingers, curled into claws, drag him out of the cross alley and back toward the opposite alley, toward where the city limits veer out to Tydon Woods and the greenbelt, what little remains. "That way spells doom."

He shakes his head. "How do you know this shit?"

"Remember when the haloband zapped you? I got zapped too. Instead of putting me in a coma, the electrical surge gives me flashes of foresight."

He grunts his amazement. "So, that's what's been saving our butts."

"Trust me. It's a curse too, Bram."

"Okay, whatever, Sis. Let's go."

We race down the alley, Karie and Rabin following our lead, closer and closer to the place we originally set out for.

Sparking light in my third eye diminishes, the bazillions of speckles washing into the background. I know we've thwarted fate, for the moment. The speckles've disappeared somehow. I learned about the third eye in our kickboxing meditations, Angelos's advanced class, though I'm no expert at any of it. Truthfully, I suck at meditation.

We come out the other end of the street. We pass an electronics shop and pause to watch the late night news flash by through the window. It hits nationwide vidcom on all wristlets. The news announcer, a lean, middle-aged man with serious face in immaculate blue suit, reports:

"Vivian Weis, ex-publicist aka PR manager for Starcom, is wanted for questioning by Starcom security and local police, on suspicion of complicity in stealing confidential company documents leading to the haloband scandal. Her son, Bram Weis, experienced acute side effects of the new device, including catatonic response, which prompted Mrs. Weis to take such action. There's been public retaliation after what critics are calling the heavy-handed beat-down of Lars Weis in his home by possible law enforcement officials, a breach of authority. An APB is out on Ellan Weis and her brother Bram, involving the death of a Starcom security agent, both wanted as key witnesses in the case of Starcom against the State re the mental health risks of haloband. Their apprehension may lead to the recovery of the sensitive documents. City police are dodging questions. They refuse to make a formal statement; however, they are taking people in for questioning."

"Bullshit," I croak.
"I know, but listen," says Bram.

"Users across the nation are experiencing unpleasant aftereffects of the haloband from dizziness to compulsive daydreaming, brain fog, memory lapses and overall 'spacing out' after extended use.

"Starcom has put all major shipments on hold. Record losses on the stock market in the last 24 hours have prompted Starcom Executives to launch a legal war against anyone who attempts to defame their product."

Fools. I want to smash the glass and destroy the screens myself. But Bram holds my arm.

"Parents complain of kids dipping into the VR, or 'tripping out on haloband'. [A mother with a distraught face appears with heavy bags under her eyes.] 'I forbade my 12-

year old son to get one as he's on a VR holiday for hours at a time. It's the worst drug of the century. I can hardly pry him away from the thing! Like he's a cocaine fiend or worse. He raises his fist at me when I threaten to take it away from him.'

"Customers are boycotting shops and regional suppliers. Department stores are ridding their shelves of all things haloband, including the glitzy ads. Angry mobs stalk the shops demanding refunds, and when they don't deliver, chairs get thrown through their windows. [The screen pans in to a mob scene, breaking glass. Police sirens wail and suspects flee while the boldest vandals are hauled away in handcuffs.] Psychiatrists say the rage is only starting… It could be the start of a civil awakening, says eminent researcher and sociologist, Dr. Franz Sairs.

"All is being investigated. Pandemonium has already hit many American cities as riots break out all over commercial centers and malls."

Karie and Rabin and the rest of us look at each other dumbfounded.

"Experts ask, is the technology safe? Cognitive scientists have said the devices place overloads on human sensory organs. While impressive as a dramatic escape from reality, haloband's command of the senses, particularly visual, is becoming a national menace.

"Under review are clinical trials that have been rubber-stamped by corporate health officials. Corruption and lobbying have certainly played key roles in the early release of Haloband. [The screen pans to CEO Stan Rane standing with a fixed grin on his face.] These are the opinions and boogie-man scares of a few overly-vocal critics.'

[Newspanel:] 'I would hardly call Dr. Sairs, an expert and PhD in the field, a boogie-man.'

[Rane shakes his head in disgust.] 'Exaggerations based on poor science and only superficial evidence.'

[The camera pans back to protesters, shouting in rage and indignation in the background. Rane holds up his hand, indicating no more questions. He turns and stalks off, surrounded by an entourage of his security people.]

I shake my head. *Pure lies.* I can only remember CEO Rane's feral grin and condescending doubletalk as he threatened me back in the white-walled D Section, not to mention his callous disregard for human life.

"There are theories of a surveillance conspiracy. A group that believes the haloband is a corporate tool to get more people hooked to the 6G web, especially the youth, as a means of mass mind control. More on that later. Stay tuned for live updates."

As the camera pans to angry civilians lined up outside the front doors of Starcom, amidst megaphone blasts ordering people to stay back or arrests will be made and tear gas used, I feel a startling wave of déjà vu—one that harks back to the uprisings of Ignatia's time.

The throbbing in my wrist has receded to a dull ache. That's good because it keeps me alert and not fall prey to exhaustion. I'm starting to flag, my step plodding a little louder, my reflexes slower on the draw, as my resources dip to new lows. The constant adrenaline, lack of food and rest, has tasked my body and dulled my mind.

No matter. I must not fall prey to weakness. I take a deep breath, dip into hidden resources and pull Bram along who's starting to feel it worse than me. Angelos's words come back to me in a hum of nostalgia. *In a tough match, evenly-matched opponents struggle for that edge, only to realize the one with resilience, who can keep his wits about him, is the one who will win.*

Okay, Angelos, all nice on paper, but I wish you were here to put that in action. My heart quickens again, with the memory of him pushed back from the barricade by apish security men. Torv tripping and falling. My heart reaches out, to all of them. Torv, Joey, the guys from the club. I hope to hell they quit the scene—Mom and Dad too, when they had the chance.

I'm in the lead, anxious to get off this narrow street. Something doesn't sit right. The shadows are too dark. Things are too quiet, as if sinister forces are about.

I am not far off the mark.

A lithe figure in a dark, unmarked vest jumps out of a window well. Jesus, some Starcom goon. He must have been lying in wait.

I kick the taser out of his upraised hand, see the snarl on his face, but am not in time to peg him with my trank gun.

I duck my head with little perceptible motion. His gloved fist grazes my chin, instead of smashing my cheek and breaking bones.

"Hey, asshole," Karie shouts to distract him. He turns while Rabin chucks a garbage can at his head. He reels back on his heels. It gives me time to clock him in the nuts with a savage front kick, then another to the gut. He's out. Face first on the paves.

I limp over to Bram who's looking ready to pass out, hand braced against the wall. I collect my breath. "Nice work, guys."

I was angry earlier…but they've made up for that. Sort of.

But across the street past the burnt-out lamppost, a driver's jumping out of his unmarked van to run me to ground. He springs in to club me in the face with enough force to make my head reel. Stars flash in my eye. He's about to taser me, snap the tape on my wrists, collect his bounty. No way. I squeeze the stinging tears out of my eyes and move in, as Angelos's taught me, bouncing light on my feet. His forearm is only half way to my wrists before I fist-jab it away and follow up with a bone-crunching kick that breaks the fingers on his other hand. The taser and tape clatter to the pavement. His eyes moon in disbelief as if wondering how a teenage girl could inflict that much damage in the space of a second and a half. Tough luck, buddy. That's the hard, violent wake-up call of a street fight. He's groaning like a baby.

"Run! Let's get the hell out of here." Rabin motions us into a side street. We scramble after him full tilt, even Bram.

A security van skids by us. We drop back behind a parked car but I think they've spotted us. I see them do a U-ey and the brake lights flare and the paddy van looping back toward us. Glaring high beams. More sirens.

We scurry into a *Lucky* corner convenience store, burst through the door. Banners and window toys jingle. It is too bright in here and my eyes squint and we're exposed to cameras. Worse, they're broadcasting our story on the overhead holo screen and flashing Bram's and my face plain as day. Feeling naked and all too panicky, I pull my hoodie over my swollen cheek and try moving to the back as unobtrusively as I can where the chip and candy aisle is. There are some washrooms at the back. Crappy hiding spots. Fat lot of good my casual walk is doing. Karie and Rabe skulk after me, thief written all over their backs. Bram takes up the rear. The cash assistant, a tousled-haired teen with a mullet cut and trendy baseball cap pushed backward, looks up from the television screen in automatic suspicion. He shouts, "Hey, you're those fugitives on the news channel they're looking for." He reaches for the alarm under the counter.

"Wait!" Bram yells.

Too late. The emergency alarm sounds. We burst out the back door. The door bangs behind us, causing the heads of customers and street people to turn. This time C-Sec officers, not Starcom men, are close by, stationed across the street. They are alerted by the disturbance. They set off after us in a run, we who must look like a bunch of petty thieves, but who are much more than that. We run down the nearest alley but we're easy prey.

The fastest officers tackle Karie and Rabin before they can react. They're down with tape around their wrists.

Bram is rasping for breath. He can't handle the pace any longer. He collapses, rolls on the paves, his grave grey eyes staring up at me, mirroring the catatonic emptiness I know too well and have been dreading for so long now.

"Bram!"

He's not listening.

"Get up, you lug!" I pound on his chest. But his expression is blank. Eyes look up at me like vacant pools. There's a hint of his breathing, but not much more. In his corpse-like unresponsiveness it's as if to tell me it's no use, to run. I get up, staggering back as I hear the thud of boots on cement. Adrenaline kicks in. Fight or flight. I'm up for a fight.

Running figures rustling in the shadows. I turn toward the cross way to face new enemies. My fists and feet are ready to kill. Two guys lurch out of the shadows.

They're dressed in dark brown leather jackets and black boots with long hair draped over the right side of their head. Something's off about them. They're not cops. The other side of their heads are shaved and tattooed with green, spidery designs. One reaches for Bram's outstretched arm while the other jogs past the dumpster and kicks at the rusty door of what must be an abandoned storage space or warehouse. He sprints back and they drag Bram down the alley past the dumpster and through the opening.

Who are they? They must have shadowed us all along like ferrets. But who? Who told them to track us...? Torv... only Torv could have told them.

"Go! Run!" one hisses at me. He lifts his hand, and I see the design of a long nail, a spike tattooed into his left forearm.

Torn as to what to do, I hesitate but the sirens only wail louder. More vested figures in black and blue are breaking out of the shadows. I can hear the silent plunk of the trank darts whistling by my shoulders and head down the moonlit alley. One buries itself in the thigh of the slower Spike savior at my back. He groans and topples over before he can duck into cover with his buddy. His comrade bravely drags the motionless body into the gap that he and Bram occupy and closes the door. I hear the clunk of a bar latching.

Now I run. Full out, my emotions a cauldron of fury and despair.

I curse myself for my cowardice, abandoning Bram, my own brother. But even as I run, my stinging eyes dry up because of what I know he would say:

"Run! Stupid fool. Dumb of both of us to get caught."

My movement is spotted. A rough voice calls out, "There she is. Get the bitch!"

I turn and fire the dart gun. *Thwack. Thwack.* Two C-Sec men in the forefront fall like logs.

I feel a stab of pain in my leg where I'd bruised it leaping for cover. I pluck out a piece of glass lodged in my shin. I put on an extra spurt of speed, suck in lungfuls of air, pushed to the point of breaking, but inspired by what I think are my brother's words. Tears become choked grief, suffocating gasps, as I hear the task force screech to a halt at the place where the Spikes dragged Bram. Everywhere shouts, red flashing lights and slamming of car doors. I shudder at what they will do to him, to me, what ordeal they will put him through, what they will force out of him.

I'm next, for taking on Starcom and dipping into the darkweb.

My calves are burning, aching feet skidding over grit and garbage, racing like the wind. Down the alley, leaping over trash cans and garbage bags overflowing from their stinking dumpster.

That's when I hear the dogs. Bays and growls. Menacing sounds, interspersed with staccato commands of their trainers.

Not more dogs?

They're distant, but not distant enough. My resolve quails. Time slows to a standstill. The nearby dumpster backs out behind a greasy spoon restaurant. Blackened brick stares up at me, seemingly a mile high. Steam is drifting out to meet my face from one of the kitchen vents. I can hear the clicking of animal claws on the damp paves, snarls and bays magnified a hundred times by the echo off the narrow stone alley.

A black Doberman is almost on me, barreling right for my vitals, teeth snapping, jowls slavering. Though my hand shakes, I stoop and aim. A dart catches the monster in the face. It whirls around, whining and pawing at its muzzle then falls flat. My heart is still thumping like a compressor. Blood pounds in my temples.

More dogs are coming. I doubt my luck to take them all down with a gun almost out of ammo, not to mention the men coming after them.

No way to outrun them.

But maybe…a wild idea strikes me on sight of the dumpster and the bags of refuse piled to its brim. An old warehouse door is twenty feet down on the same side. I run down, lash out with a kick. The rusty metal caves with a twang. Another kick. The lock around the chains break. The other dogs are winding closer. I can hear their snapping jaws and their yapping. Shit! What the hell were they seeding them with? Maybe some clothes of mine snatched from my room?

I move into the darkness, discerning vague shapes of old moldering machinery, canning equipment? Drill presses…a tannery?—I tear off shreds of my sweatshirt and hastily wipe at things to make sure my scent is plastered over several places.

I scramble back out, claw my way past the garbage bags. I make like a hobo and squeeze under the rusted green lid of the dumpster with its rusty creak. Before I tumble into the reeking slop, I wrap my sleeve around my wrist wound as tight as I can, hoping to stave off infection. I worm my way deeper, smearing myself with all kinds of disgusting refuse: bacon fat, rancid meat, moldy bread, rotten peels. I'm gagging with the hideous reek, but I force myself not to spew or cry out.

The dogs come sweeping by and leap at the steel door. I hear awful echoes. Snarling and claws raking grooves in the metal. Footfall. Shouts. Some radio chatter.

Through a crack, I glimpse the flash of several roving searchlights. Two, three? Whoever is leading the operation is pissed. Pissed to come up empty with his thirst for Weis blood not sated.

"Nothing…Keep going," says a gruff voice. "The kid must have slipped down the alley." Two sets of hands drag the dogs away. I hear more snarls and yelps.

I dare not breathe. Minutes pass. I hear the rasp of more angry shouts up the alley. Very distant now, the faint snuffling of dogs.

It worked. The foul smell must have masked my scent.

I breathe a sigh of relief. I just want to curl up here and die though. How long can I take this punishment?

A thousand pinpricks assault my body. My wrist the worse. My shoulders, knees and legs ache, they just want to shut down. But they can't. My brain spins. I dread to think of Bram, Karie and Rabin and their fate.

How long am I to stay here, alone in the dark and the stench? My only companions maggots and rats? Hours? A day? Flashing lights still strobe at the head of the alley. How can I escape this dragnet?

In sudden impulse, I push open the heavy lid. Yellow lights spill out at the mouth of the alley. I burst from my haven and hottail it down the hardtop, leaving my temporary refuge behind.

A slick sheen of rain coats the pavement, the smell of oil and dirt mingled with something else—freedom—and welcome respite from the stench of the reeking garbage. Keeping to the shadows, I retrace my steps back the way I came.

Chapter 26

Hunted like an animal. Now I know what it's like. It's a horrible feeling.

The wind has picked up. Mini dust devils swirl loose trash up the alley. New welcome drops splat on the pavement. I hold up my wrist and roll up my sleeve. The rain at least will help wash off the grimy scum and rinse my wounds of any infection. And rid me of the worst of the stinking mess from my hair and clothes.

There's a blockade ahead at the end of Vigers Ave, the greenbelt loop. Police cruisers, intercept teams, security vans, as if in anticipation of more Weis sympathizers or perhaps my next move. Surely this's all not for one teenage girl? Now that they can't track me through my wristlet, I have an advantage. I slip back behind a newsstand, blood hammering in my ears. Did they see me? So much for heading to the waterworks and the reservoir. The thought of all that liquid gives me a momentary pang for a power drink. Think again.

Where shall I go? Back to the alleys, the slums, and take my chances?

No, a sharp premonition tells me to stay away from there—the vision of me, lying bruised and battered, thrown in the back of security van, yowling and spitting like a wildcat.

To the trainyards then? My dad's voice intrudes over the cloud of my confusion. *It's the first place they'd look.*

Tydon Park then. The park was ten minutes away, a straight run up Forbes Ave.

No scary sense of alarm pings. My aching muscles loosen. My shoulders straighten.

Tydon Park is at least a half mile away. The perimeter butts up against the sparse greenwood of the main forest. If I can make it there…I might have a chance.

But my lungs and leg muscles are giving out. My calves are burning and I'm running on nothing but adrenalin and grit. Every bone in my body is crying for rest. My wrist throbs like the devil. My throat is dry as a desert.

A part of me thinks even if I escape, I will still be hunted and caught in the next manhunt. Even now, after I've come so far. But I push on, quashing that thought. It's a scared, weak part of me that doesn't believe in miracles and a future ahead. That flaw will tank me if I let it fester. Not what Ignatia or my mother would allow.

A huge empty pit opens in my heart, of emptiness over the loss of my family and acute hunger and thirst. I gave my last candy bar to Bram.

*Bram…*Where the hell is he? In the back of a Starcom ward with a haloband over his head?

I squelch the image and rein in my spinning mind.

I round a corner, pause and catch my breath. About two hundred yards away, I can see the patch of grass—Tydon Park. The tall slides and kiddie swings and sandboxes are lit eerily under the lampposts. The cameras mounted on top will detect me, but I can be out of there into the tree line before they can make use of the footage.

I hope.

In a hobbling run, I skirt the sandpits and stumble down the trimmed grass like a madwoman, even as my head swims and my mind tumbles over that last kickboxing tournament in the ring with Kojak. The same primal survival instincts kick in. There, facing a fierce opponent, ready to get my ass kicked, my muscles poise to strike. An overriding feeling of sucking it up and not backing down breaks through…that's the force it will take to win this…against all odds, to fight and stay standing.

What I wouldn't give to wake up on a lazy Sunday to the off-key hum of Dad making coffee in the kitchen and the tinkle of Mom's laughter at his dumb jokes. No haloband, no darkweb, just a hazy dream.

I reach the first trees, my lungs burning for breath. The gravel path feels good under my shoes. Sirens are a distant whine. The city patrols will be busy enough trying to control the fires and riots caused by the news coverage and the HB backlash that has erupted over parts of the city.

Chilled by that sobering thought, I groan without shame as I stretch my body which is hurting everywhere. Stooped on my haunches, I rub my sore shoulders and neck and do stretches and bends to get the kinks out. An idea pops up in my head.

I can run into the woods. The pines and their strange, fat gnarly trunks will hide me. They'd never find me. I simply have to head deeper into the forest until I get to the farthest edge and keep going into the country. I can reinvent myself, make a new life in the wilds. I'd become an outlaw, an outcast, a wanderer.

Yeah, right, Ellan. What about food? Money? Shelter? I was mixed up. A sea of roiling emotions.

Cutting out one's wristlet is like severing oneself from society—a criminal offense. They'll lock you in jail. Throw away the key.

I force my mind away from the unpleasant facts. As I stagger down the path, I tell myself to focus on surviving. The sumacs, pregnant with their seeds, waver in a vagrant night breeze. Likewise the solemn trees, even though they are my friends, look ever stranger in the dim light.

Somewhere along the course of my reverie, I hear the purr of an engine riding up the path. My heat lurches in panic and my first impulse is to bolt into the thicket, but I stay my ground, for it sounds familiar.

A deep tenor voice punches through the night air. "Get on!"

I squint under the dim moonlight. My heart does a double take. Leaps for joy. I stare, unable to move. *Torv.*

His left eye is blackened. A ragged cut angles from ear to nose parallel to the rim of his helmet. But he is intact and looking as darkly mysterious and powerful as ever. He'll have another scar. But not sure he'll care much. I know I won't.

"Quick, Ellan. No time to lose."

I don't trust my voice and limp around the side and hop on, my aching limbs operating on autopilot. I hold him tight.

He accelerates down the long access road and we leave the dim red flashing lights of patrol vehicles behind.

"I thought they got you."

"Too fast for them."

"How did you find me?"

"Call it a hunch. You always went jogging up here and I knew you wouldn't go home. Plus, remember—"

"I remember," I hiss in his ear. "Two of the Spikes helped drag Bram into a back warehouse—your friends? I don't know if they escaped. So tired of being worried sick."

"Bryn and Donnie." A sudden lurch of acceleration jerks my body back as he gears up, picks up speed. "I told them to watch out for you. Haven't been able to get through to them." Something in his monotone tells me that he didn't think their chances were good.

My vision clouds with tears again. "I had to run. I hate myself for being a sniveling coward."

"Ellan, you are a hero. The haloband scandal's been cracked wide open."

My dazed brain barely registers the words nor the smooth curve of Torv's shoulder where I rest my chin and the fast clip at which he is banking onto the highway turnpike to the A15. Light traffic: a few electric cars and gas-guzzling oldies. I clutch him tighter. There is a tense expectancy about our clean escape from Levenbrook. I want to bask in this moment of feeling safe.

Torv taps a rotor-like device on his dash. Some police scanner of sorts.

A crackle comes over the speaker.

"2-1-1 en route to Barston. Suspect clearing city limits."

"Copy, Mayberry. We will set up an intercept."

Torv swears under his breath. I cringe at our luck. Somebody must have spotted us and radioed ahead. Will they ever leave me alone?

"Hang on." Torv gears down and takes the next exit and guns the engine down the two-lane heading south parallel to the city. I feel the bite of the wind brush back my disheveled hair and the night air cool my aches and pains while his solid body on my front warms me up.

I wrap an arm tighter around his middle, feeling comfort in his presence. I just want to close my eyelids and let the nightmare wash itself away.

But that is not possible.

We are heading down Route 88 toward Roderick away from Barston. Torv swings down a sideroad, SR16.

But I can see they are on to us as red lights flash in the side mirror.

An all too familiar panic twists my gut. Torv kills the lights and we are riding blind. The quarter moon is behind cloud and it is very dark here and black walls of trees are flipping by the sides. It's dangerous. But isn't that what life is? Ignatia lived it.

Torv coaxes the bike to new speeds, outdistancing the pursuit vehicle. We must be going a hundred and ten through the thick black spring night air. The engine whines, the tires thrum on the backcountry pavement. I crush my head into the back of his neck. *Soak up, absorb his strength.* My hands circle tighter around his powerful chest and sheltering body. I know no fear, because there is no premonition in his care. No doom. Only a certainty of a future in some place far, maybe near. Wherever it is, I know we'll make it.

Denser patches of woods range to either side. I know because I can sense smaller triangles of darkness, places of hiding, between the solemn trunks that whiz by. Torv brings our speed down and pulls onto the parched grass. A small opening appears leading into the arching branches. I'm blinking in the murk. A faint trail.

"Get off." He kills the engine and we wheel the bike through the narrow opening while the C-Sec car screams by, lights flashing.

About seventy yards in, well hidden from the roadside, Torv parks the bike. He rummages in a back pannier and produces a small penlight. With a crooked grin, he turns back to scuff over the bare earth spots that leave any semblance of a tire track. Smart. He returns, laying a gentle hand on my shoulder. "We're okay now, Ellan. You can relax."

"No we're not okay," I hiss at him." They know it's you riding this bike, don't they?"

"Maybe. Why?"

"They'll track us." I hold up my wrist and peel back my hem to show the black gouge of dried blood. I'm trembling. My lip is quivering.

He grimaces, doesn't know what to make of it. Then it kicks in and his gaze goes cold. "That's messed up."

"Can you send a message out? I have to tell my mom I'm okay."

He winces anew at the bloody gash. "Sure." He taps the message in that I dictate.

"Hey, screw me. What the—?"

Security Violation.

He slaps the window closed in disgust. "Must be on to me. Bastards!"

"No doubt put you on a black list, like my mom."

"Then I'll have to do what you did."

"What do you mean? You—can't. It's illegal. They'll...they'll—"

"Shush. Shut up. I'm already up shit creek." He shakes his head with a mirthless laugh. "Always was a rebel. Hated the way things work in this society...Just an affirmation of who I am, what I've always been."

I close my eyes, as he pulls out his switchblade from his jean's pocket. I exhale a shivering breath.

"Plus, I'd do it for you."

A few grunts and grimaces later, he carves out the flesh-gobbed, button-sized communicator. He holds it up for me to see, a twisted grin on his face. He wraps the wound with his sleeve. He goes to fling it in the bushes, but I catch his hand. "No!"

He understands by my intense gaze that such a disposal won't work.

"Right." He stoops to smash it under a rock.

With that single act my heart leaps. Am I falling for this guy?

I squeeze my eyes shut, clench my fists at my temples. This was madness. I wish I'd never delved into the darkweb. I'd still be dancing at raves or jogging down the ring road and sparring at the club. But I know that's all a pipe dream now. That life is over. Like Torv, I am a rebel. Destined to be an outlaw, a whistleblower. On the run. Taking on the powers that be.

Like Ignatia.

Like my mom.

Like…Bram.

Bram. My fingers curl in claws around his arm. "Torv, we have to go back. My Mom. Dad. We have to make sure they're safe."

He pulls me into him, stops me from heading for the bike and takes my uncontrolled sobs into his neck. I can feel the rising heat of his body and the beat of his heart against mine.

"We can't." A soft grunt, almost an animal growl, vibrates in his throat. "We can't. We're criminals. Anarchists. We fired trank guns on cops. Assaulted security officers. You torched Starcom. We cut out our wristcoms. They'll string us up to dry. Willful destruction of property, assault, murder, that kind of stuff."

"I know, I know. But—"

"No offense, Ellan, but you need some serious perfume."

I laugh, choke up. "Sorry, can't help it. Had to roll around a dumpster to save my ass." I hate myself for even caring what I smell like or look like. Or how I must come across to him. My hair, wild and tangled, my clothes torn and soiled and splattered with rotten fruit and worse.

"Tell me again how you knew where I'd be?"

"The park—remember the time I picked you up on my bike and we went riding in the country?"

He cups his hand under my chin and caresses my swollen cheek. I brush my lips gently against his. A slow, timeless but agonizing moment goes by.

I sigh. "More like stalking." Though I glow with the memory. "So what do we do?"

"We ride south. We hold up, until the trail's not so hot."

It makes sense.

But there is still a lot that doesn't.

"Why are you so different now than before? I feel like I never knew you—only as the class bully."

"I'm not different, Ellan. Still a mean, ugly S.O.B. An angry kid. Just found someone I really care about. It's enough to make a person different, or seem different."

"Well, glad I've done something right." I motion to the bike in the moonlit shadows. "What's the range on this thing?"

"About 150 miles."

"Can we make it to another town, a safe place?"

"Maybe. We take it as it comes, recharge, figure it out from there. How much money you have on you?"

"Didley. Like $40 bucks."

"With my $10 that gives us $50. Not a bad start."

I shake my head, snuffle out an incredulous laugh. "Says who? That's a pretty thin plan."

"I've been in worse jams."

"Oh, yeah? Well, I haven't." I glide back and clasp him around the waist.

He turns me a wry grin. "Think of it as a new experience."

We move the bike deeper under the cover of the trees and cover up any tracks. Torv brings snacks from his pack, also a bottle of water. He hands them all over to me which I accept with a glad cry. We gather some leaves and make a resting spot in a small hollow under a birch grove. As we lie down, the night wind rustles the leaves above our head. A helicopter thrums by, or what sounds like one, somewhere high overhead. I curl up beside Torv, shivering. His body feels like a radiant furnace in my need for comfort and shelter. His firm but pliant muscles seem surprisingly relaxed considering the heap of trouble we're in.

In those moments I start to gain some clarity.

Whatever Mom has started I have to finish.

The darkweb. It can't just exist on its own. There must be others who maintain it. Maybe I can find them...

And as for these others who have rigged the game...

Who 'they' are is another story. Perhaps I'll never know. Somewhere it is larger than the police, larger than the bogus history taught at school and the 6G+ networks and radio towers. It involves Starcom, the government and maybe all the companies that still run this fractured society.

They took my family, but they can't take me.

Someday I'd make them pay. All of them.

* * *

Thanks for reading! Ellan's adventure is only beginning...

Sneak preview, **Book 2: Darkweb, Ignatia on Fire**

Forget the past. Forget the future. The healing will come, only in its own time.
Except there's no forgetting the past. The past that was part of the problem they'd tried to eliminate...

I'd become a deviant, a rebel, an invisible saboteur, a destroyer of the establishment, a nerk.

Wearing my torn leathers, army boots, long brown trenchcoat that went down to hips and past thighs, I tossed my last explosive shell in the underbrush. I'd long since hacked my hair short. Wore a khaki tuque. Camoed my face to look grimy-like, make it look darker. All five of us did: Torv, Catter, Seth, Reavin.

I was now just shy of 5' 10". And I was fast. Nobody could outrun me. Not even Torv. Ever since they'd snatched my mom and dad, I'd been on the run; fleeing from who or from what became less clear as time passed. Starcom security? C-Sec police? Government agents? I knew too much, my family knew too much. After my mom had dug up secret files on Starcom's haloband, all hell had broken loose. It was a story how top Execs had suppressed the results of the trials, lobbied and bribed the government officials to push it through, much as 6G+ and all its predecessors had gone through. Now my brother Bram was screwed up from haloband's mental effects, dead perhaps. I had used it too, but gained some strange power of foresight.

How I miss him. Yet even I do not know how to go back and get him.

Four years have gone by but not a single day passes where I fail to remember how the authorities snatched my parents and destroyed my family. How they beat and tortured them. Haven't seen any of them since. Well, I am far away from that place now, the city of Levenbrook where I grew up, but my instinct says they're gone. When I think of them, I get a warm feeling which grows cold, followed by an emptiness in my gut. If their minds are lost or controlled, they may as well be dead.

The woods here is my shared sanctuary with my travel brothers and sisters. Herein lies freedom. Or freedom from suspicion, persecution, witch hunts.

I escaped, like others did, but we are still hunted.

But we fight back.

We will hit a hundred 6G transmitters before this campaign's over. First priority is the mega radio tower that's just gone up. Far too close to our secluded camp. It must be destroyed.

As far as sabotage goes, it's a small dent, but still a strike against the crimes committed upon my family and society.

The nightmares never cease. How long must I wake up in the middle of the night bathed in sweat with terror in my eyes? My fists bunched in balls, expecting armed men in dark Kevlar to seize me and slit my throat.

Torv and I had to ditch the bike we fled on from Levenbrook that dark, moonless night. Too conspicuous a target. We fled to multiple cities, hid out in trainyards, hopping the next boxcar out of town, for rural places are much less monitored than any cities. Always southward where it is warm and easier to survive the winters. I scouted out a few, like-minded people, though these rogues, by association, were in no way easy to find. In simple words, I found my tribe.

Seth nods. "I know what you're thinking."

"Yeah, what?" I rasped.

"That the electric car could have saved us all."

"Somehow I doubt that. They would have figured out more diabolical ways to poison us and keep us enslaved. Slip chips in our bodies."

"Could be."

I thrust myself forward, my movements brisk, vengeful. Now wristlet checks in the urban centers are mandatory, as our birth records are stamped in the circuitry. An instant scan reveals all. Anybody caught without one is taken away, thrown in jail. I've got one, but it's a fake, a replacement for the one I tore out long ago on a dark rainy night. So do the members of my band. They don't work the way the security companies want them to. The Starcom bastards can screw themselves.

Torv rustles at my side, his camoed Puerto-Rican features lost in thought. I turn. Catter is not too far away, limber and wiry, her easy grin deceiving in the failing autumn light. Reavin is farther behind somewhere in the thickets, serving as rearguard in case we're being followed. He'll give a kildeer's call if he sees anything. So far nothing.

I shift the scuffed backpack on my shoulder that contains the lightweight plastic explosives. Catter carries a matching light duffel bag with the fuses.

I've gotten so confused I don't know who our enemy is anymore. Government? Global corporations? The Bogeyman? At first, it was Starcom, the 6G giant, with their surveillance absolute, their contract roster a mile long. A demon headed by Stan Rane, but now I'm not so sure. There's an underground cartel of companies that have molded this dying world we live in. Pollution hangs in the air, soil depleted, CO_2 levels higher than ever, ozone layer thin as an eggshell, weather raging out of control. People dying of sporadic epidemics, lethal contagions popping up overnight. Constant surveillance by radio towers and cellular networks everywhere. Mind control via smart devices.

The degradation of the biosphere and civil liberties started long ago. With big oil and banks at the top of the food chain: Exxon, Shell, Mobile, JPMorgan, Citibank. Then others joined the bandwagon, Huawei, Google, IBM. None of these exist anymore, except in memory perhaps. They all fell after the 'Great Calamity', but were born again into a more insidious amalgamation, Starcom and Agra. The dark web has been kind enough to illuminate the details. Such as how the historic record has been wiped clean since the deaths of the old megacorps. Brave souls paid dearly to keep the dark web alive so that those who refuse to believe or who care to dig, even at risk of imprisonment, can know the truth.

Call me paranoid or a conspiracist, but that's my take, and one shared by my allies. This band of misfits, tough ones albeit, risk their skins for an impossible cause.

However small, this last bit of defiance keeps me going day to day. I've changed my identity. To 'Ignatia on Fire', Nate for short. A tribute to Ignatia Frehan who was martyred decades ago for fighting for the truth. I saw her burned to death on darkweb coverage. Modern eyes were never meant to see that coverage, treacherous and heinous as it was, but, at the impressionable age of seventeen, it made me a believer.

Ignatia. I've taken on her spirit. They burned her with flamethrowers, but they could not kill her spirit. That fire lives on—in me. Hers was the initial spark that set me on this path, in this mess—an outlaw, neither living in this world or out of it.

"Nate, let's go." Torv's urgent voice interrupts my brooding reverie.

I must have stopped and been staring into space. Not uncommon these days. With a curt nod, not much more than a sandpiper's bob, I thread my way past shrubs and flattened grasses to the target—the tower that rises over the sun-browned pines like an alien insect.

C. TURNER, L. LASERRE

www.ingramcontent.com/pod-product-compliance
Lightning Source LLC
Chambersburg PA
CBHW031330170626
46807CB00002B/623